Black Ink Publications Presents

YOLO 3
Sun & Shyne
A Novel By
Sa'id Salaam

Acknowledgements

Bismillah Ir Rahman Ir Rahim

As always, First and Foremost All praise and worship is for Almighty God, alone, with no partners. I bear witness that there is nothing worthy of worship except Him.

Dedications

To you, the readers, thank you once again for all your love and support!

Team Salaam! Next!!!

Chapter 1

The summer before high school was a blur of activity. Killa kept his kids busy at the range, swimming pool and at the boxing gym. Although the purpose was training them for the big leagues, and Wyandanch High School was definitely the big leagues, they still managed to have a lot of fun.

Yolo had left more than enough money for them to attend any of the private schools in the neighboring towns, but she was adamant about wanting them to experience the dangerous environment. It, too, was training to prepare them for whatever they may encounter in life. The school had major drug problems, gang problems and the violence that went along with them. There was also an STD problem to go along with the school's high rate of teenage pregnancy.

Christi begged Killa to reconsider but he refused to go against Yolo's wishes. Besides, he knew that she was right. They'd raised their kids well and now they would have to use what they'd been taught. All that was left now was a trip to Jamaica Ave for school clothes.

Asad had tagged along, just like he had all summer. As a result, he too could shoot, swim and fight just as well as the twins. Shyne was forced to ride in the middle between the two boys while Christi rode shotgun next to Killa.

"Ugh!" Christi fussed at the disgusting lyrics coming out of the car's speakers. The hit song 'Bitch Suck my Dick' played at least twice an hour, every hour, to make sure to warp young minds. She couldn't take another second of it so she turned it off. "I felt like my IQ was dropping with every word!"

"Who was that?" Killa asked offhandedly. He only asked in hopes of tracking him down to murder him. That would protect not only his teens, but all teens from the foul-mouthed idiot.

"He calls himself Crack Cocaine," Shyne replied, making her stink face. She often twisted her pretty face up to show her displeasure with something or someone.

"I'll kill that dude!" Sun declared, speaking figuratively.

"Me too!" Killa said, meaning it literally. He would, too, the first chance he got. He knew his son had meant rapping so he challenged him, "Go on and spit something then."

"Un, un," Sun began as Shyne hit the beatbox. Once they were in sync, he began spitting the new lyrics he wrote over the summer. Asad wasn't particularly fond of music but was fond of the twins so he smiled and nodded along with their performance.

Shyne's lips got tired so she stopped, Sun, however, kept right on rapping. He began to show off, freestyling about everything they drove past. An hour later, he finally wrapped up his rap when his father pulled into a parking garage on Jamaica Ave.

"Twenty damn dollars a damn hour!" Killa fussed as he took a ticket and entered the garage.

"Damn shame!" Shyne tossed in. A child should never pass on an opportunity to curse in front of a parent. It's only right. Her father twisted his lips at her but didn't open them. As soon as he put the car in park, the girls got ghost.

"Y'all sure y'all don't want us to come with you guys?" Killa called after them.

"We cool!" Shyne replied over shoulder and kept pushing. She loved those dudes but did not shop with them.

The first stop was a trendy boutique where mannequins were dressed in the latest fashions, displaying plastic breast and legs in the window. Christi looked at Shyne dubiously, knowing she wouldn't wear any of the stuff inside. Yolo had raised them both and she'd raised them right. They would not be putting themselves on display like the mannequins were.

"Ooh...this...is...fierce!" Shyne proclaimed as she held a tiny skirt up to her body. She grabbed the matching half shirt and held that up as well.

"Um..." was all that came to Christi's mind. She was twenty-four and wouldn't wear it so she knew that the fourteen-year-old wouldn't. Shyne was as pretty as her mother, with a trace of her father who was also pretty in his own right. She had begun filling out and rounding off with curves.

"Too bad Asad would never let me wear it!" she said, sucking her teeth as she put it back on the rack.

"Mmhmm," Christi chuckled. She thought it was cute how Shyne blamed stuff on Asad even though it was stuff she wouldn't do anyway. Asad wouldn't like seeing her in skimpy clothes but he wasn't bossy either. Her father was though so she moved on to a rack of clothes with more cloth. "Speaking of Asad, when is the wedding?"

"After I graduate from college," Shyne replied quickly. So quickly that Christi almost started to believe that they would one day wed for real.

****

"Damn it, man!" Sun exclaimed at a sexy young thing walking ahead of them. She had big caramel calves connected to thick thighs. The short skirt came just shy of revealing her round caramel ass bouncing around under it. That was the only way that 'shy' could be used in the same sentence used to describe the girl.

"Oh my," Asad said in embarrassment. The Qur'an teaches Muslim men and women to lower their gaze, so that's what he did.

"Oh my, is right!" Killa agreed as he bobbed his head along with the booty.

"Excuse me while I go bag these groceries," Sun said and rushed to catch up with her.

Killa was impressed at how smoothly his son pulled up to and began to chat. However, had it been Shyne talking to a boy, he would have lost his damn mind. Double standard? Sure, but he didn't in-vent it. He simple enforced it. Sun and the young lady, who appeared to be in her early twenties, stopped so she could write down her number. Sun's swag was set to a thousand as he made his way back to his father and Asad.

"You know what I'm saying?" he laughed as he handed the digits to his dad to show off. Once his hands were free, he popped his collar.

"Order me a large extra cheese," Killa said, handing the number back.

"Huh?" Sun asked and looked at the number. He let out a sad sigh as he noticed the well-known number for a local pizza chain. "Aw, man!"

Asad covered his mouth, so he wouldn't laugh out loud at his friend. Sun lagged back in embarrassment, giving Killa a chance to grill the other teen. It was long overdue since he and Shyne still hadn't let up on them getting married. He had given his consent back then, assuming the kids were only joking, but that had been years ago and at present, their story still hadn't changed.

"So..." Killa began and then paused to get Asad's full attention. He knew he had it when Asad turned and looked up at him. "What do you plan to be when you grow up?"

"A man," Asad replied back instantly.

Killa frowned, thinking he was being funny. His face quickly softened as he processed the answer. Being born with a penis makes you male not a man. Having that penis and growing older doesn't make you a man either. There's a big difference between a grown ass boy and a grown ass man. Many women have children with grown boys and then wonder why they don't man up. They can't because they're not men. Men are the maintainers and protectors of women. If they don't or won't, it's probably because they're not truly men.

"Okay, so..." Killa resumed. He was impressed with the answer but wasn't going to let him know that. "What kind of job are you planning on getting? How will you take care of my daughter?"

"I'm already developing video games and later on, I'm going to sell the rights to them to major companies, In sha Allah. That means..."

"God willing. I know, but...what if you don't make it as a developer?" Killa questioned. "How will you support your family then?"

"Well, I'll be a man, so I'll do something else. Because that's what men do," Asad said, getting the father's blessing once more.

"That's all I have," Killa said. Once again, he was impressed by his children's only friend.

By the end of the day, both the trunk and the kids' laps were loaded with clothes and sneakers. Shyne had picked tasteful clothes to subdue her budding body while Sun had bought the latest fashions of the streets. They were all set for their first day of school.

Chapter 2

"A-yo, Dad, can you drop us off at school?" Sun asked, as if he hadn't already asked several times before. Ask a silly question and you'll get a silly answer. Ask the same question and you'll get the same answer.

"Nope," Killa replied. Riding the school bus was also a part of the whole experience and he wanted them to experience it. They would soon be fifteen, and sixteen the following year, where brand new cars awaited them but until then, they would be riding the school bus.

"Come on, Sun," Shyne said, glaring at her father like she wanted to fight. She didn't but she did want a ride. Have her tell it, she was too cute for the school bus.

Shyne was cute for the first day of school just like she planned to be for the last day of school and every day of school in between. Today, she rocked a white pair of pants and shirt with a pair of crispy white sneakers. The pink laces laced in them matched the pink pony-tail holders on the ends of her two Pocahontas braids hanging from her head.

Sun wore a pair of skinny jeans slung low to show off his colorful boxers that were the same color as his loud sneakers. His own long hair was pulled into a wavy ponytail and hung from the back of his head. The pair of size twelve One Ummah sneakers on his feet gave hint that he would one day be as tall as his father.

"Your balls are going to call the police on you," Shyne said of her brother's pants causing, their father to choke on his coffee.

"Don't hate," Sun said, swatting the joke away like a gnat.

"Oh my! I see that we were worried about the wrong one wearing tight pants," Christi cracked when she came into the kitchen.

"Another hater," Sun said, shaking his head sadly. "Come on."

"Bye, Christi. Bye, Daddy," Shyne relented as she hugged and kissed her father. "I love you more than the whole world!"

"I love you, too, but I'm still not driving y'all to school," he replied.

Shyne sucked her teeth and stormed out. Killa took a few more sips of coffee before he stood to leave. He may not drive them but he would be following, watching.

****

"Damn, what you got to argue about this early?" Shyne asked as they approached the school bus.

A dingy girl name Ella was all in the face of some cute girl. They traded insults back and forth while Ella's friends surrounded her. These girls were more ratchet than the one found in a tool box and didn't play fair. As soon as they had her surrounded, they pounced.

The pretty girl fought bravely but there were just too many of them. Rather than risk serious injury, she covered her face and balled up into a fetal position to deflect the blows. The brunt of the beating landed on her arms and back, saving her face from being viciously scratched and battered.

"That's fucked up," Sun growled. He was torn between the lessons he'd learned from his parents to mind your own business and to defend oppressed people. One day he would reconcile the two but today, he watched the beating.

Luckily, the long yellow school bus rounded the corner and broke it up. The pretty girl stood and dusted herself off while Ella and her crew high fived.

Sun saw how pretty the pretty girl was but couldn't help but to notice how fine Ella was as well. The skin tight jeans did more than cultivate a yeast infection. They also showed off her perfectly round ass. Her bowed legs looked like they could wrap perfectly around a back. Her short hair was gelled down to her head above a face that resembled a monkey.

"I swear, if those girls ever touch me..." Shyne snarled, stopping before finishing her violent statement. She was just like her mother and would have tracked them all down and murdered them one by one.

The twins mounted the bus and took the first open seats. The victim took a seat across from them and right behind the driver. Shyne admired her tasteful clothes and shoes, unaware that they were why she'd gotten jumped. The welfare clique always found a reason to fight the cute girls. They were all fucking privately but publicly, the pretty girls got all the attention.

A few stops later, a pretty brown skinned girl boarded the bus. She took one look at the rowdy kids in the back and sat next to the victim. Both Sun and Shyne gave her a once over. They checked out her new, clean, tasteful clothes along with her natural hair that she had pulled into an afro with a band secured around it. The girl was cute but too plain for Sun. However, Shyne saw a possible comrade in her.

The kids behind them turned the back of the bus into a party bus complete with beer, weed, music, and dancing. They laughed, joked and smoked all the way to the school. Shyne stared straight ahead but Sun couldn't help but to keep turning back to see the happenings. Those were the cool kids and he wanted to be one.

****

The kids of Wyandanch Township had been going to the same school for decades. Most of the kids were second and third generation students. Some had actually been conceived in the school while others would conceive in the school. Heads and cherries had been busted on a regular basis in its halls, stairways and bathrooms.

The school was as bad as any inner city school in any inner city. Although one could actually get a quality education there, most were more concerned with dressing fly and getting high instead. As a result, more would drop out, go to jail, give birth, or die than graduate.

All freshman shared the same homeroom so Sun and Shyne started their day together, but they wouldn't share another class until fifth period English. They would be on their own for the first time in their young lives. The dumb kids flocked to the back of the class just like they had on the bus.

"Hey now," Sun exclaimed as the pretty teacher came in and put her bag down. She didn't look much older than some of the kids who actually attended the school. As a matter of fact, a few of them were older than the recent college grad.

Miss Waters had attended this same school so she understood the challenges she faced. She'd made it out and could have gone anywhere but instead of going, so she decided to come back to help other kids make it out as well.

"Let's see here..." Miss Waters said, picking up the attendance sheet for roll call. She took a deep breath and began. "Alize Afriqa Monae Adams?"

"Here!" she called from the back of the classroom while getting felt up.

"Shyne Forrest, oh, and Sun Forrest. Sun and Shyne! That's cute. Are you guys twins?" the teacher asked excitedly.

"Yes, as a matter of fact, we are," Sun said in a deep voice that cracked his sister up.

"Born, God, Supr—I'm not calling you all of this!" Miss Waters fussed. "In here, you are Mr. Williams."

"You can just call me God, Ma. Feel me?" the teen slurred so it would sound cool. Ironically, he had just smoked a blunt to get high when the real God is The Most High.

"I most certainly will NOT," the teacher laughed and resumed her roll call.

"God still ain't found a comb," Shyne snickered to her brother.

"Or lotion, or socks, or..." Sun added and cracked up.

After a few minutes, homeroom was over and it was time to go to class. They both checked their phones, said goodbye and departed.

Chapter 3

Shyne let out a frustrated sigh as she reached first period science class. It was by far her favorite subject because of all the flammable substances. The group of goons and goonettes whooping and hollering in the back of the class threatened to ruin the experience. The thought of setting them on fire spread a smile on her face as she took the first seat. A five percenter named Dwight, but who called himself Bar-kim, thought it was for him.

"Yo, god, who that?" he asked his fellow god, which is yet another contradiction since The Real God knows everything.

"That's Shyne. I went to elementary and middle school with her," Born Supreme blah, blah, blah, blah replied.

"She fuckin'?" Bar-kim wanted to know. If so, he would move on her. If not, he would move on.

"Hell yeah! I hit that over the summer," he lied before he could stop himself. It was out now and was going to get them both fucked up.

The brown skinned girl from the bus entered the class and looked around. The only empty seats were the one next to the boys and the one next to Shyne. She took the one next to Shyne. She sat and stared straight ahead as if Shyne wasn't there. It was rude even though she didn't mean for it to be. Her own single mom had attended this very same school and had given birth to her before she graduated. Her mother had gotten stuck here but she was determined to make it out. Shyne wasn't there to make friends but she didn't like being ignored, either.

"I'm Shyne," she offered along with her hand.

The girl looked into her eyes before accepting her hand. "Bryonna," the other girl said with a soft smile.

By the end of class, they'd gleaned enough about each other to become buddies.

"That must be the no perm section!" Ella joked as she passed by.

"The Afro Puffs!" Shanika cosigned and cackled like the wicked witch of Wyandanch. That set off a round of insults and snaps that Shyne wasn't taking.

"Excuse me," Shyne said politely and began to stand. She planned on politely removing the girl's front teeth but Bryonna stopped her.

"Don't stoop to their level. Those girls will hurt themselves way more than you can hurt them!" she said, grabbing her new friend's hand.

"Oh, I doubt that," Shyne laughed.

"They ain't worth it. In a year or two, they'll all be pregnant or sick. Meanwhile, we'll be living our dreams...marriage, children, houses..."

"That's what I thought!" Ella chided when she saw Shyne sit back down. "Fuck around and get some lumps on yo' head!"

****

Sun had gym first period with the pretty girl who'd gotten jumped at the bus stop. She was still pretty despite having a fat lip and a couple of knots on her head. He noticed her but he noticed the loud ratchet girls even more. All of them wore their school issued gym shorts a size too small to show off their thick thighs and fat asses. All the boys watched them as they twerked and loud talked. That is, until a basketball came out.

Being a freshman meant Sun didn't get picked for the first game. Instead, he called next and waited his turn. When it came, he showed out, scoring six of the seven points to win the game.

"Who is that?" the basketball coach asked as he came out of his office. His assistant shrugged his shoulders since he didn't know and continued watching the show. By the end of the next game, they had seen enough and approached him. "What's your name son?"

"Sun," Sun replied and prepared for a 'who's on first' debate.

"Well, son, shoot again. Again. Back up, now shoot again. Again. Damn it, man, this kid can shoot!" the coach cheered. "You're my new shooting guard!"

"Okay," Sun shrugged nonchalantly.

The old shooting guard glared at Sun jealously. Sun had beef and didn't even know it.

****

Shyne and her new friend, Bryonna, were both honor students in honor classes, which gave them identical class assignments, so both girls had gym next period. Neither girl had nearly as much fun in PE as Sun had had.

"Okay, girls, grab a pair of shorts out of the bin and get changed!" the girl's gym instructor shouted while clapping her hands. Most of the girls rushed to the bin to comply.

"Picture that!" Bryonna frowned at the notion of using used gym shorts. Shyne actually covered her mouth with her hands and wretched at the thought. Both girls had brought their own shorts from home and quickly changed into them.

"Wow!" Shyne grimaced at the ghetto girls with used shorts pulled so tight into their used crotches that their ass cheeks were hanging out the bottom.

They moved from the dressing room to the gym where the boys were.

The ratchet girls immediately began to put on for the boys. They shook, popped, locked and dropped it low to a lukewarm audience. Most of the boys had already had sex with most of the girls and so they didn't have much interest. In fact, Shyne and Bryonna got more attention sitting on bleachers. Once again, a bouncing basketball stole the attention of the boys in the class and they hit the floor.

"Excuse me, young ladies," Coach Jan said, smiling at the rarely used phrase to describe students.

"Yes, ma'am?" the two girls sang, proving they were worthy of the title.

"How would you two like to join the junior varsity cheerleading squad?" she cheered like a cheerleader herself.

"A cheerleader?" Shyne asked to be sure she heard her correctly. "Like, in tiny skirts, kicking my legs and doing flips and splits?"

"In front of men?" Bryonna tossed in. She loved to dance but putting for a bunch of men was out of the question.

"Yes!" she cheered and clapped happily that they got it. "I would like it to be classy this year."

"NOT!" the two new friends announced in unison and high-fived.

Coach Jan slinked away over to the ratchet girls. They wore short skirts and kicked their legs open for men daily, so why not do it with some pom-poms.

****

It wasn't until lunch that Sun and Shyne finally met back up. Sort of, since both were with new friends. Sun and the school's point guard James had linked up. Sun immediately looked up to the seventeen-year-old junior. Shyne and Bryonna were joined at the hip. Both girls bypassed the cafeteria line since they'd both packed their lunches.

"Them bitches think they all that!" Shanika pouted when Shyne pulled a thick turkey sandwich from her lunch bag. The chips, pudding and soda that followed only made things worse.

"Bitch got lettuce, cheese, and tomato! She trying me!" Ella said as she grabbed her tray with the cardboard cutout fish plank.

Bryonna added even more fuel to the hate when she removed a tuna sandwich with all the extras from her bag. To make matters even worse, neither girl ate all of their food. The bread ends and chip crumbs they threw away were a slap in the face to the hungry girls watching.

"Yo, that's a pretty little bitch right there!" James cheered when Shyne and her friend walked by.

"Who?" Sun wondered, looking past his sister. James couldn't have been referring to his sister as a bitch or pretty. He'd never considered his sister as being pretty since she was his sister. She was just Shyne.

"In the white," he said, staring at the back of Shyne's loose fitting pants in search of her booty.

"Yo, that's my sister!" Sun said hotly. He wanted to hang out with the cool kid but Shyne came before anything and anyone else.

"My bad. She cute, though," James said, saving the friendship for now.

****

Sun and Shyne shared a fifth period health class. She and Bryonna were already seated when he came in. He saw them and made his way over to check on her.

"Sup, Shyne?" Sun asked instead of greeted. He'd already seen several fights and a robbery and wanted to make sure his sister was cool. He'd assumed that she was since he didn't smell any smoke.

"I'm good. This is my friend, Bryonna," Shyne replied.

Bryonna perked up and smiled at her friend's handsome brother. How cool would it be if they all hung out together and one day got married?

"Sup?" Sun said and then walked away without waiting for a response or taking a second look.

"What's wrong with him?" Bryonna reeled from the snub.

"He stupid! Your pants aren't tight and your chest isn't out, so he don't even see you," Shyne said, twisting her face at her brother like he stank as he headed back to the back with the rest of the cool kids.

"Anyway, you have a boyfriend?" Bryonna asked.

Shyne's face changed immediately along with the subject. "No, I'm engaged," Shyne smiled, holding up her left hand as if she had a ring on it. "How about you?"

"I just turned fifteen, what I need with a boyfriend? The only thing a boy has to offer is something I don't want. Won't have me stuck in this town forever. Most of these boys will be dead or in prison before we graduate," Bryonna explained. "What I need a bad rep or a baby daddy for?"

Shyne nodded along as Bryonna preached to the choir. Bryonna was repeating all the same things that Yolo and Christi had already drummed into Shyne's head. Memories of her mother put a smile on her face and muted her friend's tirade.

Good parenting made the girls content to be kids as well as look forward to the future. They had their whole lives ahead of them and wouldn't mess it up now. Most of the other girls would have at least one baby before they graduated. Some wouldn't even graduate. Instead, they'd drop out and settle for being on welfare, food stamps and living in subsidized housing. Having an apartment and food would give them a party place where they'd drink, smoke and fuck themselves to even more problems. More drugs and dicks would lead to more problems in the form of more kids, addiction and diseases. Some would graduate from forties and blunts to lines and crack pipes. A few would even end up selling heads and tails on Straight Path alongside mothers and aunts who'd also gone that route.

The boys wouldn't fare much better either. Being hip and cool was more important than staying in school. That's why none of their favorite rappers encouraged it. Instead, they promoted reckless sex, excessive drug use and crime. The same fuck shit that had morgues and prisons filled to the rafters. Yet Sun was in the back of the class hoping to be down with them.

Chapter 4

"There they go!" a homely girl named Kelly shouted as she pointed out Shyne and Bryonna as they emerged from inside the school.

The girls got in line to board the bus for the ride home. The cool kids hung back so that they could have an audience as they swagged to the back of the bus. Kinda like the *Soul Train* line.

"It's about to be on!" Ella said, punching her fist into her other hand. The girl was still hot about that turkey sandwich Shyne had eaten at lunch. Ella led the charge as the bus pulled up. When the door opened up, she shoved past Shyne to get on.

"Bet!" Shyne laughed and accepted the challenge. She counted the six girls that followed Ella and put them on her list as well.

"They're going to jump us," Bryonna groaned. The word 'us' proved that she was indeed a true friend. A fake one would have put some distance between herself and Shyne.

"Ain't enough of them," Shyne laughed. She didn't mind fighting but if they jumped her, she was going to kill all of them. The Plexiglas knife she had in her purse hadn't set off the metal detectors but it was still deadly.

"Them bitches got me fucked up!" Ella hooped and hollered on the ride home. She was trying to hype her friends as well as herself up for a battle.

Meanwhile, Shyne, knowing what was to come, wore a sarcastic smirk. This was one of life's be careful what you ask for moments.

Shyne didn't have to get ready for battle because she stayed ready for everything. Sun was near the back of the bus and heard the plans to jump his sister and her friend. Once it popped off, he would spring into action. He would fight a toddler if it fucked with his sister.

Students bypassed their own stops hoping to see the fight. Most of the girls on the bus had been bullied or beaten up by Ella and her crew at one time so they hoped to see her finally get whipped. Today was their lucky day. The boys, on the other hand, tagged along in hopes of seeing some titties.

"Just get behind me," Shyne told her friend who looked confused by the order. "Trust me, I got this."

"Okay," Bryonna shrugged and followed Shyne's direction.

"Talk...shit...now!" Ella shouted, punctuating each word with a hand clap.

"I knew it. I just knew it," Killa mumbled to himself when he saw his daughter in the middle of the commotion. He let out a sigh and turned on the video camera on his phone.

"I'll fight all y'all myself. Give me a one," Shyne dared. "Line up, unless y'all scared."

"Scared! Sca- bitch!" Ella shouted and pranced around, putting on a great show. "Bitch, let's get it!"

Shyne smiled as Ella put her hands up and her friends lined up six deep. She knew the girl couldn't fight by her stance and the way she held her hands. This was going to be ugly.

"Ugh!" Ella shouted as she launched a wide, looping punch at Shyne. It was so slow that Shyne had time to giggle at it before ducking under it. She then unleashed left and right hooks to the girl's body that caused her to lift up off her feet.

"Shit!" Killa laughed as he filmed the brutal beating that followed.

Shyne threw punches in bunches that left the bully lumped up and leaking. Finally, Ella tossed her hands up in surrender. Shyne had to fight the urge to really hurt the girl. She only spared her because of the line behind her.

"One down...six to go," she said, challenging the next in line to step up. She did and got knocked out cold by a kick to her chin. "Two down...two to go? What happened to the rest of them?"

"They ran," Bryonna laughed.

The two that remained charged at Shyne. She could have and would have whooped them both but Bryonna joined in the fray. The boys finally got to see some titties when they beat the girls out of their clothes.

"*World Star!*" Killa laughed and uploaded the video.

****

"How in the world do you get into a fight on the first day of school?" Christi wanted to know.

"It's just what we do," Shyne cackled. "For real, for real, they asked for it."

"Begged for it," Sun added. "Dang! It's on the internet already! How'd they get it so fast?"

"Ion know," Killa said with his hands up as if he really didn't know. Everyone in the room squinted at him and saw through him. "At least you guys set the tone early."

He was right, too, because the mean girls fell back from picking on Shyne and Bryonna. Now it was, "Hey Shyne! Love your shoes, Shyne! Tell your brother I said hello, Shyne!"

Shyne set the tone for herself early. Knowing that she would fight and could fight prevented anyone else from picking on her. Next came Sun's turn.

****

It was the start of basketball season and Sun was making a name for himself. He made the most of the first practice and impressed the coach. The coach may have been impressed but the old shooting guard, not so much.

"Nigga ain't all that!" T-Dub growled form the bench where Sun's playing had sent him. No sooner did the words leave his mouth than Sun drained a long three-pointer.

"He's pretty good," Cheese blurted without thinking. He knew his partner was a hater and haters needed company–with their miserable asses.

"Thomas! Come check Forrest," the coach called, putting T-Dub on the spot. Sun made mincemeat out of the boy trying to check him so he called for more help. "Double team him."

They could've triple teamed him and it wouldn't have helped. He got it honestly since Killa was a beast with a basketball back in his day. He was quite the shooter before he became a shooter. To make matters worse, the cheerleaders worked overtime to catch his attention.

"Give me an S..." Ella moaned and gyrated her hips as she began spelling Sun's name. She then bent over and stole his attention by jiggling her ass cheeks.

"I'll take that!" T-Dub laughed and stole the ball. He only got to dribble it once before Sun took it back.

"Beep-beep," Sun laughed like the Road Runner and took off. T-Dub made the mistake of trying to block the shot and got dunked on.

"Oh shit!" the whole gym shouted and cheered. Sun cheesed while T-Dub turned red.

"I want a one!" T-Dub announced, swinging as he said it.

Sun was slow to react and got popped in the mouth. He was mad at himself for allowing himself to get hit and took it out on T-Dub.

"And you got one," Sun said as he threw up his hands. As soon as T-Dub put his up, Sun dipped low and scooped him off his feet.

"Oh shit!" the crowd repeated when Sun slammed the boy on his head.

"Hey!" another coach shouted as he ran over to confront Sun. "How would you like to join the wrestling team!"

Chapter 5

Times flies when you're having fun and the school year was over in a blur. Shyne grew even lovelier and curvier by the day and her father hated it.

"What are you eating?" Killa frowned as Shyne breezed through the living room. She wasn't allowed to wear little shorts or tank tops outside but it was her daily uniform around the house.

"Regular food," Shyne said in her fussy little manner.

"Well, stop!" her father demanded. "I don't want no more food in this house!"

"That's the one you need to be worried about!" Shyne said when her now six foot tall brother walked into the room. "Always talking to that nasty girl Ella and hanging out with those older boys!"

"So snitches still get stiches, or that over?" Sun asked their father.

"I ain't snitching! I'm just telling daddy he's gonna be a grand-daddy soon."

"Man, I didn't touch that girl!" Sun declared.

He and his sister continued to go back and forth.

"Excuse us," Killa said, dismissing his daughter. Shyne stuck out her tongue at Sun as she left the room. "You got some ass yet?"

"No," Sun giggled refreshingly.

Killa was proud to see that his children were still children. He'd noticed the changes in Sun as he pulled towards the streets. Killa knew it was a rite of passage that he would have to go through.

****

"You coming to the store with us?" Asad asked when Sun joined him and Shyne downstairs.

"Huh?" Sun replied to stall for an excuse. He couldn't find one so he told the truth. "James is coming to pick me up to hang out."

"I don't like him," Shyne warned of the older boy.

"You don't have to. He's coming to get me, not you," Sun shot back in defense of his friend. A horn blasted, signaling his ride's arrival, so Sun took off before she could reply.

"Come on, Asad. You can buy me some candy, chips, a soda, and..." Shyne fussed.

"Yippee!" Asad cheered sarcastically. They left the house just in time to see, smell and hear Sun ride off.

"You smoking today?" James checked like he did every day while extending a blunt.

Everyday Sun declined and turned him down. Every day, that is, except today.

"Why not?" Sun reasoned. It was summertime, the radio was playing Crack Cocaine's latest single 'Smoke One' and his mentor James was smoking, so he took the cigar and took a pull.

"Easy, yo!" James laughed as Sun choked and gagged. He patted his back as if it would help. "You gotta take light tokes."

"Okay," Sun said and tried it again. This time he was able to get a decent pull and hold it down. A smile spread across his face as the warm glow of THC rushed through his being. He was in trouble now but he wasn't the only one.

****

"A-yo, god! Ain't that the bitch from school?" Bar-kim asked Born when he saw Shyne and Asad approaching the store.

The strip mall contained a corner store, barber shop, dry cleaner, and a Chinese restaurant. Its close proximity to the expressway made it a favorite spot for the dope boys to trap. That's why Bar-kim and Born Supreme were out there twenty-four/seven. Funny how gods had to sell crack to eat.

"Yeah, that's that bitch! Yo, I know son she with, too. He used to go to school with us. He's artistic or something," Born recalled.

"I don't care how good that nigga draw, I'm tryna bag the bitch wit' him."

"Oh boy!" Shyne groaned when she saw the dudes staring at her. Asad was somewhat sheltered so he didn't register the brewing storm.

"What's wrong?" he asked, looking around to see what he'd missed.

"Nothing. Let's just get our stuff and go home!" she spat hotly.

"Peace, Ma, what's good?" Bar-kim demanded as he stepped in front of Shyne to block her path.

"You can't want peace if you're blocking my path," Shyne growled.

Asad looked from face to face to face, trying to figure out what was going on. He knew Shyne well enough to know she was mad. "Excuse us," Asad said politely because he was polite.

It's so unfortunate that people took a person's kindness for a weakness. What was coming their way was neither kind nor weak.

"Who you talking to, my nigga?" Bar-kim shouted aggressively. Born got into an aggressive stance as well.

"Look, we're not trying to get into a fight!" Shyne warned as she attempted to step in front of Asad.

"Sometimes you have to fight," Asad told her, just like her father had told him, and pulled her behind him instead.

"What's up? What's up?" Bar-kim shouted, hopping up and down to hype himself up. The commotion drew a crowd just in time to see two people jumped by one.

Asad threw a four punch combination that rocked Bar-kim to his core. Born wanted to run but knew the consequences of that. He let out a sigh and threw a punch so it could be said that he tried. Asad snatched his arm out of the air and twisted it until snapped.

"That's enough, Asad!" Shyne pleaded when he went back to Bar-kim.

"Some...people...really...really...need...their...asses...kicked," he said in between stomps and kicks.

"Well, yeah," Shyne laughed at the familiar advice of her father. "Go on and do you."

Asad had just finished up when she came back out of the store with her candy and soda. The fake gods helped each other up and then used each other as crutches as they limped away.

"I know where that nigga stay," Born whimpered. They couldn't beat him with their hands so they went to get their guns.

****

"Who lives here?" Sun asked when James pulled to a stop in front of a rundown house on the Southside of town. Before James could reply, Ella stepped out on the front steps.

She wore a half shirt that showed off the stretch marks that marked her stomach that were quickly overshadowed by her heavy set of braless titties above them. Below them was a fat crotch that was put on display by a pair of tight shorts that fit her snuggly. Another girl about the same age and wearing similar clothes stepped out next.

"A couple of freaks. Smoke a blunt with them and they'll fuck."

"O-o-o-o-o-k-k-kay," Sun stammered at the reality of him getting ready to lose his virginity. It was cool since he didn't want it anyway.

"Bet. I got the moms, you take Ella," James announced. He'd had sex with them both before so knew that the mother was a little freakier.

"Sup, Sun?" Ella sang, batting her eyes as they entered the living room.

The dirty floor and raggedy walls quickly stole Sun's attention—he and Shyne were quite sheltered so he'd never seen anything like it before. If he thought the walls were raggedy, just wait until Ella took him into her room.

"Huh?" he asked when he realized that Ella had spoken. She repeated the greeting and Sun greeted her in turn. Blunts and beers rotated the room while a Crack Cocaine CD played in the stereo.

"Come on, Monae," James announced as he stood. He then took her by the hand and led her into her own bedroom.

"Come on," Ella demanded happily. She jumped up, causing her girl parts to jiggle, which sealed the deal. She began to strip as soon as they entered her room.

"Um...," Sun said in confusion. He meant to ask about a condom but her naked body stole his train of thought.

"Um is right!" Ella sang happily when Sun stepped out of his clothes. She helped him inside and popped his cherry.

"It's so hot!" Sun proclaimed. He couldn't say tight since it hadn't been tight since before she had her second child.

"Thank you," she giggled at the compliment like she deserved it.

Instead of thanking her, he should've thanked the Chlamydia that she had festering inside of her since it's what raised the temperature. It didn't take long for Sun to go stiff and grunt as he filled the girl with his swimmers. They'd both given the other something to remember themselves with.

Chapter 6

"Ooh! Ooh! Sun, you should've seen it!" Shyne shouted excited-ly as her brother came in grinning from ear to ear. The combination of weed and vagina had him giddy.

"Seen what?" he asked, looking back and forth between Shyne and Asad who never looked up from the laptop.

"Asad whooped their asses! Both of them! He was like...Boom...Bam!" Shyne said, demonstrating kicks and punches. "So much for them being gods!"

God got a black eye today!" Sun said, shaking his head.

Shyne scrunched her face up when he came closer. "You stink!" she said, sniffing. "Like...the girl's locker room."

"Huh?" Sun shot back and took off up the stairs to shower. He returned a half an hour later to find Shyne alone. "Where's Asad?"

"He went home," she replied.

A moment later, all hell broke loose outside.

"That's him," Born said, sounding like one of the *Fat Albert* kids, courtesy of the fat lips that Asad had given him.

"Where?" Bar-kim asked, trying to see out his eyes that were swollen shut from that same whooping.

Asad heard a car behind him and turned to look. He took off running just as the fake gods opened fired. The real God didn't de-cree for him to die today, so all the bullets missed him. Stray rounds damaged cars and houses as Asad zig-zagged towards his house.

"What is all that noise?" Christi demanded when the sound of gunfire interrupted her studying.

"Sounds like a mac," Shyne guessed.

"Nah, a tech nine. Oh yeah, and a mac," Sun said correctly. Thanks to their father, both were virtual weapons experts. "Oh shit!"

"Asad!" Shyne screamed and took off. The girl wasn't even armed as she tore down the street to check on her fiancé.

"Shit!" Sun fussed at not having time to grab the only gun in the house he knew of. He dashed out of the house to catch up with his sister. They made it to their friend's door together and began to bang.

"Asad! It's us! Sun and Shyne!"

"Th-th-they tr- tr- tried to sh sh shoot m-m-me!" he stuttered as he opened the door. He looked around before snatching his friends inside.

"Are you okay?" Shyne shouted into his face as she inspected him. She didn't find any bullet holes in front so she spun him around. There were no bullets in his back either, so she spun him around again and embraced him.

"Who was it?" Sun demanded. Asad tried to speak but Shyne was squeezing him too tightly. "Chill, Shyne, he's turning blue!"

"It was those guys from the store! They were shooting while another guy was driving," Asad recalled. "They were in a white Jeep with the big white tires!"

"Infinite!" Sun nodded. He knew Born's older brother drove that truck.

Asad escaped Shyne's grip and went for the phone.

"Who you callin'?"

"The police!" he shot back, making a face to convey how silly he thought the question was.

"No!" Shyne protested and snatched the phone. "Don't call the police, I'm calling my daddy!"

"Daddy! What's he going to do? Tell jokes until they die?" Sun replied. "Look, dad isn't like us. He soft. We need to handle this ourselves."

"Yeah, you right. Daddy ain't gon' bust a grape," Shyne fumed. "Asad, you stay inside until it's safe."

"Okay," Asad agreed quickly since that was already his plan anyway. He hugged his friends once more before they left.

"Late, as usual," Shyne pouted as police cars descended around a neighbor's house. The small cottage was riddled with bullet holes from one end to the other.

"I hope Miss Smith is okay," Sun said of the sweet old lady who lived inside. She wasn't, though, because one of the rounds had killed her as she sat inside on her sofa. The twins slipped into the gathering crowd and watched as her body was removed.

"Bastards need to burn in hell," a lady fussed when the frail lady's body was carried out in a body bag.

"Oh, they're gonna burn alright!" Shyne growled.

****

"What the hell you gonna do with that?" Sun snapped when Shyne produced a Super Soaker water gun. He figured it out for himself when he smelled the gas. "Oh."

"Oh is right! Infinite is first. I want Bar-kim and Born to know that death is coming!" Shyne snarled wickedly.

"Yup, and it ain't shit they can do to stop it!" Sun agreed.

Shyne had actually selected Infinite to go bye-bye first because he was the easiest to get to. His job as the night clerk at a gas station made him a sitting duck. He sat inside a bulletproof booth so he couldn't get robbed.

The twins had to wait until the wee hours of the morning to make their move. Not only would Christi be sleep, there would also be far less people out. At two in the morning, only crack addicts and rats scurried about and neither made good witnesses.

Being too young to drive forced Sun and Shyne to have to ride their bikes over to the gas station. Sun had a pistol in his pocket while Shyne had the water gun filled with gas strapped to her bike. They wisely used the back streets as they weaved their way across town.

"Right here," Sun ordered and pulled over a block before they got to the gas station. A quick walk through the woods would put them behind the gas station.

"He's in there!" Shyne smiled when she saw Infinite's truck parked out front. She pumped the water gun and began to creep forward until Sun stopped her.

"Wait...someone is in there," Sun whispered when he saw Infinite looking down as he spoke.

"Suck...that...dick!" Infinite demanded as he thrust his hips. The crackhead below gagged loudly as he slammed down her throat and into her tonsils. The end was near and he came with a grunt and some curse words. "Shit! Fuck! Damn!"

"Ten dollars," the crackhead requested as she stood and extended her palm. She displayed a yellow smile at the green bill that she'd used to buy a white rock. "Thank you."

"Yo, say thank you, god! You know the black man is god..."

"Uh...yeah right," the woman laughed as she left the booth. Even the crackhead knew that men are not god.

"Nasty!" Shyne said when she saw the woman leave. She waited until a car came and left before making her move. Infinite was watching a replay of the blowjob on his phone when she strolled up and began spraying gas into the money hole.

"Bitch! Fuck you doing?" he screamed when the liquid hit him. The smell hit him next. "That's gas!"

"Ding, ding, ding!" Shyne cheered and clapped. Sun stepped forward holding a lighter in his hand.

"What the fuck y'all think y'all doing? Y'all know who I am? The god Infinite Knowledge Wisdom Understanding..."

"If you were really God, you would have seen this coming," Sun said and flicked the lighter into the slot. It didn't light but it didn't need to. The spark alone was enough to ignite the booth into flames, causing the inside to practically explode.

Shyne was mesmerized as she watched the burning man howl as he bounced around inside the booth. He fumbled at the door in an attempt to get out. When he opened it, Sun raised the gun to shoot him, but Shyne stopped him.

"No! Let him burn," she hissed. Sun lowered the gun and made his escape back through the woods. He'd made it all the way back to their bikes before he realized that he was alone.

"Damn it, man," he fussed and ran back to get his sister. She was still standing over the flaming corpse when he grabbed her hand. "Come on!"

"One down, two to go," Shyne announced as they rode their bikes back home.

Chapter 7

"News from Wyandanch Long Island. A man was found burned to death inside of a gas station. Police say it was intentionally set and are investigating it as a homicide."

"These damn kids," Killa sighed knowingly. He'd put two and two together and it added up to Sun and Shyne. Her more likely than him since it involved fire. News had already reached him about someone shooting at Asad so it didn't take a rocket scientist to figure it out.

"Who?" Shanice rolled over and asked. Anytime Killa stayed in the Bronx with his older children, he spent time with the pretty lady. A good deal of that time was spent inside of her vagina.

A whole year had passed after the double death of Yolo and Sincerity before he touched another woman. Shanice lived in the same projects, which made it easy for him to slip away.

"Nothing. I gotta go back out to the Island," he sighed. Pulling double daddy duty was daunting. Especially since he couldn't get his children to get along. They'd picked up their mothers' rivalry and held on to it tightly.

"Well, get you one for the road," she offered and flipped over. She assumed the face down doggy style position and Killa slid in behind her. He got them both one for the road then hit the road.

****

"Daddy's here," Sun announced when he heard a car pull into the driveway. Shyne beamed brightly at the mere mention of the man. Sun was just as crazy about his father but was too cool to show it.

"Sun, Shyne," Killa called out as he stepped inside. Usually the twins would have rushed in and thrown a parade but they were getting older now.

"Sup, Pops," Sun swagged in and gave him a pound and man hug like they were homeboys. Sun pulled back and nodded at his father proudly. Killa knew then that his son had busted his cherry. He also noticed a tinge of discomfort or his face just past the smile.

"What's wrong?"

"Ion know, Pops. My..." Sun groaned, reaching for his crotch until Shyne breezed in to greet her daddy.

"Hello, Father," Shyne attempted but couldn't. She busted out in a huge smile and rushed over and hugged his neck. "Hey, Daddy!"

"Hey, baby," Killa said flashing that killer smile. "You must have run of deodorant?"

"Huh?" Shyne reeled and pulled away to smell her underarms. Of course, she was fresh and clean and realized that he was teasing. "Daddy!"

Killa engaged in small talk to catch up on his week away. One week was spent in the city with grandma and the boys and the next here with Christi and the twins. Once the jokes were out of the way, he got down to business.

"So, what happened with Asad? Why in the world would anybody shoot at him?" he asked, genuinely confused. The kid was one of the nicest people he'd ever met in his life. He had no doubt that his own children were better because of him.

"He whoo-,"

"Beats me!" Sun cut in and cut off his sister. She wanted to brag on her boo for defending her but it could connect them to the get back.

"Probably mistaken identity," Shyne tossed in when she caught on.

Killa nodded in approval to the answer but wasn't finished yet. "Oh, did you guys hear about someone getting burned up at a gas station?" he asked, looking directly at Shyne. It had her name written all over it.

"Yup. Dude was a real scumbag! He got what he deserved," Sun growled, telling on himself. Killa furrowed his brow when he turned to look at his son. Sun had busted two cherries in one day.

Shyne jumped in to kill the awkward silence. "I heard he got burned over ninety-five percent of his body!" she said and cracked up. Killa and Sun looked at her, each other, then back to her. "Get it? He was a five percenter? Burned over ninety-fi- y'all so wack!"

"Anyway," Killa said shaking his head. "It was real sloppy, though. Straight amateur hour."

"It was? How?" Sun asked, sounding wounded. He just knew it was a clean hit.

"It was a gas station! Cameras everywhere. That whole thing was caught on tape. They got a good selfie of whoever started that fire," he shot back and watched his kids squirm. Shyne was about to open her mouth and ask for a lawyer until he continued. "Luckily, the computer burned up along with everything else. Murder is no place for luck!"

"No such thing as luck, just divine decree. Everything that has happened or will happen has already been written," Shyne preached.

Killa and Sun took a moment of silence to process the jewel she'd dropped. Finding nothing to refute it, they nodded in agreement and accepted the truth.

"Proper planning prevents penitentiary stays," Killa freestyled. "See, now what they should've done was get a pretty girl to lure their victim somewhere secluded. Nice and quiet, no witnesses or cameras and did the do. But, what do I know?" Killa retreated upstairs to let his kids ponder over his suggestion. He stopped short and listened for their reactions, with his nosey ass.

"Pops talking like he know the streets," Sun chuckled but still juggled the words in his head.

"I know, right!" Shyne laughed. "Actually, though...it's not really a bad idea. Boys lose their minds over girls. I wonder why?"

"I mean, it makes sense but...where we going to find a pretty girl? Christi is pretty but she ain't bout that life."

"Sun! Really?" Shyne huffed indignantly.

"Sun, what? Wait...you?" he frowned at the suggestion. "You're not pretty! You're Shyne! But...that just might work!"

"It will work! I'll catch them on the block and lure them to the park...," she said, laying out the plan while Sun and Killa nodded. "Leave it up to daddy to come up with a plan! I wonder why they call him Killa."

"Probably cuz he be talking people to death," Sun cracked and cracked up. Shyne joined in and snickered at her comedian father.

"That's what's up," Killa laughed to himself as he went upstairs. His children had no idea who or what he was and that was just fine. They would find out soon enough. They were just like him and one day they would join the family business.

****

It had taken five years after Yolo's death for Killa to sleep in the bed they once shared. The sheets were the only thing that had been changed. Everything else was exactly as Yolo left it when she'd set out to kill Sincerity. Except for the diary Shyne had claimed but didn't read and the .40 cal Yolo had kept under her pillow.

Killa smiled at the fond memories of the vigorous sex they'd shared as he waited on his children to sneak out. Once the hard working Christi fell asleep, they would make their move and so would he.

"Eww!" Shyne grimaced at the thot in her full length mirror. She shook her head at the nipples poking out through the halter top that showed off her belly. She pulled her panties out her butt but the tiny cut off shorts forced them right back in. After pulling a wig on, she crept downstairs to meet her brother.

"What the hell you got on?" Sun growled in a whisper. He loved seeing girls dressed slutty, except for his sister, that is.

"Bait," Shyne shot back in a whisper. "Now let's hurry up so I can get out of this crap!"

"I'm telling Asad!" he huffed and led the way outside. He hopped on his bike and rode off towards the ambush spot.

"Tell him! He ain't my daddy!" Shyne said defiantly after her brother was out of earshot. She pulled her panties out once again and walked towards the store.

Sun had their only gun but Shyne was just as deadly with the butterfly knife she had in her purse. In fact, they were better off getting shot by Sun than stabbed by Shyne. To her dismay, she only saw Bar-kim standing on the block. She waited for him to finish selling a rock to a rock head then made her move.

"Peace, g-g-g-g," she stuttered, but couldn't get the word out. He was a man, not God, so he wouldn't be called God by her.

"Sup, Ma. Oh shit!" Bar-kim smiled then flinched in fear when he noticed who she was. He shot his eyes around, hoping not to see Asad with her. He was real tough when he was with his friends or firing from a speeding car but alone, he was pussy.

"I said peace! I come in peace," Shyne sang, holding her hands up. It took everything she had and more not to laugh at him when she saw him in the light. The light skinned thug had a swollen purple jaw and a black eye with a bright red blood clot in it. The boy's face had more colors than a box of Lucky Charms.

"O-o-okay," he said, scanning the streets to be sure. Once he was, he turned on the charm, tried to that is, because how charming can you be with a black eye and a fat lip?

"Where's yo' partner?" Shyne asked, hoping to kill two birds with one stone. Actually, kill two thugs with multiple shots.

"He with his baby moms. He told me you let him tap that," Bar-kim said, licking his lips. He winced in pain when his tongue hit the split.

"Hit what?" she asked naively. She was familiar with the phrase but was totally confused at how it could apply to her.

"That fat little ass you got on you," he said, reaching out to turn her sideways so he could get a good look at it.

Shyne flinched at his touch and almost pulled the knife. A last second glance around saved his life when she saw cameras. It didn't save it for long, though, because he was still dying tonight.

"Oh yeah...um...you wanna...um," Shyne stammered, trying to get the words out. "You wanna tap it, too?"

"Hell yeah!" he shouted back and snatched her by the arm. He was leading her down the block so quick that she had to jog to keep up. "Ain't nobody at my crib!"

"Wait! Let's go to the park instead. I, um...I like to do...it...outside."

"Okay," he said and switched direction. He didn't care where he did it as long as he got to do it. Shyne finally understood the power of the P.

"Come to poppa," Sun chuckled from his hiding spot as his sister led their victim into the park. The full irony of the statement escaped him.

"Over there," Shyne said, directing him towards the pavilion closest to the woods.

"Let's get it!" Bar-kim said, pulling his dick out. Shyne snatched her head away before the sight of it reached her eyes.

Sun popped up and fired off a couple of rounds into his torso. He knew Bar-kim carried guns so he didn't play with him. Killa would have had a wisecrack or two if it were him. Bar-kim landed on his ass as Sun stepped from the woods. He raised the gun to his forehead and...

"Wait!" Shyne yelled. "Hold on. Tell my brother what Born told you."

"Who?" he whined. Hot lead had a way of making people forget shit. At that moment, he didn't even remember ever meeting anyone by the name of Born.

"Your friend, Born! Tell him what he said!" Shyne said as she flipped her knife open.

"What, that he hit that?" Bar-kim quickly remembered.

Sun actually growled like an animal upon hearing the assault against his sister's honor. He wasn't the only one.

"Okay, bye-bye," Shyne said and cut his throat from ear to ear. "Let's go."

"Let's," Sun agreed. He then pulled his bike from the woods and waited while Shyne climbed on behind him. Bar-kim choked himself trying to keep his blood in his body as the twins rode away.

"Amateurs," Killa fussed as he lowered himself from the rafters of the pavilion. Bar-kim looked relieved to see someone until he saw the gun in his hand.

"You have to excuse my kids, they're just getting started," he explained before he emptied a full clip into his face and head. "Now that's how it's done!"

Chapter 8

Sun awoke the next morning feeling like a champ. Two of the three people who'd violated his family were now neighbors in the morgue. It was just a matter of time until the last one joined them. His thoughts shot to Ella and her pizza oven vagina as he marched down the hall to the bathroom.

"Yeeeooww!" Sun screeched as he tried to pee. Instead of urine, nothing but flames shot out. He grabbed his penis tightly to shut off the fire and ran down to his mother's room, where his father now slept.

"A-yo, Sun," Killa said, twisting his lips at his son standing there with his dick in hand. The cold sweat on his pained face said all that needed to be said. Killa keeled over with laughter.

Christi and Shyne heard the commotion and came running to investigate. Sun turned away as his sisters came into the room and looked around.

"We heard a woman scream," Christi said as she looked around.

"That was no woman," Killa cracked up all over again. He was laughing so hard that Shyne and Christi backed out the room and left the father and son alone.

"Dad, I'm on fire! I need some ice or...or...or a fire extinguisher!" Sun pleaded.

"No Sun, go get dressed. You need a doctor," Killa advised as he rolled out of bed. "Nothing flammable, though."

****

"So...got hold of a bad piece of pussy, huh?" Killa asked, breaking the silence as they rode up Straight Path to the clinic.

"It sure felt good," Sun recalled, still squeezing himself through his pants. "Guess I should've used a condom, huh?"

"Yes, I guess you should've used a condom!" Killa agreed. He was happy to see his son had learned from this lesson. Sometimes it takes a man's dick to be turned into a flamethrower for him to learn. Killa parked in the lot and took his son inside the clinic.

"Dang!" Sun proclaimed at how packed the waiting area was. Wyandanch was dealing with a nasty case of Chlamydia being shuffled around town like a dirty deck of cards.

"A-yo, Sun!" James called across the waiting room, holding his hand up. "She got you too?"

"Go on," Killa urged when he saw that his son was conflicted. "I'll be at the house if you need me."

"Okay," Sun said and gave him a pound. He waited until he left before walking over to his friend. "Sup, yo?"

"Would say I'm chillin' but my dick is on fire. Woke up and found it melted to my leg!" the point guard joked.

"Man, Ella gave me something," Sun moaned as he sat beside him.

"Like moms, like daughter. Her moms burnt me, too," James sighed.

"Speak of the devil," Sun announced as Ella and her mother were escorted in by a health department worker and police officer. Their names had been given by so many teens and men that a production warrant had been issued so they could get treated.

"I knew that pussy felt a little too hot!" James said, shaking his head.

"Yo! You heard about that dude Bar-kim?" Sun asked. He wanted to get a feel for what the streets were saying. He held his breath as he awaited an answer.

"Yeah, I heard he got his head cut off!" he exclaimed. The thing about rumors is that they get bigger as they traveled. Sort of like an avalanche. Everyone who passes it adds a little bit more to it.

"I heard he was beefin' with them dudes in Amityville," Sun said, adding his contribution. In doing so, he shifted the blame to the next town.

"That's what I heard, too!" James announced. It wasn't a lie since he had really just heard it.

An hour later, both left with doses of antibiotics in their asses and complimentary condoms in their pockets. The two smoked a blunt of loud and hit the park.

Born and five or six other five percenters stood under the pavilion where their partner had been killed. They blew trees and poured out some liquor on the bloody concrete in his behalf. Had Sun been armed, the town would have been short five or six more five percenters.

"Can't believe my sister got a baby by that lame," James griped, looking over at the guys.

"Who?" Sun asked.

"Born. Made her name him Born Supreme Wisdom Junior. I just call him Junior," he answered. "You would think a god could buy some diapers.

"Word, word," Sun nodded thoughtfully. "Where he stay?"

****

"Heads!" Shyne called out hopefully as her brother flipped a coin in the air. It was the only way to settle the debate over who got to murder Born. Shyne was hot about her name being slandered but Sun was even hotter. He felt like it was his right to kill him since men are the protectors and maintainers of women.

"Damn it," he fussed when the quarter landed on heads. "Two out of three!"

"Not! He's mine," Shyne smiled, rubbing her hands together deviously. "Now, how should I give it to him?"

"It's gotta be brutal," Sun suggested while their nosey father eavesdropped.

"Oh, it will be," Killa said as he walked away.

The kids would have to wait until everyone went to sleep before they could sneak out. Then they'd have to ride their bikes over to the Southside to break in and kill the teen.

Not Killa, though. He didn't need have to sneak out and he had a car and plenty of weapons.

"Eenie, meenie, miney, moe," Killa sang over a display of pistols. He smiled when the nursery rhyme ended on a .50 caliber Desert Eagle. It really doesn't get any more brutal than that. "I sure hope none of his friends are over," Killa lied as he rode over to Born's house. In truth, he hoped that the liars were having a meeting so he could murder them all. They were supposed to be gods so they could just resurrect themselves.

Killa counted six heads as he drove slowly by the house. He circled the block and came back around to park in the driveway. He shoved the hard cannon into the pizza delivery hot box and approached the door. The chatter inside ceased when he rang the bell.

"Who?" Born barked and grabbed his pistol from the coffee table. Killa just shook his head at the glaring contradiction. If this dude was god, wouldn't he already know who was at the door?

"Pizza!" Killa shouted and prepared to shoot through the bag.

Born snatched the door open with his gun by his side. That really wasn't a good place for it. Killa could have gunned him down but held back.

"One large pepperoni!"

"Gods don't eat no swine!" Knowledge shouted, causing Wisdom and Understanding to nod along with him. Born sat the gun down and sat.

"They must have screwed up the order," Killa guessed as he eased his way inside. "You guys can have it free then."

"Well, now that's a different story!" Wise said, jumping to his feet.

Killa tugged on the trigger. The huge round ripped through the hot box, picked Wise up and slammed him into the wall. Knowledge, Wisdom and Understanding tried to run but Killa made them turn flips as he shot them.

"Wait!" Sincere pleaded with his hands up.

"Nope," Killa replied and sent a slug through his palm and into his face.

"Peace, god," Born begged as Killa reloaded a fresh clip. He was shaking so hard, his gold chains rattled. "Peace!"

"Nah, pieces!" Killa corrected and proceeded to take him apart piece by piece. Shot him in his arm, leg, leg, arm, and head. So much for that black man is god bullshit.

****

Killa was amused to see the look of bewilderment on his kid's faces the next morning. The twins had snuck out last night and rode their bike across town to find nothing but a crime scene. All the yellow tape and black body bags made it looked like a Pittsburg Steelers game.

"Morning, guys...what's wrong?" Killa asked as if he didn't know.

The twins looked at each other knowing that they couldn't tell the truth. "Um...cramps," Shyne said and held her stomach as she walked out.

"Yeah, cramps," Sun repeated and did the same. Their father's laughter rang in their cars as they went back upstairs.

"You guys can be so weird!" Christi declared.

Chapter 9

Bryonna and Shyne walked up to the corner store for chips, soda and candy, all things that would put pimples on their pretty faces. News of the murders of Bar-kim and Born provided a job vacancy that was quickly filled by other dealers. A group of teen thots pranced to and fro looking for attention.

"Eww," Bryonna groaned at seeing jiggling butt cheeks in front of them.

To make the scene even more gross, the girl turned and showed a slight baby bump under her halter top. That was bad but it got even worse when the girl turned and saw Shyne.

"Hey, Shyne!" Ella cheered and bounced. She bounced a little too hard, causing one of her titties to pop out. Shyne spun around, looking to see who else was named Shyne, but Ella ran up and hugged her, killing those hopes. "Hey, sister-in-law!"

"Sister-in-law?" Bryonna laughed then processed what it could mean. "Eww!"

"Um..." Shyne replied since she had no idea what she meant. She did know that the girl's deodorant wasn't working so she squirmed out of her musty embrace.

"Where's my boo? I keep calling him but he don't never answer his phone! I need to talk to him A.S...um...T," she declared, putting a hand on her stomach.

"I-I-I," the stunned girl stuttered.

Bryonna caught Shyne when her knees buckled. They both watched Ella swing her butt cheeks as she pranced away.

"Let's go to your house!" Shyne's friend said, turning her body in that direction.

"I need to go to the clinic! That girl touched me," Shyne reeled.

As they turned to leave, they saw an associate of theirs leaving the pharmacy. The girl looked right through them as if in a daze. She stepped off the curb right into the busy traffic.

"LaDonna!" Shyne screamed as cars skidded and swerved to avoid her. She and Bryonna risked their own lives to snatch her back on the sidewalk.

"What...the...heck...is wrong...with you?" Bryonna shouted in her face.

It took a few blinks for the girl to focus.

Shyne immediately assumed she was on drugs and got mad. Her small circle of associates didn't do drugs, boys or anything else that could dim their bright futures. Birds of a feather flocked together and there would be no chickens in her flock. Bryonna saw that LaDonna was distressed and pulled her along with them.

****

"Excuse me, guys. Let me talk to my brother for a minute," Shyne said when they reached her house. Sun was just leaving the house to get in the car with James when they arrived. "Sun! Hol' up, I need to holla at you for a sec!"

"Nah," Sun laughed. Her little friends were cute but square and he had no time for squares. Not in a town full of girls ready to turn up. And turn up they did. They turned up pregnant, turned up with STDs and some turned up dead.

"Yeah, alright. I got you, Sun." Shyne nodded wickedly as she turned back to her friends. She led them up to her room then turned to LaDonna and demanded, "What the hell is your problem?"

"Shyne!" Bryonna frowned at the outburst. "You see she's upset!"

"Look," LaDonna said in a hoarse whisper as she dug into her pocket. What she produced caused her friends to reel backwards as if it were a snake.

"Aww, man!" Shyne whined at the positive pregnancy test. "What about college? How could you do this?"

"It's not like I had a choice! My father doesn't ask if he can come in my room in the middle of the night and molest me! He just does it!" She got out and broke down crying. For the next few minutes, the three girls cried a river.

"So, why didn't you tell your mother?" Shyne wanted to know. Her face was beet red but it wasn't from embarrassment. It was pure rage.

"My mother!" LaDonna huffed indignantly and rolled her eyes. "Remember that crackhead that pushed the other crackhead down to get in the car with that white man?"

"Yeah?" she replied. The town had been turned into a hoe stroll with all the crack whores competing for tricks—dick sucking had become a competitive sport.

"No aunts? Grandma? Nothing?" Bryonna asked.

"Remember the crackhead who got pushed down? That was my aunt. My grandma lives in North Carolina but my father said I can't go."

"Why would he?" Shyne growled with smoke coming out of her eyes. She didn't need a crystal ball to know she would be moving down south soon because her father wasn't going to be around much longer.

"So, what are you going to do about, you know?" Bryonna asked.

"I went to the drug store to get that abortion pill but they wouldn't sell it to me. They said I'm too young. You have to be over twenty-one."

"I'll take care of that," Shyne offered. "I'll take care of everything."

****

Sun came sneaking into his window just after 2AM after a night of sex, drugs and hip hop he was ready to hop in bed and get some sleep. Too bad Shyne had other plans.

"What the?" Sun asked as he felt a strange texture on his bed. He didn't like the answer Shyne gave when she flicked the lighter. The toilet tissue she'd lined his bed with caught fire and burned quickly

"Te-he-he," Shyne giggled as her brother beat the flames with his pillow. "Got time to talk now?"

"Daddy!" Sun yelled. A moment later, their famous father stuck his head in the door.

"What are you two...," Killa began asking. He smelled smoke and directed the question to his daughter. "What are you doing?"

"She tried to set me on fire!" Sun demanded. "Tell her to stop!"

"Tell him to stop snitching," the defiant girl said, mocking her brother's whiny tone.

"Shyne, stop trying to set your brother on fire," Killa said dryly before going back to bed.

"Shyne, are you crazy?" Sun wanted to know as he knocked the ashes from his bed.

"Yes, but what's your excuse. How could you get that, that...girl pregnant? I don't want a thotler for a niece, crawling around twerking in a too tight diaper!"

"You been in my weed?" he accused and checked his stash. "I don't know what you talking 'bout!"

"Ella! She claims that you're her baby daddy!" Shyne shouted, causing her brother to wince and grab his crotch at the mention of her name.

"Shyne, that girl screwed half of Wyandanch. Ain't no way she pregnant by me!" he assured her.

"I'm not letting her have no baby by you!" she warned. "I'm not!"

****

"Come on, Shyne. Let's go driving," Killa called once Asad arrived. They'd all gotten permits and it was up to him to teach them to drive.

"Um, you guys go 'head," she replied, raising everyone's suspicious. She usually bullied the boys into going first so not going at all was odd.

"Go on. I'll take her in my car," Christi suggested. She could tell the girl had something on her mind. Her hunch was proved right as soon as the guys left the house.

"Um, Christi, I, um, I need to talk to you about something," Shyne began. "Only, you can't tell anyone. Especially my father!"

"Shyne, you are my sister. I love you, you can tell me anything," Christi assured her.

"Good. I need you to get an abortion pill for me. I...what are you doing?" Shyne asked when Christi pulled out her phone.

"Calling your father!" she huffed. "I can't believe you!"

"Chill, Chrissy! It's not for me!" Shyne shouted snatching the phone away. "I can't tell you the whole story, but you just have to trust me."

"I trust you. I do. Good thing, too, cuz I was gonna jump on Asad when they got back!"

****

"Go faster! Why you driving so slow?" Sun whined from the backseat.

"I'm doing the speed limit!" Asad shot back, keeping his eyes on the road.

"You only have to do the speed limit when you see police! Tell him, Dad!"

"I will not!" Killa shook his head. "Remind me never to let you borrow my car. Oh wait, you just did!"

Killa directed Asad to drive to the park where he beat the boys in a two on one game of basketball. He was getting older but definitely still had. He let Sun drive home where a surprise awaited.

"Wait the..." Asad exclaimed from the backseat when he saw the girl waiting on the front steps. The exposed flesh under and below her skimpy clothes made him blush. Killa, too.

"Please tell me she's here for you and not your sister!" Killa pleaded.

"I don't know why she's here for me!" Sun replied.

Shyne came out wearing a smug smirk on her face. "Hey, Asad," she cooed and batted her eyes. Killa twisted his lips at being greeted second. "Hey, Daddy. Oh, Sun, I invited your friend over."

"You play too much!" he shouted as his family left him alone with Ella.

"Hey, baby daddy," Ella sang, smiled and bounced happily. She had no idea who'd impregnated her this time, but out of all the men and teens she'd recently slept with, he was the nicest. Not to mention one of the few to actually enter her without a condom.

"Um," Sun replied since he couldn't think of anything else to say.

"Want some pussy?" she offered since it was the only thing she had to offer. Deciding to drink, smoke and turn up had destroyed the infinite potential she was born with. "We can go on the side of the house."

"Um," he repeated while shaking his head no. The thought of burning again made him cringe.

"Guess what I'ma name our son! Sun!" she cheered and clapped.

Shyne eavesdropped and giggled at his dilemma. It was quite funny to her, but there was no way she was going to allow Ella to have a baby by her brother.

Chapter 10

Shyne had decided to murder LaDonna's father a half a second after she told her about him molesting her, and since her mother hadn't protected her, she was going to get it, too. Being a crack whore made her easy to get at. Her dangerous profession had turned deadly.

The clever girl used money as bait, literally, since she'd put a twenty-dollar bill on a fishing pole and now waited in the wooded area adjacent to the trap. It didn't take long for her prey to show up.

LaDonna's mother hopped out of a trick's car and spit his salty semen to the concrete. She planned on taking the ten bucks she'd earned straight to the dope man. Later on in the night, she would cut out the middle man and suck the dope man off for a rock or two.

"Huh?" the addict asked when the twenty landed in front of her. Most of her money came with dicks attached, so she didn't mind the string. She bent down to pick it up but Shyne reeled it in a little. The crack head gave chase just like planned. The cat and mouse game ended at Shyne's feet. "That's mine! I saw it first!"

"Pick it up then," Shyne shrugged.

As soon as the woman bent down, Shyne slipped the garrote over her neck. To Shyne's surprise the woman was more concerned with clutching the bill than the fact that death was creeping into her life. She died with the money clutched tightly in her hand.

****

"I can't believe your father let you spend a night out," Bryonna exclaimed as they prepared pallets in Shyne's room.

"Don't believe it, cuz he didn't. He's drunk as usual, passed out on the sofa. He'll figure it out when he wakes up for his midnight snack and I'm not there," LaDonna sighed.

"Bastard," Shyne growled. She could barely contain her rage until she could carry out the next part of her plan.

"Sorry to hear about your mother," Bryonna tossed out.

"I'm not. My mother died years ago when she hit that first rock. That shell that was left walked by me a many a times and didn't even see me."

"Well," Shyne began, then stopped since she didn't have anything nice to say. The woman died as undignified as she'd lived. "Oh, here."

"Is this it?" LaDonna asked and popped the pill into her mouth and swallowed it dry.

"Girl, here!" Bryonna fussed, passing her a glass of water.

"That's it. We had to buy two since they come in pairs," Shyne explained. "Guess the next one is for those girls who use abortions as birth control. Anyway, I'll get us something else to drink."

Shyne came back with punch laced with sedatives. After presenting the drinks she turned up the music so that they could turn up. The three modest girls danced and giggled to the latest tunes. As planned, the exertion sped up the effects of sedative. Soon, all three girls were blinking and yawning. Two were sleepy, one was faking.

"I'm so sleepy," Shyne said, fanning herself with her hand.

"Me...too," Bryonna managed through a deep yawn. She didn't even try to fight it. She just curled up on her pallet and went to sleep. LaDonna followed suit and stretched out and drifted off.

"Showtime," Shyne cheered in a whisper. She slipped some jeans over her nightclothes and prepared to go out into the night. Although there wasn't much preparation since all she did was load her gun. She eased out of her window and dropped down. Right next to Sun.

"Where you think you going?" Sun demanded, sounding like an older brother. It didn't matter that he was only a few minutes older, he was till her big brother.

"Where I'm not going is to some skeezer's house to smoke and drink my brain cells away and have sex and..."

"Oh," Sun said embarrassed, then he noticed the pistol. "You need me to come?"

"No, I got this," she growled and set off. LaDonna only lived a few blocks over so she left her bike. Sun left with James to go smoke, drink and have sex with some skeezers.

Shyne had borrowed LaDonna's keys so let herself in. Her friend's father was snoring loudly on the sofa just like she'd described. She started to murder him on the spot then changed her mind. Instead, she picked up an empty can from the skeletal remains of a twelve pack and tossed it at him before running down the hall. Once she reached LaDonna's room, she ducked under the covers and waited. She didn't have to wait long.

"Huh?" the drunken man asked in a drunken stupor. He rubbed the place where the can had hit him while looking around the empty room.

Finding nothing, he debated on whether to get another twelve pack or some pussy. Pussy won out, as it always did, and he hoisted himself off the sofa. He used the fact that he wasn't the girl's biological father as justification for raping her. It was a secret that her mother had taken to the morgue with her, that and the twenty-dollar bill that they couldn't pry from her hand. At least if they had trap houses in hell she could cop a rock. The slab next to her was currently empty but she was about to have some company.

"Hey, sugar," the drunken man slurred as he opened the door. Naked except for his socks, he leaned against the doorframe in a sexy pose.

Shyne peered through the dark and was disgusted by the nappy chest hairs over the pot belly over his big thick erection. She blushed at the sight of his penis and gripped the pistol under the girl's girly blanket.

"Let me get a lil taste," he said, approaching seductively. He then climbed on the bed and crawled forward.

"Okay," Shyne giggled as she fired into his smile. She raised the pistol a little more and fired into his bald spot, blowing his brains onto his back. "Damn pervert!"

****

"Good morning, sleepy heads! You girls been snoring like chainsaws!" Shyne said when her friends finally awoke late the next morning.

"I'm still sleepy," Bryonna complained and yawned. Neither girl had ever used drugs so the sedatives had knocked them out for the count.

"Me, too," LaDonna co-signed and rolled over to go back to sleep.

"Y'all get your butts up so we can eat and hit the mall!" Shyne ordered.

Her groggy friends got up to comply with their leader. Knowing it would take a minute, Shyne hopped on her bike and set off. She had one last bird to kill with her last stone.

"Shyne? Hey, sis," Ella greeted when she opened the door and saw her. "What's up?"

"Nothing much. I had an extra, um...xan...molly...ecstasy pill," she said, fumbling through the little drug knowledge she possessed.

"Looks like an oxy!" Ella smiled gratefully and popped the pill in her mouth. Shyne waited for her to swallow before smiling happily. Her work was done once the abortion pill went down the girl's throat.

"Okay, bye-bye," she sang and rode her bike away.

Chapter 11

Christi and Herbert had worked side by side for a little over a year. They spoke casually and stole glances when they could. She was so focused on work and raising the kids that she never dated. The now thirty-year-old virgin was now starting to feel the pressure.

"Let's grab a bite some time," Herbert finally suggested. The tall handsome man was unmarried with no children, which made him a perfect candidate.

Christi didn't go on many dates because of her high standards which included no wives, no girlfriends, no baby mamas, drugs, alcohol, or drama. Those who actually got a first date with her never asked for a second since she wasn't fucking.

"Yes!" she blurted before her mind could say no. It was already in the air so she went with it. "Sure, why not?"

The future couple exchanged phone numbers to set a future date. After a couple of weeks of conversation, it was time to spend time together. Instead of dinner and a movie, she invited him home to meet the family.

****

"How do I look?" Christi asked nervously as she prepared for her date. Who better to ask than Shyne, the in-house diva?

"Turn around," Shyne ordered as she scrutinized the cute dress. "Make sure you ain't showing off no booty!"

"Yeah right," she laughed. Having so much more to offer than tits and ass meant she could dress like a lady and still impress. "I think you're going to like him. I think I like him."

"Don't worry about me. It's Dad and Sun that you need to worry about!"

Killa and his son sat stone-faced in the living room awaiting her date's arrival. Both had other things to do but had put them off to screen the suitor. Sun was meeting up with his friends while Killa had to go kill someone. He'd tracked down one of the pedophiles from the laptop in New Jersey and planned to pay him a visit.

"I got it!" Killa announced when the doorbell began to chime. He marched over and snatched the door open, startling Herbert.

"Hello, I-I-I. um...um," he stuttered and stammered when the big pistol in Killa's hand made him forget why he was there.

"Oh my gosh! Stop it! I'm so sorry," Christi cried, coming to his rescue. She moved Killa aside and escorted him inside. "Don't pay my father any mind. He's..."

"Crazy," Killa interjected.

"And it runs in the family!" Sun added, rising to his full six-foot stance.

"I...um," the man repeated. "Nice to meet you all."

"Nice to meet you, too," Shyne spoke up since the males wouldn't.

The mood lightened immediately once Killa and Sun departed. They sat at the rarely used dining room table for a home cooked meal.

"That was wonderful," Herbert complimented after swallowing the last bite of salad.

"Now for the main course," Christi said proudly. If he loved her mixed salad, he would lose his mind over her baked ziti.

"I'll help you," Shyne announced and went into the kitchen with Christi.

Herbert locked in on her backside as she walked away. She was young, just like he liked them. Herbert stole glances at Shyne every chance he got. Every time she looked up, he looked away. Still, he made her uncomfortable with his creepy looks

"That was great!" Herbert complimented once more. One, because he wanted to be polite and two, because it really was.

"Now for dessert!" Christi cheered happily. If the way to a man's heart was truly through his stomach, then she was halfway there.

"I'll help," Shyne offered again to get away from the man's stares.

"I got it. Keep Herbert company," Christi ordered and floated into the kitchen.

"You're very pretty," Herbert said just above a whisper so that Shyne could her but Christi couldn't.

"I know but if you hurt my sister, I'm going to set you on fire," Shyne replied matter-of-factly.

"I like it hot!" he replied and winked.

Christi returned with her homemade pound cake before Shyne could respond.

"I hope you like it," Christi said as she placed a slice in front of him.

"I do," he said, staring at Shyne's breasts. He couldn't say that he hadn't been warned.

****

Christi was all set on her date so Killa set off on his. The 1-800-Killa website kept him so busy that he hadn't had time to get to the names on the laptop that Shyne had given him. So when someone named J.R in nearby Deer Park posted that he had a six-year-old for sale, Killa couldn't pass it up.

"Two years ago, a friend of mine asked me to say some MC rhymes, So I said this rhyme I'm about to say..." Killa rapped along with the vintage rap song as he rode towards Deer Park. He was still undecided on an exact manner of the impending murder but the raincoat he'd brought along with him meant that whatever the method, it would be brutal. He had his black bag containing all kinds of deadly devices to choose from with him as well.

Killa arrived at the well-appointed home and came to a stop. He used a disposable cell phone to announce his presence before heading up the walkway. The door opened just as he reached it.

"J.R?" Killa asked in confusion.

"You were expecting a man?" the fifty something white woman said with a husky laugh. She was tall, tan and sported a low cut.

"Pedophilia is a male dominated industry," Killa replied. Not that it mattered because she was going to die tonight. He followed her in and took the seat offered. "So...what you got?"

"A beautiful six-year-old. Blonde, blue eyes...," she rattled on in delight. Boys of that age were in high demand, which created a bidding war which Killa won with a twenty thousand dollar bid.

"Is he from the area?" Killa pried, seeking more information. He knew there was a network of these monsters and planned to murder each and every last one of them.

"Daycare! We set up a daycare center using fake names, fake business license, fake everything! Once we get enough children enrolled, we take them, all of them. We rake in millions!"

"Wow," Killa croaked. This was even bigger than he'd imagined. He had heard enough so he went into his bag. Instead of cash, he came out with a pair of brass knuckles on each hand.

"What is that?" J.R asked as Killa stood. She did not like the answer.

"Argh!" Killa grunted as he socked the woman in her jaw so hard it broke on both sides.

"Mm...mm...mm," the woman pleaded as she tried to crawl away. Killa followed and flipped her over with a kick to her mid-section. He sat on top of her, pinning her arms at her sides with his legs.

"Fuckin' monster," he said with a left and then a right. He called her every bitch in the book while he beat her face in. "Un uh, don't die yet!"

The woman continued to let out low moans as Killa searched the house. A large collection of dildos and strap-ons in a bedroom brought a smile to his face. He grabbed the biggest three and went back into the living room.

"Mmm...mmm," J.R moaned as Killa viciously snatched off her clothes. Her tan body was the same complexion as his except for the white triangles at her crotch and tiny titties. She moaned even louder when he rammed a dildo inside of her unused vagina. It was far too thick and long to fit easily inside of her so he gave it a kick. Her shattered mouth opened, letting out a scream that was so high-pitched it couldn't be heard by human ears. However, all the dogs in the area barked like 'what the fuck.'

"I bet," Killa laughed and flipped her onto her flat stomach. Another high-pitched complaint escaped when he shoved the next dildo up her rectum. Another kick sent that one deep into her digestive track. She squirmed in pain as he flipped her back over. "One last one."

"Argh!" J.R gagged from the dildo in her larynx. Killa put his full weight on it and choked the life out of her. Once she was gone, he found the child in a back bedroom. He collected him and a computer on his way out.

"Close your eyes," he said, covering the boy's eyes as he led him pass the disfigured body. He sat him on the steps and used the throw away phone to call 911.

Chapter 12

"Happy birthday to you! Happy birthday to you...," Killa sang as his twins came downstairs on their sixteenth birthday. That put their dear old dad at forty-nine years old. He was still fit and trim enough to pass for thirty-five and make passes at twenty-something year old women.

"Yesss! You know what this means!" Sun said, rubbing his hands together and rushing to the door.

"Keys, please," Miss Shyne demanded with a huge smile. All three had been promised cars for their sixteenth birthday. Asad had received his two weeks prior and had already traded his learner's permit in for a real driver's license.

"Hey!" Sun protested when he didn't see any new cars in the driveway. "Where are our presents?"

"Same as every year," he shrugged nonchalantly.

Every year of their lives had been marked at Chuck E. Cheese. They were a bit old for the mouse but all of them loved the games. Especially Killa, who held the family record at the basketball game.

"Aww, man!" Shyne moaned and stomped her feet as she stormed upstairs. "Christi!"

"She's not here," Killa called out behind his frustrated daughter.

"She probably with that dude," Sun fussed with a slight snarl. His big sister was crazy about Herbert and he didn't like it one bit. Sun was a player himself and it takes one to know one.

"She's still dating that dude?" Killa asked, glancing at his watch as if it counted months instead of hours.

It had been almost three months of nonstop dinners, movies, text, calls and emails between Christi and Herbert. Christi was totally in love but still held tightly to her virginity. It slipped away a little more by the day as he did and said all the right things. Everything that is, except I love you.

"Yeah," his son sighed. He blew his breath once more before heading upstairs to get dressed for Chuck E. Cheese.

****

"Can we go now?" Shyne whined as her father held the door open for her. He made sure to always treat her like a lady so she would never accept anything less.

"We just got here!" Sun answered for his father. He hadn't wanted to come either but now that they were there, he figured he may as well play a few games.

"There's Christi," Killa said pointing towards her and Herbert at their reserved table.

"Happy birthday to you! Hap—"

"Yeah, yeah, yeah, happy birthday," Shyne cut in and cut them off dryly. "When's the cake so we can blow out the candles and blow this joint?"

Killa and Sun raced to the basketball game to compete like they did every year. Meanwhile, Herbert locked in on Shyne's breasts. She felt him staring and crossed her arms as she fell into the booth.

"Let me so order some pizzas," Christi offered. Shyne tried to get up to join her but she waved her off. "Keep Herbert company until I get back."

"You look pretty," Herbert offered with a wide smile.

"How can you tell?" Shyne spat since he was still looking at her chest. "I'm up here!"

Herbert laughed and fed her more compliments until Christi arrived with the food. Sun had an extra wag in his swag as he and his dad returned to the table.

"And the new...champion is..." Sun proclaimed raising his hands in victory.

"Sun Forrest," Killa sighed in a ho-hum manner. He'd never admit it but he'd let the kid win. Everything he did with his kids had a purpose, an ulterior motive to be revealed when the time was right.

"Get away from me!" Shyne growled and took a swipe at the large rat delivering their flaming birthday cake. One side was her favorite, strawberry, while Sun had chocolate.

"Easy, little mama. Make a wish and blow out the candles," Killa ordered.

"I will not," Shyne huffed. "I'm not wishing nothing! You said if we ask, ask Allah and then you."

Sun nodded in agreement to the sound advice he'd given them their whole lives then blew out the candles without making a wish. The whole wishing upon a star and four leaf clovers had never made much sense to them. They knew that they had a Lord and took all their request to Him.

"As salaamu alaykum," Asad greeted as he appeared.

"Wa alaykum as salaam," Shyne smiled and batted her eyes.

Almost everyone got a kick out of her blushing except Herbert, who wanted the girl for himself. Once he conquered Christi, she would be next.

"Time for gifts," Killa announced as the rat returned with two large boxes.

Neither was large enough to have a car inside so Shyne sucked her teeth. Sun would be content with anything so he tore into the one with his name on it. He snatched the lid off the top and stuck his head inside.

"Hey!" he protested, paused and tripled checked the box before he proclaimed, "It's empty!"

"Check the lid," Christi offered knowingly. Sun obeyed and found a car key taped to it. He didn't say another word before running outside to see what it belonged to.

"Mmhm," the diva hummed and opened her box. She politely plucked the key from the lid and stood to leave. "Thank you."

"No, thank you," her father replied in response to the kiss on the cheek. He followed her out to the parking lot where matching SUVs awaited.

Killa made sure that they were identical. They were both black and had the same bells and whistles. That should have prevented the twins from arguing. Should have, but didn't.

"Why she get the one on the right?" Sun pouted. It didn't make much sense but it was all he had.

"You wanna go for a ride, daddy?" Shyne asked as she approached her new truck.

"Sure!" Asad and Killa answered at the same time.

"Um, I'm sure she meant you," Asad offered embarrassed.

"I'm sure. But you kids go on. I'll see you at home," he said.

"Well, I'll see you tonight," Herbert offered, indicating that he was leaving.

"Okay," Christi sang, fluttering her eyes.

Killa shook his head at the display. He wasn't feeling dude either but had to let the grown woman be a grown woman.

Chapter 13

"That was nice," Christi said appreciatively after the last bite of dessert. The wonderful restaurant was draped in darkness except for candles at each table.

"Anything for you. I...love you," Herbert said with a straight face. Mentally, he patted himself on the back for the flawless delivery.

"I-I...love you, too!" she confessed. "Been loving you."

"So, you want to go home now or hang out with me?" he offered.

"With you," she replied quickly. She knew what going home with him entailed and she was ready. Yolo had taught her to save herself for love and marriage, so if he loved her, marriage had to follow.

The couple held hands in his coupe as they rode to his condo. Herbert was the perfect gentleman as he opened doors for her to get out of the car then again to enter the unit.

"This is nice," she gushed while looking around the well-appointed condo. He replied by putting his tongue in her mouth. They stood there kissing and touching. Her panties got so wet so quickly that she was slightly embarrassed. She hoped they didn't squish when she walked.

"Come on," Herbert suggested as he broke off the kiss. He took her by the hand and led her into his bedroom.

He gently laid her on his bed and quickly ducked under her long, flowing skirt. She was relieved when he pulled her soaking wet panties from her body. He ducked back between her legs and licked her to the point of no return.

"Oh my!" Christi marveled at how well he licked and lapped at her lonely vagina. She tried to hold off the mounting orgasm but that only made it worse. She came with a screech that sounded like an Indian war cry. Herbert's mouth filled with her juices as she came. He spat them back between her lips where they were needed.

"Take a deep breath," Herbert advised as he worked his swollen dick head between her outer lips. He then eased by her inner lips and into her brand new vagina. It was only then that he realized that she hadn't been playing hard to get, she was a virgin. Was, because he was now deep inside of her.

Christi felt more pain than pleasure but still felt good about her choice. She her mind drifted to plan their future as he continued to stroke her. Herbert had recently switched jobs but that was okay. She would stay home until the twins went to college then...

"Shit!!!" Herbert grunted and gasped as he came inside of her. It was at the moment that he remembered not putting on a condom. He pulled out and skeeted what was left onto her stomach. Classic case of too little, too late.

"That was nice," she lied while rubbing his back soothingly. The faces he made when he came looked like he was in pain. She damn sure was.

"Mmm," he grunted and rolled off of her. She admired his fine body as he marched into the bathroom. The puddle of seeds he'd spit on her stomach had grown cool so she used a napkin to wipe it away.

"Want me to join you?" she called out when she heard the shower come on.

"Nah," he replied dryly and stepped under the hot water. She went back to planning their future life while he prepared for the rest of his night.

A few minutes later, he dried off and came out of the bathroom. Christi blushed and turned her head away from his swinging dick. It was only visible for the time it took to walk into his walk-in closet. A few minutes later he came out fully dressed.

"I gotta run out, so...I'll, um...call you, um...later," he said.

Christi frowned and blinked as she tried to process the words and their meanings as if he'd spoken Farsi. He'd spoken English, but that meant he was putting her out after making love to her. She may have been new to all of this but she was pretty sure that it wasn't supposed to go like this.

"Hello?" Herbert asked almost sarcastically, waving his hand.

She had been stuck in her thoughts for several minutes without realizing it. "Oh, um, well. Okay, I guess, um...call me, um...tomorrow," she stammered as she looked for her panties. A wave of shame swept over her so she decided to leave them and rush to her comfort zone. She need not worry about the panties since they would find a home in Herbert's growing collection.

Have him tell it, Shyne's were next.

****

"Hello, Herbert! It's me, Christi. I'm not sure if you're getting my messages so, um...well, anyway...um...give me a call," Christi said on his voicemail for the fiftieth time. She shook her head at the pleading she heard in her voice.

Shyne did too when she walked in on the tail end. "Mmhm," Shyne said with a snarl. She had been watching her beloved big sister moping around for weeks now and didn't like it one bit. She'd assumed that Herbert was the cause but Christi wouldn't admit it. The second she did, it would be 'flame on!'

"Mmhm, what? Everything is fine. Are you ready for school?"

"Yes, ma'am. Eleventh grade! Yes, it's almost over!" Shyne cheered.

"Did you decide on a major yet?" Christi asked, relieved at the change of subject. It had been over a month since Herbert had chumped her off and days since her period should have started and didn't.

"Either a doctor or a lawyer. Everyone needs doctors and our brother is definitely going to need a good lawyer one day," she laughed.

Christi laughed too since it felt better than crying.

****

"Sun Forrest, that's a pretty name," the pretty teacher admired as she called roll. The thirty-year-old Miss Rowland put the teen girls in her class to shame. Her round ass filled out her classy skirt like a basketball. When she erased the board, it shook like it was nervous.

"Right here," Sun said, dropping his deep voice a notch and making it sound even deeper. Raising a hand would have sufficed but he stood so that she could get a good look at him.

"You most certainly are there," the teacher said flirtatiously, looking him up and down.

"Damn thot," Ella spat jealously. Sun was kind to the girl but never touched her again. However, that didn't stop her from cock blocking every chance she got. Even though she already had four, she looked at him as her baby daddy that got away.

"Wow," Bryonna laughed at the pot calling the kettle black. "I'm telling Shyne."

"Tell her to give you some Chap Stick too cuz your lips ashy," Sun laughed. He laughed even harder when she poked her bottom lip out trying to look and see if it was.

"Mr. Forrest, I need to have a quick word with you," Miss Rowland announced as the bell rang.

"Bet you do," the arrogant teen said as the class filed out. "How can I help you?"

"By not cumming too quickly," she said, pressing a folded piece of paper into his palm. He knew without looking that it was her number so he put it into his pocket.

"I won't, but you will," he smiled before turning on his heels and leaving. He wasn't the only pretty teen being hit on by a teacher.

****

"Miss Forrest, may I have a word with you?" her chemistry teacher asked as the students filed out. All the fast ass girls flirted with the handsome teacher but Shyne was focused on her favorite subject. Besides, she was so committed to her fiancé that his good looks didn't even register.

"Sure! What's up, Mr. Mallory?" Shyne bounced, all bubbly from the lesson.

"How would you like some extra credit? A referral from me would like good on your college applications," he advised.

"I would love it. I'll do whatever you want!" she gushed naively.

"That's exactly what I wanted to hear. We'll get started next week."

Shyne felt eyes on her from behind and in front as she walked out of the class. Her fat little ass was well concealed under her baggy pants but the teacher stared anyway. She was more concerned with the pair of eyes looking directly at her.

"What?" Shyne demanded as she walked up on Dianne. They weren't friends but didn't have beef either so the staring needed to be explained.

"What did that pervert want?" Dianne demanded. He'd ran the same extra credit game on her last year. She got the referral letter but it had cost her virginity.

"Pervert?" Shyne reeled. She spun around and saw the teacher still staring at her greedily.

"Extra credit? College referral?" Dianne replayed his spiel.

"Yup, yup," she beamed brightly. "He got the right one now!"

****

"This don't make no sense!" Bryonna griped as she and Shyne sat on the gym bleachers.

"None!" Shyne agreed of the sweltering heat. The A/C didn't work, along with a host of other items in the dilapidated school. Bricks crumbled from the façade while lights flickered from the faulty wiring.

"There she go!" Bryonna said as Ella snuck off into the boy's locker room with a boy.

"Baby daddy number five," Shyne teased. She added another when another boy followed them inside. "Correction, make that five and six."

The Ella train ended just before the end of gym class. Luckily for her, too, because she had enough semen inside of her already. She was first in the locker room as well as the first in the shower.

"I'll wait," a girl said, shaking her head at Ella taking a disposable douche with her. Little did she know, the nasty girl had just saved her life. As soon as Ella turned the knob, she was electrocuted by a current running through the water pipes.

"Help her!" Bryonna shouted helplessly as the girl fried right in front of them. Shyne held her back from running inside, knowing she would be electrocuted as well.

"Someone's going to pay for this," Shyne growled.

The girl died a horrible death that she didn't deserve. It was nowhere near as horrible a death as whoever was responsible had coming.

Chapter 14

"Christi, you in there?" Shyne called from the hall doing the 'I gotta pee real bad' dance. Christi didn't answer, so Shyne turned the knob and went in. Christi was still seated on the toilet rocking back and forth in a catatonic state. "What's wrong?"

Christi didn't even register her sister's presence. She just kept rocking, clutching something in her hand. Shyne got no resistance when she pulled it from her hand. It took a few seconds for the pink plus sign to register.

"Oh no," Shyne wailed and began to cry. Christi instantly snapped out of her trance when she heard her sister in distress.

"What's wrong?" she asked, forgetting she was the one with the problem.

"You're pregnant? By that, that...," Shyne said, trying to pick the right word to describe Herbert.

Christi popped an abortion pill and gulped it dry. "Bastard!" Christi tossed in. "Low down, dirty dog. He played me all that time just to get me in bed!"

"Wow!" was all Shyne could come up with. "Well, he can't say that I didn't warn him!"

"Where are you going?" Christi called after her little sister as she marched down the hallway.

"To keep my word!" she said over her shoulder without breaking stride. She'd told him she would set him on fire if he hurt her sister. Shyne was a lot of things but a liar wasn't one of them.

****

"Sun Forrest," Miss Rowland called out as she took roll in the motel room.

"Right here," he replied as he stepped out of his boxers and into his birthday suit.

"You certainly are here," the teacher marveled as she fondled his dick. A smile spread on her face as it grew long and stiff in her hand. Sun smiled when she knelt down and wrapped her lips around it.

The teacher taught him that the second nut takes longer than the first by sucking the first one out of him and swallowing it down. She worked him long enough to make sure he stayed hard before rolling a condom on him. She guided him onto the bed and inside of her comfortable vagina.

"That's it...right...there," she said, guiding him to a perfect stroke. She came over and over again as he pumped away inside of her.

"Can...I...cum...n-n-now?" Sun asked after an hour of slow stroking. In which time, he'd brought the woman to several orgasm of her own and couldn't hold his own much longer. She answered him by squeezing her vagina tightly around his shaft.

"That's it," she cooed, rubbing his back as he filled the condom. "Very good. We'll have to do this again sometime."

"Anytime!" he cheered.

They shared a shower before leaving to go back to their separate lives. He to go smoke and brag to James about the older woman and her to go brag about her latest young conquest to the group of pedophiles she belonged to. The semi-nympho woman loved sex with men, women and young boys. The younger the better.

****

"Is that..." Sun frowned as he passed by a gas station back in Wyandanch. He busted a U-turn and whipped into the station where Shyne was filling up gas cans. "What are you doing?"

"Keeping my word!" Shyne spat as she continued to fill the cans.

"Wait! Tell me what's going on," Sun demanded, pulling he nozzle away from her. Shyne knew when not to defy her brother and this was one of those times.

"He hurt Christi," she began then filled him in on the deception, minus the result.

"Shyne, you can't murder a man cuz he hurt our sister," he stated plainly.

"Why not?" Shyne pouted.

"Because I am!"

Shyne followed her brother home so that they could devise a plan. They found their father in the den watching his favorite show, *The First 48*, and joined him.

"Sup, Pops?" Sun said, taking a seat on the loveseat while his sister kissed Killa's cheek and cuddled up under him. Shyne felt like the crook of his arm was the safest place in the world. Actually, it was because the man would literally murder the whole world before he let any harm come to his family.

"Sup with you two?" he asked in reply. The man was smart enough, as well as intuitive enough, to know that something was amiss. Christi was walking around like a zombie, Sun was home and his baby girl smelled like gas.

"Chillin," Sun said nonchalantly. "What they got going on?"

"This thug about to snitch on himself and all his friends," he said of the teen of the screen.

"Nuh uh! He look like he 'bout dat life," Shyne proclaimed.

"Oh, they all be 'bout dat life until they get in dat room," Killa laughed. "They gone give him a cigarette and he gone sing like Patti LaBelle!"

"Can I have cigarette?" the thug asked the homicide detectives. They gave him one and offered a light. The teen took one long drag and exhaled the whole story.

"See, what fucked them up was their phones. They should have gotten some throwaway phones to lure their enemies out. Police got caller ID, you know," Killa informed. He kissed his daughter's forehead before standing and leaving the room.

"You know what!" Sun snapped as a bright idea came to him. "We need to get a throwaway phone and lure dude where we want him."

"You think!" Shyne said, shaking her head.

****

"Who is this?" Herbert read aloud as a text from a new number appeared on his phone. He smiled at the unknown and typed. He smiled at the reply.

Who do you want it to be?

"Gina," Shyne said out loud as she typed. Sneaking into Christi's phone provided his phone number and address. Sun looked at Google Maps of his home while his sister baited the trap. "How old are you?"

'3-delete-25 and you?' Herbert texted. He'd started too high and dropped off ten years.

'14' Shyne typed back. He took the bait and rattled off a flurry of predator's questions.

'You have a boyfriend? Ever had sex? Seen a penis before?'

"Whoop, there it is!" Shyne announced when the inevitable dick picture popped on the screen. The prudish teen passed the phone to her brother. "He wants to see..."

"I got it!" he exclaimed and went into his phone. He took out the SD card and popped it into the throwaway phone. Shyne just shook her head as her brother swiped through a large collection of vaginas.

"Just nasty!" Shyne blushed. "How do they even do that? She must have three hands! She must have just given birth!"

"Here we go!" Sun said, settling on a picture of a pretty shaved vagina and sent it to Herbert.

'You ever let a man eat it?' Herbert shot back. He texted with one hand and freed his erection with the other. The next pictures were of him stroking himself.

"I know how this ends," Sun laughed and texted him goodbye. The fish was firmly on the hook. All they had to do now was reel it in. In the meanwhile, they had a funeral to attend.

Chapter 15

"I'm not going," Sun suddenly announced. He and Shyne were dressed in all black ready to say goodbye to their fallen classmate.

"What do you mean you're not going?" Shyne whined. "That girl loved you, you know!"

"I know and that's why I'm not going," Sun spat back and marched upstairs. He was thirty-eight hot about the girl's senseless death and wanted to lash out at something or someone. Shyne felt the same way.

"Sup with him?" Killa asked as Sun stormed passed him on the stairs.

"That girl died for nothing. That raggedy ass school falling apart and killing people," Shyne growled. Killa was pleased to see that his children hated injustice and corruption just as much as he did.

"I know, baby girl," he comforted with a hug.

Christi came down wearing a black dress and the same blank expression she'd worn daily since being tricked out of her goodies. Too bad that life doesn't have rewind or do-overs and that you can't unfuck someone.

"As salaamu alaykum," Asad greeted as he walked in the front door.

The family, minus Sun, greeted him back as they set out to the graveyard.

****

"Wow," Christi exclaimed at the large turnout for the girl's funeral. Wyandanch was essentially a small town and they showed up to send the girl off.

Ella's mother stood with her sons while holding her baby girl in her arms. Her eyes were beet red from tears of sorrow and the blunt of good weed she'd smoked. A flamboyant man giving a speech had everyone's attention; especially Killa's.

"Who is that?" Killa hissed. The gator boots, silk suit and diamonds he wore just irked him. He reminded him of that nasty ass Reverend Cash from down in Atlanta.

"That's Mr. Edwards, our principal," Shyne answered. "Supa Fly."

"I didn't know being a principal paid that well," Killa said, tallying up the man's jewels. He had on a ten-thousand-dollar watch, twenty-thousand-dollar chain, two-thousand-dollar boots...

"It doesn't," Christi replied.

The man had sparked Killa's interest but he wasn't the only one who had. A beautiful woman stared at Killa with a bewildered smirk.

"And who is that? In the little black dress?" Killa asked, joining the woman in a staring contest. She only won because he dropped his eyes down to her protruding breasts that were threatening to pop a button and break free.

"Miss Rowland, the algebra teacher," Shyne spat as if her name had a bitter taste to it. She knew that the grown woman was having sex with students, including her brother. To her, there was no difference between a male pedophile and a female pedophile and she was right.

"I like algebra," Killa mumbled and rejoined the staring contest. He didn't hear another word as he envisioned all the positions he would put the pretty woman in. Pretty much the same positions his son was putting her in.

"Daddy! Daddy!" Shyne called, trying to get her father's attention back from the slut.

"What, baby?" he asked without even looking at her.

"It's over. The girl is in the ground. It's time to go," she advised.

"Okay, one sec," he replied as the woman made her way towards him.

"Miss Rowland. I teach at the high school," she introduced with a pretty manicured hand.

"Killa, I um..." Killa caught himself before he said something nasty. Shyne shook her head at her father as he flirted. Killa and the teacher exchanged numbers with tacit plans to exchange bodily fluids the first chance they got.

"Um, Dad, there's something you should know about Miss Rowland," Shyne said as they drove away from the cemetery.

"Yes, Shyne," he sighed in a condescending manner. "What is it, baby girl?"

"Nothing, don't worry about it," she said, deciding to let him find out the hard way.

****

"Sup with that fish?" Shyne asked when she caught up with her brother.

"Ready to be reeled in," he replied deviously then laid out his devious plan. The black hearted Casanova had made a date with his death.

Later than night, Sun drove his vehicle to the park. He let his sister out to wait and went to his hiding spot. Killa used the GPS unit hidden in his son's car to follow his children to the future crime scene. Once there, he posted up in the woods with a sniper's rifle to lend a hand if needed.

"Ugh!" Shyne fussed as her panties rode up in her butt. She never could understand how the slutty girls could stand it. The itty bitty shorts were uncomfortable on so many levels. Sun had the gun but she carried her trusty butterfly knife in her bra.

"You look stank," Sun snickered from the darkness of his hiding spot. The plan was for him to jump out and shoot Herbert as soon as he arrived.

At least, that was the plan.

"I know you ain't calling nobody stank!" Shyne laughed. "Speaking of stank, where's your girlfriend Miss Rowland?"

"She had to grade tests tonight," he replied with the excuse she'd given him. His voice dropped off to a whisper when he saw a car pull up. "He's here,"

"He's staying here, too," Shyne growled to herself. Shooting would be too quick and easy and she wanted the man to suffer the same way Christi suffering. With all the thots, hoes and whores, he had to go after good girls. No, he was going to die a very violent death.

Herbert parked and scanned the area. He saw Shyne waving in the dark distance and smile. His dick got harder with every step he took towards who he thought was a fourteen-year-old virgin. He was in for a shock when he reached the pavilion.

"Shyne? You're not fourteen!" Herbert proclaimed, sounding disappointed.

"No, but I am a virgin," Shyne replied and restored his smile. It didn't last long as Sun rustled the bushes as he joined them. Herbert turned to investigate and Shyne attacked.

"Aaah!" Shyne shrieked as she jumped on the man's back. She then wrapped her legs around his torso and an arm around his neck. That freed her other hand to work her knife.

"This girl!" both father and son sighed as Shyne stabbed the man in his face and neck. Herbert took off running, bucking and spinning trying to dislodge the girl.

"Yee-ha!" Shyne yelled like a cowgirl on a wild bronco. She wore a huge smile as she hung on with one hand and kept stabbing him with the other.

Herbert skeeted blood with each heartbeat as he ran to his car. Killa peered through his scope to get a clear shot, but couldn't. Neither could Sun as he ran behind them. The man reached his door handle just as death finally wore him down. He sank slowly to the ground as he panted his last few breaths.

"What are you doing?" Sun demanded as his sister struggled to pull him inside his car. She had to get in first herself to drag him inside.

"Keeping my word," she replied between grunts before turning her attention back to the dead man. "Told...you...I...was...going to set...you on fire...if you...hurt...my sister!"

Shyne used her knife to hack a piece of his shirt off, took it around to the gas tank and shoved it inside. After lighting it, she slowly back peddled to a safe distance while Sun got his truck.

"Come on!" Sun demanded as he pulled up and flung the passenger door open.

"Wait," Shyne pleaded as the fire slowly started. A minute later, a satisfying explosion made her smile. She wasn't the only one smiling.

"Just like yo mama," Killa chuckled and went to his car. He was late for his date.

****

"Miss Rowland," Killa greeted as the teacher let him in. She wore a see-through gown so he could see exactly what he was getting into.

"Call me Alicia," she smiled as he ran his eyes over her body.

"Alicia Rowland. Why does that name sound familiar to me?" he asked with a perplexed frown. His dick was far too hard for clear thought so he shook the question off.

The woman shrugged off his question and walked away. There was no need for an invite because he followed. She dropped the gown as she went up the stairs, giving her guest a clear shot of her bald box. When she reached the room, she crawled to the middle of her bed and put her ass in the air.

"Damn!" Killa marveled as he watched the plump vagina swell and glisten as he stripped. He wore nothing but a condom and his socks as he climbed on behind her. The woman arched her back, making her pussy pucker for penetration.

"Damn it, man," she moaned as her vagina guest slid in to the bottom of the well. He backed out slowly and plunged back to the bottom. She approved of the stroke by cumming and coating his dick with creamy goodness.

"Turn over," Killa directed as he pulled out. He'd long stroked her to several orgasms and now it was his turn.

"Hurry up! Put it back in!' she pleaded and flipped onto her back. She lifted her legs onto his shoulders so he could get every bit of her. The teacher grimaced and grabbed handfuls of her sheets as Killa pounded on her cervix.

"Grrr...Grrr!" Killa growled when he reached the point of no return.

"Aaah," she said, offering her tonsils for target practice. Killa scrambled to get the condom off to take her up on her offer. He then shoved his dick into her mouth until she gagged and let go.

"Shit!" he cursed as he came down her throat. He stayed in her mouth until he went limp and pulled out. "I gotta go."

"Aww!" Alicia pouted. The freak could have gone ten more rounds but Killa was done. He wouldn't allow her to think it was anything more than it was.

"Yeah, I know but I gotta..." he said getting dressed.

"Okay, just lock the door behind you," she sighed. As soon as he hit the stairs, she pulled a vibrator from the nightstand and fucked herself again.

Killa stepped out of the house and came face to face with his son.

Chapter 16

"Dad?" Sun blinked, trying to make sense of why his father was here. He figured it out when the sweet scent of the woman whose house it was wafted into his nose. "What are you doing here?"

"I'm sure it's not what it looks like," Killa assured him.

"It looks like you just had sex with my teacher!" Sun shot back, sounding wounded.

"Oh well, I guess it is what it looks like then," his father chuckled. "Oh, wait, did you have like a crush on her or something?"

"CRUSH? More like I been crushing that since the semester started. I can't believe you!" Sun whined and stomped back to his truck.

"Don't be mad at me!" Killa called after him. "If you wanna be mad at someone, be mad at her for all of your brothers and sisters she just swallowed!"

"Is everything okay?" Miss Rowland opened the door and asked. Killa turned and stared at her breasts as if they'd spoken. "Care for seconds?"

"Technically, it would be sixths, but yes," he said and stepped back inside. Her bedroom was way too far to walk to so they fucked in the foyer. Since he was way up inside of her, decided to pry for a little information. "Sup with Supa Fly? The principal?"

"Mmm, Mr. Edwards? Mmm," she replied as she slowly rode and wiggled on his dick. "With his...mmm...crooked...mmm...ass."

"Crooked?" he pried and gripped her ass. "How so?"

That good dick in her eased the way for her to tell all she knew. She knew plenty since the principal was skimming money left and right. Most notably, he'd created a fake contracting company and gave it the contract to fix the school's faulty electrical wiring.

"So, he's to blame for that girl dying," he surmised.

"Yeah, I guess he is. Somebody should report his ass!" she growled. The growling increased with her strokes until she came once again.

Killa got another nut of his own then got dressed to leave. He planned on reporting the principal the first chance he got. Only he wasn't telling the cops, he was telling Shyne.

****

"Sup, yo," Killa greeted his son when they met in the kitchen the next morning. Sun just nodded his 'sup' and continued shoveling cereal into his mouth. "Word, it's like that?"

"We cool," Sun said dryly and kept right on eating. "We ain't gon' fall out a bi- um."

"Bitch. I didn't know you was hitting that but she did. She's a bitch and what did your mother teach you about bitches?" Pops demanded.

"My mother said bitches ain't shit so find a lady," Sun said loud and proud. Many people remember Yolo as a lovely little lunatic but to Sun and Shyne, she was just mommy.

"What language!" Christi said, sticking her fingers in her ears as she came into the kitchen. She was all smiles and laughs after hearing about Herbert's demise on the news. His death had breathed new life into the woman.

"My bad, sis," Sun said then turned back to his father. "You can keep that thing we was talkin' 'bout."

"What thing?" Shyne's nosey ass asked as she breezed into the kitchen.

"Nothing," her father told her and then went back him, "Nah, we can share."

"Can we go to the range?" Shyne asked in her daddy's little girl voice. It had always worked before and of course, it worked again today.

"Sure. You guys get ready," he said and went upstairs to get ready himself. A half an hour later, he, Sun, and Asad were still waiting for the little diva to get dressed. She finally came down a half an hour later.

****

The family shot a variety of guns while at the range. The shooting turned competitive when Sun called his father out. He was not ready and got spanked pretty badly.

"Cool!" Asad cheered when Killa shot a smiley face into the face on the target sheet.

"We need one of these for the house. You know, for protection," Shyne said when it came time to return the rented guns to the counter.

"Yeah, better make it two," Sun nodded in agreement with her.

"Protection, huh?" Killa pretended to ponder. He even scratched his chin as if he were really tossing the idea around. "Nah, but I will get you both one of those."

"A stun gun! What we supposed to do with a stun gun?" Shyne protested.

"Um, stun people,' Killa laughed. "These things aren't toys! If someone happened to be in a puddle or...a shower...they would get electrocuted!"

"Electrocuted?" Shyne asked.

Her father filled them in on the principal's embezzlement that had ultimately cost Ella her life. Shyne immediately started planning to murder him and knew just the way to get even doing it. Killa smiled inwardly as he watched his daughter drift in a murderous day-dream.

A smile spread across her pretty face when she came out of it. "Yeah, get it!"

"Get two!" Sun said, wanting in on whatever his sister was plotting. The twins drew near as their father made the purchase.

"Daddy be giving us all kinds of ideas and don't even know it," Shyne whispered.

"He's so green," Sun snickered. "If he only knew." But the truth was, if Sun and Shyne only knew.

"Dead man walking," Shyne growling as Principal Supa Fly walked by in a new pair of gator boots with gold tips. "Gold is an excellent conductor, you know."

"I do. Let's get him," Sun suggested eagerly. He didn't wait for her reply to put their plan into motion. He pulled the fire alarm while Shyne slipped into a janitor's closet.

"Flame on!" Shyne giggled as she flicked the lighter. The rags soaked in cleaning supplies quickly went up in flames.

"Evacuate in an orderly fashion!" Mr. Edwards instructed as he clapped his hands and pointed. Being the principal meant he had to be the last one out of the school in a fire drill–sort of like the captain of a ship.

The smoke indicated this was no drill so the students and the staff quickly exited the building. The only ones left when the overhead sprinklers cut on were a man in gator boots and a set of twins in rubber rain boots.

"Hey! You two! What are you waiting on?" the principal barked. It could go down in history as the bark before the spark.

"You," Shyne said, flashing a smile as he stepped into a puddle. She raised the stun gun and fired the two barbs into his chest.

Meanwhile, Sun had stepped out and also fired his own stun gun into his back. Eye contact between the twins triggered them to pull the triggers that sent a thousand volts of current into the body they were attached to.

Mr. Edwards seized in place as the electricity made him do the Harlem Shake. His Jheri Curl sizzled and caught fire from the oils and activator in it. He stopped doing his dance when his black heart stopped.

Sun and Shyne quickly disconnected the electric wires from the dead man. They shared a high-five and then retreated from the building like everyone else.

****

"Oh...my...goodness!" Christi exclaimed at the morbid news reported the principal's death. She was shocked but everyone else in the room wore satisfied smirks on their faces.

"That's the same thing that happened to Ella," Sun said almost defiantly.

"Karma is a bitch," Killa tossed out even though he didn't believe in it.

"So is payback," Shyne mumbled under a smile, confirming to their father that they were indeed behind it. Killing bad guys had actually become the family's business.

Once the nightly news came to a depressing end, the family prepared to end their day. For Christi and Shyne, it meant baths and bed. However, for Sun and Killa, it meant tits and ass.

"Call it in the air," Killa called out and flipped a coin.

"Heads!" Sun called, hoping for some head before getting some tail. His father caught the quarter and flipped it onto the back of his fee hand.

"She's all yours," he conceded when it landed on heads. He went on up to bed while his son went off to bed his teacher.

Chapter 17

"I can't believe we're seniors! Can you believe we're seniors?" Bryonna screamed when Shyne pulled into the school parking lot. It was the first day of their last year at the rundown school. The new principal hadn't fixed shit, either. There were still floods, power outages and a host of other problems.

"I can't believe Sun is," Shyne replied as her brother sped by with a cheerleader in his truck.

"I can't believe he likes that girl!" Bryonna spat, sounding more than a little jealous. It was a silly statement since the girl was gorgeous, but Shyne knew that her friend had a hopeless crush on her brother.

"Well, she's definitely his type," Shyne huffed when the girl's head disappeared from view. "Nasty!"

"I can't believe he doesn't have ten kids by now," Bryonna sighed. She knew that she couldn't compete with his other girls because she wasn't doing what they did.

"Chile, please! I don't want ten baby mamas I gotta burn up...I mean, beat up," his sister said, correcting herself. She hit her remote locks and led the way into the school.

The girls hit the office to get their twelfth grade schedules.

"Aww, shoot!" Bryonna griped when she saw her class assignments. "I got that creepy Mr. Mallory for first period. I don't wanna have to deal with that man right after breakfast.

"Just ignore him. That's what I did. And don't fall for the extra credit bull he's promoting," Shyne warned. She'd spared the man last year by switching classes but needed it to graduate herself.

"If he tries that crap with me, I'll make sure that he never teaches again," Bryonna vowed out loud.

Meanwhile, Shyne made an inward vow to herself. If he tried that crap with either of them, she would make sure he never breathed again.

****

"Very nice. Good job," Mr. Mallory exclaimed, looking down Bryonna's shirt instead of at her project.

"It's not in my bra!" she spat and pulled away. It was bad enough that she was struggling in the class but his creepy come-ons made things even worse.

"No, I suppose it's not. You know, I can give you an extra credit assignment that will give you an A+ for the semester," he offered. All the teachers gossiped enough for him to know that she needed a scholarship to attend college. He planned to use that as bait to get her home.

Mr. Mallory graded Bryonna's test, quizzes and assignments on a curve. A curve that led directly to his home. By mid-terms, the girl was desperate enough to listen to what he had to say. The decision weighed heavily on her mind.

"What?" Shyne demanded across the lunch room table. She made sure to bark at Bryonna so she wouldn't try to hold out.

"If I fail chemistry, I'm not going to get a scholarship. If I don't get a scholarship, I can't go to college. If I don't go to college, I'll be stuck here in Wyandanch. If I'm stuck here in Wyandanch, I'll end up a baby mama on WIC, welfare and weed!"

"Um..." Shyne replied and took a minute to process it all. She flipped the words around, added and then subtracted them until she came up with an answer. "Mr. Mallory! What did he say?"

"All he wants is for me to dance. Not even naked. Just twerking. The same stuff we be doing at your house," she whined.

"Yeah, but we be in my room with the door closed!" Shyne shot back. "You know what? Don't even worry about that class or Mr. Mallory's nasty ass!"

"That's easy for you to say. You got a scholarship, your mom left you money and your dad got your back! What I got? Who gone look out for me?" she yelled and broke down.

"Sun and Shyne, that's who!"

****

"Sup, yo?" Sun asked when he caught up with his sister at home. He sensed her distress the moment he walked in. Shyne had her murder mami face on, so he knew something was up.

"Somebody messing with my girl!" she spat hotly.

"Who?" Sun asked, ready to whoop whoever's name came out of her mouth.

"With all the thots and hoochies in school, why he wanna go after the good girls? Why he wanna corrupt chicks with morals? I mean, who does that?" Shyne said, stringing her brother along.

"WHO?" Sun demanded as he followed the string. Her anger slowly transferred to her brother. "WHO?"

"Mr. Mallory, the chemistry teacher. Gon' tell her that if she twerk for him, he'll give her an A and a letter of referral. He tried me with the same spiel last year," she said, sealing the deal.

The last statement was literally the final nail in his coffin. She knew it, too, and stifled a smile.

****

"We need a plan," Shyne suggested as she trailed the teacher.

"Yeah, plan," Sun muttered from the passenger's seat. They'd followed Mr. Mallory from the school out to the nearby town of Deer Park. "Plans are good."

The teacher pulled into the driveway of a well-kept ranch style house. He was totally oblivious to the danger in his rearview mirror.

Shyne crept slowly by to memorize the address and check the surroundings. However, her impatient brother had other plans.

"Let me out!" Sun demanded. He popped the passenger's door and began getting out while the car was still moving, so Shyne had no choice but to hit the brakes.

"I come from a land down under, you better run, better take cover," Mr. Mallory continued singing along to the song playing on the radio as he walked towards his front door. He was so into singing the song that he didn't even hear Sun rushing towards him with the .40 cal in his hand.

"You shoulda ran and took cover," Sun growled before firing a round into his back. The first shot ripped through his spine and dropped him. The next shot to the back of his head severed his soul from his body. The last twelve shots were just to reiterate that men are the protectors and maintainers of women.

"Nice plan!" Shyne quipped when her brother jumped back into the passenger's seat. She glanced in every direction as they made their escape.

****

The new chemistry teacher took a purely professional interest in Bryonna. She kept her afterschool to tutor her so she would improve. She broke it down in a manner that she could relate to and got her grades up. By the end of the school year, she had scholarships and acceptance letters from schools all over the country. She wasn't the only one.

"I got UCLA, too," Asad announced as the four close friends compared college acceptance letters like they were baseball cards.

"Bet you ain't got Spellman!" Shyne teased, showing a letter from the all-girls college in Atlanta.

"Bet you don't have Morehouse!" he shot back, holding up a letter from there.

"Well, I'm going to USC," Sun stated plainly. He had received a scholarship to play ball from a bunch of schools but he would definitely be the starting shooting guard there.

"I'm going to Atlanta College," Shyne declared, casting the den into silence. Asad flipped through his letters and found his acceptance letter from there, too. He had a full scholarship from Autism Speaks, as well as another for academics since he was a math wiz.

"Atlanta College it is, then!" Bryonna cheered, holding up her letter from there as well.

All eyes turned to Sun to see what he was going to do. Atlanta College already had a star guard which meant he would be riding the bench.

"Guess I'll see you guys on Christmas break then, cuz I'm going out west," he insisted.

There was a brief pause as if the world had stopped then the room erupted in laughter. No one believed for a second that he would leave his sister, not even him.

"Now that that's settled, we gotta get ready for prom," Shyne cheered.

Asad just shook his head at his unpleasant duty. He didn't like music much and he hated large crowds, but Shyne got what Shyne wanted, so he would be her escort.

"Do you have a date?" Sun asked Bryonna.

"No!" she shouted hopefully then held her breath so she could say yes when he asked. The boys in school had no use for a good girl, so no one had invited her. She had planned to go with Shyne and Asad.

"Figures!" he cracked and cracked up. He left the room still laughing at the mean joke.

Bryonna stuck out her bottom lip and middle finger at his back.

"He's such a jerk!" Shyne fumed. "Makes me sick!"

Chapter 18

"What?" Asad finally asked when Killa kept staring at him. He was quite dapper in his tux with his long hair freshly braided and pulled into a ponytail.

"I'm just saying," he said like he'd said something.

"Here she comes!" Bryonna announced as she came down the stairs ahead of Shyne. She was cute, too, in a long, flowing gown that matched the band in her hair.

"Drama queen," Christi laughed as she filmed her descent. Shyne waved her hand like the queen of Zumunda as she came down.

Killa nodded in approval at the tasteful prom dress that both covered and concealed his teenaged daughter. Her natural hair was in two thick braids along her head like an Indian squaw. Both Asad and Killa noticed her glossy lips. They looked at each other and then shrugged a tacit 'no comment.'

"All that gloss better still be there when she come home," Killa whispered to Asad, who just giggled. "Seriously, I mean it."

"Oh Lawd!" Bryonna sighed when the music began. If they thought Shyne was a diva in need of a grand entrance, Sun was even worse.

Sun had thrown on the old school Big Daddy Kane classic 'Smooth Operator' as theme music to make his entrance. He danced his way down the stairs while Christi filmed it on her phone. The party was broken up when the limo honked its horn to announce its arrival.

"You guys still need to pick up your date," Christi reminded Sun.

"No, I don't. She's already here," he replied. All faces frowned in confusion until he extended his hand to Bryonna.

"Aww!" Christi and Shyne sang as she accepted it and stood.

"I still ain't fucking," she warned under her breath.

"So, I am," Sun laughed and escorted her outside. Killa and Christi snapped last minute pictures as the couples set off for the prom.

****

"This is unacceptable!" Asad huffed when they stepped inside the sweltering gym. The school districts of nearby Deer Park and Dix Hills had both rented ballrooms for their students' proms, but not Wyandanch. They held their prom in the school's rundown gym. It wouldn't have been so bad had the A/C been working.

"I'm sorry," one of the teachers working as a chaperone said as she wiped sweat from her own brow. "They need to tear this school down and start over!"

"They need to burn it down!" Bryonna pouted. Thankfully, she and Shyne didn't have perms to sweat out.

"Don't give Left Eye any ideas!" Sun laughed.

"Anyway..." Shyne sighed like she wasn't a firebug. "Let's dance."

"O-kay," Asad huffed. He didn't really want to but he was a man of his word. He'd told Shyne she could have whatever she wanted when they were seven years old and he'd meant it.

"Come on," Sun ordered Bryonna, who looked at him like he was crazy. He caught on and softened his tone and asked, "Dance?"

"Okay, but no grinding," she giggled.

The two couples danced close enough that Shyne and Bryonna could talk about and laugh at their ratchet classmates.

"Girl, what is she wearing?" Shyne asked, pointing with a nod at a girl twerking in a tiny dress.

"Nothing!" Bryonna shot back.

The dress had ridden up over the girl's ass and one of her titties had popped out from all her movements.

A loud creaking sound was heard over the thunderous sound system. Everyone looked around except for Asad who looked up. He shoved his fiancé and friends out of harm's way just as a large beam dropped from the ceiling.

"Oowww!" the girl in the Betty Rubble dress screamed when the steel beam fell on her leg and trapped her ankle.

The party was officially over after the near death accident. The fire department had to use the Jaws of Life to free the girl's leg. She was taken to the hospital while police evacuated the condemned building.

The foursome had the limo for a few more hours so they went to Lindenhurst Diner for a late night snack. They ate, talked and cracked jokes until it was time to go. Sun picked up the tab for everyone's meals. Bryonna lived on another block so she would be the first to get dropped off.

"Walk her to her door!" Shyne insisted and pushed her brother from the limo. He caught up with Bryonna and walked her the rest of the way to her door.

"I had a great time! Thank you," she said sincerely.

"Me, too. You're not as nerdy as you look," he chuckled playfully.

The moment turned awkward as they reached her door. Bryonna closed her eyes, puckered her lips and leaned in for a kiss. That's exactly how Sun left her.

"I hate you!" Shyne declared when he reached the car. She said it loudly to be heard over Asad's laughter.

Asad was next to be dropped off. He shared a fist bump with Sun and Shyne before getting out. The siblings watched until he disappeared into his house before going home.

"You guys have fun?" Christi beamed when the twins came in. Killa had his ear to a police scanner so he already knew about the accident.

"We had a blast," Shyne declared with a wide smile to prove it.

"Yeah, it was fun," Sun cosigned. "Welp, I'm about to turn in."

"Me too," Shyne, Killa and Christi all said.

Only Christi actually went to bed, though.

Killa snuck off to bone the freaky teacher, Sun changed out of his tux and set out to bone one of his many girls, and Shyne slipped out, too, with a bone to pick with the school district.

The clerk at the gas station couldn't tell that Shyne was filling gas cans instead of her truck. She really appreciated Obama when the four five-gallon cans came to just under forty bucks. It was money well spent in her eyes.

"The roof, the roof, the roof is on fire!" Shyne sang and giggled as she drove back to the high school. "We don't need no water..."

The locks on the school's doors didn't work either so Shyne had no problem getting in. It took a whole hour and several trips to evenly distribute the gas around the school. She made sure to cut the gas line in the kitchen and to the furnace before leaving. A trail of gas out to the parking lot gave her enough distance to safely start the fire.

Shyne smiled and flashed back over the last four years of her life at the school. It hadn't been all bad but it would soon to be all over. She gave a final salute and lit the fuse. The fire traced the line of gas from the parking lot back into the school. An orange glow filled all the windows as the fire quickly spread. Once it hit the gas tank, the school exploded.

"W-w-what w-was t-t-that?" Miss Rowland asked behind her. Killa was delivering perfectly balanced back shots when the explosion shook the house.

"My daughter," he said, shaking his head. "Just like her mama!"

Chapter 19

"Um, you know they not going to wait on you two!" Christi yelled upstairs to the slowpoke twins. Graduation started in an hour and they were still not ready.

Asad had aced his testing for homeschooling and would be allowed to walk across the stage with his graduating class. Only a depressing twenty-five percent of the freshman who began with Sun and Shyne had made it to see graduation day. Some were in the eleventh grade. Some were in prison while others were dead. Some were at work while others were in the streets. There was even one in labor with her third child.

"Daddy not even here yet!" Shyne whined as she came down in a pair of capris and a t-shirt. Her cap and gown were neatly pressed and hanging in plastic.

"He is now," Christi replied as Killa pulled into the driveway.

A minute later, he came in with a surprise.

"Hey, Daddy," Shyne smiled. Her face suddenly changed when she saw the danger. She tried to run but was too late and she was snatched off her feet.

"My great granddaughter!" Grandma Deidra squealed as she pulled Shyne into a deadly embrace.

Everything bean to go black as she struggled to break free. Luckily, Sun came down and saved her life. It almost cost him his own life, though.

"Oh sh-," Sun exclaimed when his ninety-year-old grandmother moved with the speed of a python and coiled her arms around him and squeezed. "Argh!"

"We better get a move on it," Killa suggested to spare his son. "I have one more surprise later."

"Okay," Shyne huffed, still trying to catch her breath. She and Asad rode with Sun while Killa chauffeured Grandma and Christi.

Since Wyandanch no longer had a school, the graduation was held at the nearby Farmington College. The two hundred or so students who worked hard and stayed down proudly walked across the stage. It was mainly good girls who had been focused on their futures. Sun still stared at booties under gowns.

"Sup, Pops?" Xavier greeted as he and Rico arrived. Technically, he wasn't his father but he was Pops, so he'd agreed to come see the twins get their diplomas. It was an effort, however, to have peace and get along.

"Sup, guys?" he greeted back with a hug. "Oh, your sister is up!"

"Shyne Forrest," the new principal called out when he reached her name. The family erupted in applause as she crossed the stage to graduate.

"Thank you," Shyne smiled and curtsied as she accepted her well-earned prize. She turned to her family and frowned. Shyne squinted to make sure that she saw who she thought she saw and then attacked.

"Shit!" Sun fussed as his sister dove off the stage and went after Rico and Xavier. Asad shook his head and jumped in. It was Sun and Shyne, so he had no choice but to join in the fray.

"Are you serious right now?" Christi asked incredulously as the children brawled. "Do something!"

"I am!" Killa replied and stood up and began recording the action. "World Star!"

Christi and Grandma helped the security guards separate the combatants. Once it was over, the graduation resumed so everyone else could get their diplomas as well. Xavier and Rico went back to the city while Asad and the twins got set for their last summer in Wyandanch. Once they left, they had no intentions on ever coming back.

****

Sun decided to spend his last Wyandanch summer getting as much Wyandanch booty as possible. Like the say goes, 'mo' booty, mo' problems' and the summer was filled with plenty of each. A coalition of boyfriends and baby daddies was formed to combat their common foe; Sun Forrest.

"A-yo, fuck that nigga Sun! And I don't care nothing about no karate, either!" Markel lied. He did give a fuck about the karate. That's why he beat his girlfriend up instead of confronting Sun. The nosey nigga had gone scrolling through her phone gallery and found her taking selfies with a dick in her mouth. A few pictures later, he'd seen Sun smiling down at the camera.

"Word is bond! Fuck some karate! I bust my gun!" Grip bragged.

He was a well-known shooter around town. Grip would shoot dudes in the leg or the ass if he had beef with them. What he didn't know was that Sun bust his gun, too. The difference was that no one lived to talk about it.

"We need to jump his ass," Cap whined. He'd seen Sun's car at his baby mama's house one time too many.

"Yeah, yeah, yeah!" Ronnie, Ricky and Mike all agreed. All of them had lost vagina time with their girlfriends and baby mamas due to the handsome playboy.

With that, a plan was hatched to catch Sun alone and jump him. Jumping off a building would have probably been an easier and safer idea. Markel's girlfriend Shay was known to have the best head in Suffolk County so her throat would be used as bait. She was slightly chubby, kind of cute and had a set of lips that could cool a whole pot of soup with one blow. She also had a nice, thick tongue that made her talk with a lisp, which made her sound like Cool G Rap, but it was an added bonus when it came to blow jobs.

'WYD?' Markel texted Sun from Shay's phone. Sun swerved in his truck from seeing the girl's lips pop up on his screen. Markel had beat her up and taken her phone before forcing her into her own bedroom while he and his goons laid in wait for their victim.

'Thinkin' 'bout you' Sun texted back. It wasn't a lie since she was suddenly on his mind. He was supposed to be headed home to go to the movies with Asad, Shyne and Bryonna but they were about to get stood up. First things first and good head came first.

'Come see me.' Markel texted back with his girl's favorite saying.

'Only if you gonna suck my dick! Now ask can you suck it.' Sun demanded even though he had already changed directions and was headed to her house.

"Man! What kinda fuck shit he be on?" Markel fussed.

"What?" Mike asked seeing his frustration. "Get him over here!"

"Yeah, yeah," he griped and typed, *'Can I suck your dick?'*

'Yup, I'm outside.' Sun texted back as he shut off his vehicle.

"Yo, he here! Hide!" Markel urged in a whisper. His friend dipped behind a sofa, into a closet and in the hall.

"A-yo!" Sun called out as he knocked on the door. The doorbell no longer worked from all the traffic to her tongue.

"Come in!" Markel called out in falsetto.

His voice was so high that his friends frowned, wondering if he did it on a regular. There was a brief pause as Sun got ready, then he came in.

"Look what I got for you," Sun called out into the dark as he stepped inside and closed the door behind himself. His smile disappeared the moment the lights came on. Then again, what's to smile about in a room full of angry thugs and you have your dick in your hand? "Sup?"

"What it look like, my nigga?" Markel shouted and stepped forward.

Grip was the first to attack and later he'd be the first to die. He tried to sneak Sun from behind but Sun heard him. He dipped under the wild blows and launched an uppercut that lifted him off his feet. The other five quickly moved in and jumped on him. Sun would have beat them all in a one-on-one, but the six on one was too much. He realized his best choice was to drop low and cover up. Trying to fight exposed him too much so he got into a ball to deflect the blows. Luckily for him, the blunt and menthol smoking goons didn't have much wind.

"Now keep your dick out my girl!" Cap demanded as he delivered the final kick. The last lick meant he would be the last one to die. Sun peeped through his defenses to make sure he got a good look at everyone who participated in the beat down. He added Shay to the list as well, that is, until she came out from the back and explained herself.

"I'm so sorry!" Shay whined sounding like a *Fat Albert* kid from a swollen lip.

"You set me up!" Sun growled as he checked to make sure he still had all of his pearly whites. They were all there but his lip was split and he had lumps on his head.

"No, I didn't! He beat me up, too! Oh, he'll fight a girl but gotta get his friends to fight a guy!" Shay said in her own defense. "I don't even go with him! He claims me and won't leave me alone!"

Sun saw the tears and believed her. Her face was pretty beat up too so she wasn't lying about that part. She took the ice pack from her own face and put it on Sun's

"Help me up," he grunted then stood on his own instead. He felt a little wobbly and leaned on the wall. Shay helped him to the sofa.

"Want some head?" Shay offered since it was all she had to offer.

"Head!" Sun reeled. That's what had gotten him in this trouble so he definitely didn't want any. "Nah, I'm about to leave."

Sun rose to his feet once more. He steadied himself and then walked to the door. He pulled it open only to see his ransacked vehicle in flames. He let out a deep sigh and went back to the sofa.

"Call me a cab," he said since Shyne and Asad were out. "I guess I'll take that head after all."

Chapter 20

"Seven dollars," the driver announced as he pulled to a stop in front of Sun's house. Sun shook his head at his father's car in the driveway and leaned to the side to pullout his wallet.

"Shit!" Sun fussed when he realized his wallet was gone. He felt the bare spot where his necklace once lived and it was gone, too. "A-yo, hit the horn."

The driver complied and blasted his horn a few times. An irritated Killa came out and frowned. He saw his son in the backseat and made his way over. The frown deepened when he saw the lumps and bruises on his child.

"Keep it," Killa said, handing the driver a twenty and pulled the door handle to collect his child.

"Shukran! Jazakallah khair!" the happy driver cheered.

"He said..." Sun began to translate until his father replied to the man in Arabic.

"Afwan, wa anta," he said, welcoming the man and returning his prayer. Jaza'a was one of his favorite Arabic words. It means recompense, just reward for either good or bad. The driver's statement of Jazakallah khair meant 'may God repay you with good.' Killa was going to repay whoever had harmed his son with extreme bad. The worst.

"Thanks, Pops," Sun offered once they got settled into the den. He grabbed the remote and turned it to sports as if there was nothing else to say.

"Well?" Killa demanded waiting on the rest of the story. "You come home without your truck and your ass kicked and all you got is 'thanks, Pops'?"

"Street stuff, Pops. You wouldn't understand," Sun explained.

"Try me," his father replied. He was amused how green his kids thought he was. They would find out in due time.

"Bunch of haters mad cuz I fu-...um...bagged their birds. Tricked me over a girl's house and jumped me. Set my whip on fire, snatched my chain."

"And what are you going to do about it? Call the police?" he dared.

Sun opened his mouth to tell the truth: that he was going to hunt them down one by one and murder them, but Shyne came in the door.

"Daddy, I'm home!" she called out to stop the clock. High school grad or not, that ass still had to be in by curfew. She followed her ears to the den where her family was.

"Mmhm," Killa said, looking her up and down as she came over to hug him.

"Yeah, right. You ain't got to worry about me," she declared and turned to her brother. "Now, him... What happened to you? Who did it?"

Killa saw a flash of Yolo in her eyes and smiled. His daughter was a lunatic just like her mother and he was cool with it. He saw his son glance at him, letting his sister know that he didn't want to speak in front of their father. He took the hint and rose from his seat.

"I'll let you guys talk," Killa said and left the room. He walked out of sight and leaned in to eavesdrop, with his nosey ass.

"It was Market, Cap, Grip, Ronnie, Ricky, and Mike," Sun announced.

"You got jumped by New Edition?" Shyne demanded with her hand on her hip. She vaguely recalled some of the names from school but couldn't place faces with them.

"They gon' be the Late Edition when I catch them," Sun growled. He planned to put them all in the past tense. Shyne twisted her lips and shook her head while he told the whole story.

"So that chick Shay set you up?" Shyne asked, ready to go kill her.

"Nah, I really don't think," he replied, hoping his vision wasn't blurred by that good head. "She was pretty beat up herself."

"It's gonna be a crazy summer!" the crazy little girl said with a crazy smile on her face.

Her crazy father smiled, too, as he listened to his children plot revenge.

****

"It's here! It's here!" Sun shouted when he pulled the insurance check from the mailbox. He jumped up, clicked his heels together and ran inside the house. Dad, it's here!"

"'Bout time," Shyne griped. She was tired of driving her brother around town. It wasn't so much the errands as it was the fact that he wanted to stop and talk to every girl he saw.

"A'ight, a'ight. Get ready so we can go to the Bronx," Killa said and got ready himself. His Dominican partner had a used car lot on Jerome Avenue that specialized in tag jobs. Stolen cars would get new VIN numbers from wrecked cars. The check from his truck would go a long way at the lot.

"I need something sexy," Sun said more himself than his father as they rode. "A vagina finder."

"A cat mobile?" Killa chuckled but his son didn't. "Get it? Cat mobile like *Batman*...you wack!"

"Eww, that's wack!" Sun grimaced at a beat-up looking hooker on Jerome Ave. "Who would pay for that!"

"You would be surprised! They get a lot more than they pay for, too. A hundred percent of the prostitutes on this street test positive for HIV," Killa explained. "These women and teens are the real walking dead. Men get a quick nut for a couple of bucks and then go home to infect their wives and girlfriends."

"That's fucked up," Sun blurted before he could stop himself. The curse was already out so he left it alone. His father nodded in agreement because it was fucked up.

"Here we go," Killa said, breaking the silence when they approached his friend's lot.

"That's it right there!" Sun shouted. He jumped out the car before it even stopped. He stumbled, rolled, then popped up, and ran over to a jet black Benz.

"Sup, Killa?" the owner greeted his old friend with a warm smile.

"Sup with you, Manny?" he replied with a pound and hug. "I see my son found something he likes! How much?"

"For ju, papi...give me twenty," Manny said, giving him half off his price which was half off what it was worth.

"Bet!" Killa cheered at the discount. He spotted a dark sedan with tint that looked like a cop car. It would be perfect to do dirt in. "What you want for that one? And I need it with all the bells and whistles. Oh, and a couple cherry bombs."

"Give me two for the car and the bells and whistles are on me."

"Can we go for a test drive?" Sun asked as he came over. Manny called for the keys in rapid fire Spanish, sending a man in motion. He returned a minute later and handed them over.

"This is smooth," Killa admired as they floated up the Avenue.

"Hells yeah! I gotta have it!" the teen pleaded.

"No doubt but, uh...it's flashy. This is why you got your ass kicked. Niggas spot your whip at all the girls' houses. You need a spare car. Something low-key, dark with tints," the father taught the son. Killa could see the wheels turning in his son's mind. When they returned to the lot, Sun spotted a car that fit the description.

"So, we gonna write it up?" Manny asked when they returned.

"Um, yeah," Sun replied and turned to his father. "Why don't you run and grab us some lunch while I handle this?"

"Okay," Killa said, trying not to laugh as his son attempted to dismiss him so he could talk business with Manny. He even pulled a few dollars out to pay for lunch.

"How much you asking for the blue sedan? I got a check for twenty-five," Sun explained.

"I'll let you get it for two, so you got three bands coming back," Manny replied.

"Check it, I don't want my pops to know about this, though. He kinda green, you know," Sun leaned in and whispered.

"Your father, green? Wow!" Manny exclaimed. He, of course, knew better. "Um, okay. I'll leave it on the block for you then."

"Bet. Me and my peeps will come scoop it tonight," he said. They concluded the deal just before Killa returned with Mickey D's.

"All set?" he asked, turning blue from sucking one of those thick ass vanilla shakes.

"All set," Manny and Sun replied.

The two shook hands and departed to Long Island. Sun opened up his new whip on the expressway and left his father in the dust.

Chapter 21

"And you came up with that on your own?" Shyne asked dubiously as she drove Sun to pick up his other car. She squinted at him to make sure he was really him. "Maybe you're not retarded."

"Nope!" Sun said proudly. His father had planted the seed about the spare car so well that he really thought that it was his own idea. He pulled their shared gun from under the seat and cocked it when he saw the familiar 'Welcome to The Bronx' sign.

"Damn shame!" Shyne fussed as a young prostitute tried to flag them down while another one chased after a car like a dog.

"You don't know the half!" Sun exclaimed. He filled her in on what his father had told him about the HIV rate on the hoe stroll.

"And these broads know they got that shit and passing it around," Shyne growled. She was disgusted at first. Now she was plain mad.

"Yup. Oh, there it go!" Sun declared when he saw his vehicle parked on the curb.

"Check it out good before we pull off!" Shyne called to her brother. He complied by kicking the tires as he walked around to the popped the trunk.

"Oh shit!" Sun shouted, wide-eyed with excitement and shut it back.

"Don't tell me you bought a car with a body in the trunk," she said, getting out to see what he was so excited about. He was too stunned to speak so she took the keys and opened the trunk for herself.

"Yoooooo!" she said, bouncing happily. Inside the trunk were two Mac 10 machine pistols. Both had an extra clip and long silencers. Even better were the two grenades. "One for me, one for you!"

"Nuh uh! You can get a Mac but the grenades are mine!" Sun protested, with his stingy ass.

"I'm telling daddy!" Shyne whined.

"And just how does that go?" Sun quipped. "Daddy, Sun won't give me a grenade. And he gon' say, Sun, share with your sister. Give her a grenade!"

"Yup!" she said over his laughter. She was right, too, because that's exactly what he would have said. Those were the cherry bombs to go along with the bells and whistles he'd asked for.

"Here, girl!" Sun said begrudgingly and gave up one of each. Shyne smiled happily and took her new toys to her truck. She couldn't wait to try them out.

Sun drove behind his sister up Jerome Avenue to the expressway. He saw her brake lights come on as they passed the congregation of hookers. She drove half a block more then pulled over.

"Shyne, Shyne, Shyne," Sun said, shaking his head when it dawned on him what she was up to. It wasn't a bad idea so he pulled over to join her. She approached the hookers from one way while he came from the other.

"Looking for a good time?" an elderly hooker asked Shyne as she approached. She and the other whores cracked up at the joke but come to find out, the joke was on them.

For the record, it's never a good idea to tease a deranged teen holding a Mac-10 behind her back.

"As a matter of fact, I am!" Shyne smile as she whipped the gun out. The fully automatic gun spit so silently that they didn't know what hit them.

It looked like a hooker dance off as the .45 ACP rounds made them do The Harlem Shake, Wop and Running Man. They turned to run but Sun opened fire from the other direction. Both guns clicked empty and both teens reloaded.

The sound of stiletto heels click-clacked on the sidewalk as the Macs clapped at their backs. By the time they emptied their next clip, thirty prostitutes lay dead or dying. They wouldn't be spreading anymore diseases.

"Now that's what I call a public service announcement!" Shyne cheered.

****

"Sometimes the best way to get some get back is to wait, rock 'em to sleep so that they think the beef is over," Sun replied when Shyne wanted to know why the dudes who'd jumped him were still breathing. He'd gotten the advice from his dad but left that part out.

"Um...okay," Shyne agreed since it made perfect sense. She squinted once again and sure enough, it was her brother. Maybe he wasn't really retarded after all. Maybe it came and went like a rash, or maybe...

"What?" Sun protested as Shyne stared at him trying to figure him out.

"Nothing. Just handle your business before I do," she warned.

"Leave them alone! I got this. Chill and watch me work!"

And work he did. A month had passed since the attack before he went on the attack himself. Grip was the first to swing so he was going to be the first to die. Having no car forced the broke man to walk everywhere he went. That made him an easy target. Sun knew the dude had a reputation as a shooter and would probably be armed, so he came hard when he came.

Suga, Grip's baby mama, had the body of a super model but the IQ of a doorknob. Her self-esteem wasn't much higher because she was jet black and all media outlets said you had to be light skinned to be pretty. Every music video show mixed women she looked nothing like. Every urban book she read had half Black, half Asian chicks with long, sinuous hair. As a result, she fucked for compliments. Sun told her she had a nice ass in gym class and she thanked him by giving him some ass in gym class.

Suga lived on the opposite side of town, which meant Grip had a long walk to her place. Not a good idea when you're being stalked by a killer. He was exposed in so many places that Sun had a hard time picking an ambush spot. A wooden area near his own home was finally selected. Sun parked his sedan and waited. He didn't have to wait long.

"Lookie, lookie," Sun cheered when he saw his victim ditty bopping right towards him. The car was so plain that most people walked by without a look. He slowly lowered the tinted window as Grip approached. "Yo, Grip!"

"Huh?" Grip asked, turning to Sun. His mind didn't have time to register the gun before it spat at him.

'Pst' the silent gun whispered a round into his forehead. Sun pressed the gas, leaving the dead man backpedaling. He tripped on death and fell in the middle of the street.

Sun parked the hooptie in its spot a few blocks from home. He made the short walk home and went inside.

"One down," he told Shyne and gave a wink like their father didn't understand. Killa just shook his head like, 'if these kids only knew.'

"Who you calling?" Shyne frowned, hoping he wasn't crazy enough to brag to anyone else. Asad was their closest friend and he had no idea what they did.

"Suga. I'm going to comfort her during her time of grief," he laughed. Actually, it was more of a relief than it was a grief for the girl.

"Use a condom!" Killa and Shyne both called after him as he left the room.

****

Ronnie, Ricky and Mike weren't New Edition but they were cousins so they were almost always together. That meant that Sun could kill three birds with one stone, or grenade. He stalked them for days looking for the perfect time to strike. It came late one Saturday night.

Ronnie had three bucks to go with Ricky's two dollars and Mike had stolen a ten from his mother's purse. The grand total of fifteen bucks meant they could buy a dime bag of reefer, cigars and two forty ounces of malt liquor. They didn't want to share with their girls or baby mamas so they headed to the park. Once they got good and high, they would go lay-up with their women.

"Yo, I'ma go fuck the shit outta baby mama once we finish," Ronnie declared between tokes of weed.

"Word!" Ricky co-signed. That's pretty much all he ever said anyway.

"Meka on the rag and bitch still don't suck no dick, so I'ma go home watch some porn and jack this dick," Mike announced.

They were chopping it up real good when they heard a metallic knock on the glass window. The three men strained to see through the smoke and darkness. Ronnie rolled a window down and couldn't believe his eyes.

"Is that Sun? Let's whoop his ass again!" he suggested and hopped out. His cousins followed him and came face to face with a Mac-10.

"My nigga, Sun! Yo, you smokin', yo?" Mike cheered as if they were the best of friends. A Mac-10 with a silencer on it will make a nigga want to be friends.

"Don't mind if I do," Sun said, accepting the blunt. He gave it a sniff to make sure that it wasn't laced with anything. He made sure that it didn't spark, sizzle or give off any strange smells before he took a pull.

"Yo, you know we really wasn't with that shit," Ricky offered. It didn't make much sense since they were involved in the beat down but when someone has a Mac-10, you gotta say something.

"Eh," Sun shrugged. "Which one was your girl? I got confused."

"Meka, my baby mama!" Mike said defiantly.

"You had a baby by that thot?! You should do like I do and bust her in her mouth. Here, let me show you," Sun laughed and showed the video of the girl who didn't give head giving him head. Mike wanted to swing on Sun but, he had that Mac.

Sun went on having Show and Tell about all their girlfriends. He'd had sex with all of them since the attack and made sure to get it on tape. The boys had no choice but to sit there and take it since Sun had a Mac. They were relieved when the blunts were finished so the show would be over.

"Yo, you need a ride anywhere?" Ronnie offered since Sun had approached on foot. The dark sedan was parked nearby but was almost invisible in the darkness.

"Nah, I'm not tryna go where you guys are headed," he replied. They missed the veiled threat and piled back into the car. Ronnie got behind the wheel, Ricky slid into the passenger's seat while Mike hopped in the back and Sun jumped on top of the hood.

"Get off of there!" Ricky shouted as Sun raised the gun. The fully automatic weapon opened up huge holes in the windshield as he sprayed the front seats. Ronnie and Ricky were killed almost instantly but Mike survived by ducking behind the seat.

"Good news or bad news?" Sun called into the survivor. As his gun clicked empty.

"Uh, good news?" Mike asked hopefully.

"Well, the good news is I'm out of bullets. This..." Sun paused to pull the grenade from his pockets. "This is the bad news."

Sun pulled the pin with his teeth like he saw in the movies and tossed it inside. However, he didn't take cover like they did in the movies. Instead, he stood there and watched. The device exploded, lifting Sun off the hood and flying into the air.

"Amateur," Killa said, shaking his head from his hiding spot. The grenade shredded Mike and crew up. Sun, on the other hand, ended up with a broken arm after landing with a thud.

"Shit!" Sun cursed as his broken arm dangled uselessly. He winced in pain as he hobbled to his car. It was a struggle to drive with one hand but he managed to make it back to his parking spot. He looked like the Hunchback of Wyandanch as he hobbled home.

"What's wrong with you?" Shyne fussed when he came in in distress. Shyne looked and sounded just like their mother in that instant.

"I broke my arm!" Sun said, trying to lift it. "Can you fix it?"

"I'm pretty sure I can," Shyne guessed. "I may have to operate, though."

"Okay. Let's go in the kitchen," Sun said. He was in so much pain that he would've agreed to almost anything. Luckily for him, their father came in when he did. Shyne wanted to be a doctor one day but wasn't one today.

"Come on, we're going to the hospital," Killa said in a tone that left no room for argument or protest.

Shyne helped her brother outside and into the back of the car. She got up front and rode shotgun next to her daddy. A few hours later they returned home with Sun's arm in a cast.

Chapter 22

Summer was drawing to a close and Sun was still in a cast. It drove Shyne crazy to see Markel still walking around in her brother's chain. The thought of him getting away with it was something she just couldn't live with. Sun was ready to let it go but not Shyne.

Shyne was once cool with Markel's girlfriend Shay. She was actually a part of the good girl clique until she went bad. Once a good girl goes bad, she's gone for good, or until she's ready to redeem herself.

The chubby girl was taunted and teased about her big lips and lisp in elementary and middle school. Once she got to high school, everything changed. She started drinking, smoking and traded Shyne and company for a crew of ratchet girls. Next thing you know, she was fucking and sucking with the best of them. Markel claimed her as his own and whooped her ass anytime she broke up with him. Come to find out, she was a victim, too. More like hostage, really.

Shyne decide to drive over to Shay's house with the intention of beating her up. She wasn't going to kill her but she did plan to blacken her eyes and swell up her big lips even more. That was the plan until Shay opened her door.

"Bit- Dayum! What happened to you?" Shyne asked, going from one hundred to zero instantly. Both eyes were black and her top lip had black stitches in it.

"Come on in," the wounded girl sighed and walked inside. Shyne watched her as she plopped down on the sofa before she entered and closed the door behind herself.

"I know you came to beat me up but before you do, you should know that I didn't set your brother up. Markel beat my ass and took my phone."

"Who did this to you?" Shyne asked compassionately. She may have been a little lunatic but she hated injustice.

"Markel, who else? I believe it turns him on to jump on me. He always be wanting to fuck as soon as he's finished," she answered.

Shay was so relieved to be able to vent, she broke down in tears. Shyne took her in her arms and rocked her until she got it all out. They sat there for hours talking like they used to. Shyne encouraged her to follow her dream of joining the Air Force and Shay had unknowingly given up all kinds of valuable information on Markel. Shyne knew enough about his life to end it.

****

"Shyne who?" Markel frowned as he took the call on his cell phone.

"How many girls name Shyne do you know?" Shyne spat back. She stopped short of calling him a stupid name to match the stupid question.

"Only Shyne I know is a pretty little bitch that ain't fucking!"

"Damn, I call to get with you and you insult me!" Shyne said, feeling genuinely insulted. Good thing she was going to kill him anyway. "I'm feeling you, though."

"Me! Why?" he asked. At least he knew he wasn't that handsome, didn't make any money or have anything else of benefit.

"Cuz Shay said you got a big dick," Shyne said truthfully. She could hear him smiling through the phone. It wasn't true but he sure enjoyed hearing it.

"Get you some then!" Markel said, sticking his chest out proudly.

"Come get me!" Shyne replied. She gave him directions to her house even though she wasn't home. She was parked down the block so she couldn't miss the show.

"I'm taking your car, Ma!" Markel announced and took her keys from her purse.

She shook her head at her sorry ass son as he departed. The wannabe rapper didn't put gas in her car or contribute anything towards the household. All he did was promise that one day he was going to blow up. Little did he know, today was that day.

"Raggedy ass car!" Markel griped when he saw a puddle of fluid under the aged vehicle. He noticed the smell of gas, too, and hoped that there was enough in the tank to make it to his destination. He didn't, however, notice the thin wire attached to the door as he snatched it open. It pulled the pin form the grenade Shyne had stuffed into the headrest.

"Wait for it," Shyne giggled and counted down along with the timer on the grenade. "Four, three, two...Dayum!"

The blast lifted the vehicle off the ground when the device exploded. Markel's brain matter flew like confetti from the window. The gas caught and saved his mother from the expenses of having to have him cremated. Shyne watched the fire until she heard sirens approaching and went home.

****

"Man! That's fucked up! I told you I had them!" Sun whined when Shyne came home.

"I don't know what you're talking 'bout, Willis," Shyne said, holding her chin up defiantly. She managed to contain a goofy smile to the corner of her mouth.

"Yeah, you do! You smell like gas! I know you did it," he whined.

"Did what?" their nosey father asked as he came into the room.

"Nothing, Pops. Some street stuff, you wouldn't understand," Sun said, frustrated.

"Say word," Killa laughed and walked back out. He went just far enough to hear yet not be seen. He gleaned all he needed to know about the remaining victim and headed out. "I'ma show y'all how it's really done."

****

Sun and Shyne were still arguing days later about who would get to kill Cap. Dumb ass hadn't put it together that all his friends had been brutally murdered, so he continued about his daily routine, making himself an easy target. He was the last to strike Sun and in turn would be the last to die.

"Just gonna stand on the corner and sling rocks while my children plot your death," Killa said as he watched the dealer deal. He'd borrowed one of the officer's personal cars from the police substation for the night. It would have a little something extra in it when he returned it.

"Got dubs, dimes, nicks and three-dollar hits!" Cap announced to all the cars that pulled into the parking lot. A car stopped and he stuck the top half of his body into the window to make a sale. The car pulled off and the next one pulled up.

"Got dubs, dimes..."

"Nicks and tres. Yeah, yeah, yeah," Killa cut in, cutting off his sales pitch. "Give me five dubs."

"That's, uh...um...five, carry the one...seventy-five dollars," Cap said and stuck his head in. He was so focused on the hundred-dollar bill that he didn't notice Killa slip the metal ring over his head until it was already on. "What's this?"

"The DC 2000," Killa said and hit the switch. His head did a little flip before landing upright in the passenger seat. It stared up at Killa so he continued explaining as he drove away. "My baby mama actually came up with it but when I saw it, I had to have it."

The headless body sank down and sat on the curb. A few junkies actually tried to buy crack from it and got mad when it wouldn't reply. Killa returned the borrowed car to the substation parking lot and walked back to his own car. To his surprise, his kids were still arguing about who would get to kill the last man.

"Tails!" Shyne yelled as Sun flipped the coin. They watched anxiously as it tumbled in the air.

"Heads," Killa laughed at his inside joke as he went upstairs to bed.

Chapter 23

Summer went out with a bang because Sun set out to bang all the Wyandanch girls he'd probably never see again in life. Both he and Shyne knew that they wouldn't be coming back there to live. They had no idea where their final destination would be, but they knew that it wouldn't be Wyandanch.

Killa sprang to have the twins and Asad's cars shipped to Atlanta, along with all of their personal affects. Bryonna joined the family for the flight down south. Neither she nor Asad would be returning either.

"You really don't have to come, you know, Pops. I got them from here," Sun said for the tenth time.

"Mmhm," Killa chuckled. It translated to 'yeah right, picture me sending my eighteen-year-old children off to a strange city all by themselves.' Atlanta is a very dangerous city but so were his kids. He was afraid for the city of Atlanta, not his children.

"I just hope you didn't get us a raggedy apartment!" Shyne fussed, scrunching her face up in disgust.

"Mmhm," Killa repeated. This time, he meant 'picture me putting my children in some bullshit.' It can't be pictured because he wouldn't do it.

Once they reached Atlanta, the extended family loaded into a rental. They reached downtown and Killa pulled into an underground parking lot that shut Shyne up. The diva had no complaints as they rode the elevator up to the tenth floor. Killa paused when they stepped out to decide which way to go.

"You forgot where it is?" Shyne said, shaking her head.

"Be easy, you know he's getting old," Sun whispered as if their father was hard of hearing. He shook his head and turned left.

"After you," Killa announced as he opened the door and stepped aside so the four freshmen could enter.

"I got the master!" Shyne shouted as she took off in search of it. Bryonna shrugged an 'oh well.' She was too grateful to not have to live in the dorms to worry which room she got. The sofa in the living room would have been fine with her.

"Hey! There's only three bedrooms," Sun said, scratching his head. He had no intentions on sharing a room with anyone.

"Asad and I can take the master and you guys can get a room to yourselves," Shyne said as if that settled it.

"Un, no," Killa laughed. "The master is for Christi. She's driving down tomorrow. You girls pick a room. Boys, follow me."

Killa walked Sun and Asad back down the hallway where another three-bedroom unit awaited. The smart father had purchased the two units knowing that they would double in value by the time his kids graduated college.

"I get the master!" Sun yelled when they entered a unit identical to the ones the girls had. Killa had made sure to furnish them exactly the same to cut out the bickering.

"The master bedroom is for the master; me!" Killa laughed and went to his room.

Asad and Sun flipped a coin for the other rooms and put their bags away.

****

Basketball season hadn't begun yet but Sun was already on pace to break the freshman record for fucking. The Benz turned out to be a real cat mobile. He did well in his classes but spent all of his free time on a panty raids.

Asad settled into his classes and quickly excelled in them. Not only was he excelling in school but a major game manufacturer had taken an interest in one of his games, so his free time was spent working the bugs out. Once he did, it would be worth millions.

Bryonna and Shyne had flip-flopped majors. Now Shyne was going into pre-law while Bryonna had decided on pre-med. They were both on their way to being honor roll students but they still twerked to music in the privacy of Shyne's room.

Meanwhile, Killa did what killers do and scanned his 1-800-Killa site for people in need of killing. He also scanned the names of the pedophiles listed on the laptop he'd gotten from Shyne. He had future plans for them. That is, until he found one he just couldn't resist.

****

A sexual predator was in a group chat bragging about how he used his karate classes to lure young girls into grownup positions. The thirty-year-old handsome black man could have easily attracted women his own age but he preferred them young, eleven or twelve to be exact. And that was why Killa preferred him dead.

"Good morning, Daddy," Shyne sang as she let her father into the condo. He made it a point to eat breakfast with the girls as often as he could.

"Morning, sweetheart, Bryonna and Christi," he greeted as he walked in to the smell of cinnamon rolls and turkey bacon. He took a seat at the table and began to pout.

"What's wrong, Daddy?" Shyne said, ready to kill whoever had upset her father. Killa knew it, too, and that's why he was putting on.

"Just was reading about this karate instructor who has been molesting little girls. He beat a couple of cases in Texas then moved here to Atlanta and is at it again," Killa sighed helplessly.

"Sho-nuff?" she asked as the wheels began to turn in her head. "Where is he?"

"He has a school on Memorial Drive," he replied and produced a flyer. On it was his handsome face along with the address to his school. Killa just happened to leave it on the table when he left.

****

"Ki-ki-ki," Shyne practiced giggling in her mirror. She pulled her hair into pigtails and tied ribbons to them in an attempt to look like a twelve-year-old. At eighteen, she wasn't far off anyway and could have easily passed for a preteen.

Most twelve year olds didn't drive so she parked a few blocks away from the strip mall where the karate studio was located. She walked over and arrived a few minutes before closing.

"Well, hello there...?" the instructor smiled when Shyne entered.

"Shyne," Shyne said truthfully as she discreetly scanned for security cameras.

"Well, Miss Shyne, we're about to close so have your mom bring you back tomorrow."

"My mom is at work. I came by myself," Shyne replied shyly.

"W-w-wh-what about y-y-your d-dad?" he asked, getting an erection in his karate pants.

"Never met him," she shrugged. "Can you teach me karate?"

"Um...yeah...I...um," he stammered as he locked the front door. Shyne was as happy as he was since now they wouldn't be disturbed. "Sure, come on into the studio. The first thing we need to learn is wrestling."

"Not blocks?" Shyne asked since she knew better. She realized she'd let the cat out of the bag and tried to fix it. "Cuz the girls at school be hitting me."

"Um...okay. I'll show you a few blocks, and then wrestling," he agreed. He couldn't wait to wrestle the girl down and rape her. However, it was not to be. "Use your arm to block."

The teacher threw a soft jab that Shyne knocked away before firing an uppercut to his mouth that split his lips. "Like that?"

"Bi- Uh," the man frowned as he looked at his own blood on his fingers. He threw a harder punch and got hit even harder in return. "Who...are...you?"

"I told you, Shyne," she growled and got into a fighting stance.

"Oh, okay. I see what this is," he nodded, bowed and then got into a stance of his own and prepared for battle.

Shyne quickly found out that dude didn't know a lick of karate. It was all just a ruse to put him in a position to molest kids. He should've picked being a clown or something else because Shyne commenced to beat the man to death. Every time he tried to throw a punch, Shyne slipped it and hit him with a flurry of punches and kicks of her own. Once she'd softened him up, it was time to break him down, literally.

"Is that all you got?" Shyne snickered.

He frowned at the insult and threw a wild blow just as she'd expected. She grabbed his arm and locked it in her own. She dropped to the ground and rolled until his arm was twisted behind his back.

"Owweee! You're going to...," the man yelled but was interrupted by the loud snap of his arm breaking. "Yeeoooweee!"

"Yeah, yeah, I know," she said dryly and twisted the other one. It snapped too, giving him two broken arms. Next she put him in a leg hold and snapped his knee.

"Help! Help!" he yelled and tried to crawl to the front door. Shyne followed behind looking for something to beat him with. A pair of nun-chucks on the wall caught her eye and brought a smile to her face.

"Ha-yah!" Shyne said in her Brue Lee voice as she swung the device. The crack of his arms was nothing compared to the sound his skull made when she hit him. She hit him again and again until his head caved in. She stood over him and gave his dead body a bow. It was now time to go.

Chapter 24

By sophomore year, both Shyne and Bryonna had gotten internships in their chosen career fields. Shyne had taken a position in a law firm to get some practical experience while Bryonna worked in the school's clinic and got in everybody's business.

"Um...gonorrhea. No, wait, um, chlamydia," she bet the other intern when a pretty girl came in.

"Nah, she look like she got Zika!" the girl laughed. They giggled but quickly straightened up when she arrived at the desk. "Can I help you?"

"I doubt it," the girl frowned as if the two were beneath her. "April Hill, I'm here for my follow-up."

"The doctor is expecting you. Second room on the right," Bryonna said cheerfully despite the snub.

"I do hair, you know," April advised, frowning at her natural hairstyle before sashaying to the back.

"Um...that's not hair, that's plastic," her friend whispered and cracked up again.

"Miss Hill, have a seat," the doctor said stoically.

"Hurry up because I have a date tonight," she huffed. The woman was too occupied with herself in the mirror to see the grim look on the doctor's face. It was just as grim as the news he had.

"Okay, well, the results of the test you took are in. I'm sorry to inform you, but you are HIV positive."

"Okay, thank you," April said as she stood and began to walk away.

He'd seen plenty of strange reactions to this diagnosis but none as strange as this.

"Mmhm," she shrugged like it was no big deal. "I gotta get ready for my date. A big spender, he may get him some."

"Some what? Miss Hill, it's a crime to have unprotected sexual contact with anyone once you've been informed that you're HIV positive! Also, by state law, we require the names and numbers of anyone you've had sexual contact with in the last six months."

"You and me both," April laughed. "Don't nobody do names and numbers. We be too busy turning up! I can give you their IG names."

"Wow!" Bryonna said when the doctor relayed the strange encounter with the strange girl. She'd seen the girl around campus, always with a different guy on her arm. It wouldn't be long before she saw her with someone she knew personally.

****

"Excuse me, Miss!" Sun called out to the fat ass that passed by. He caught up with her and spun her around to introduce himself.

"Do I know you?" the girl asked, feigning indignation at him grabbing her arm.

"Not yet but you 'bout to," the smooth player shot back then flashed that killer smile that he'd inherited from his father. "I'm Sun."

"April," she said, smiling up at the handsome young man. She was pretty sure she hadn't fucked him yet but she planned to the first chance she got. They exchanged social media contacts with plans to hook up. As soon as Sun turned, he came face to face with Bryonna.

"What you doing with her?" Bryonna fussed.

"Nothing yet, but as soon as I scoop her up, I'ma do all kinda stuff to her. Course, you wouldn't know nothing but that," Sun teased. Ironically, he liked that Bryonna was a good girl and he had no use for a good girl. Not yet, anyway.

"Do you know who she is?" she demanded, putting a hand on her hip.

"Um..." he paused to check her username. "Wet-Wet69!"

"Sun! Leave that chick alone! She nasty! She dirty! She..."

"Just like I like 'em," Sun chuckled and walked off.

Bryonna was at a loss since she didn't want to lose her job by violating their policy on patient confidentiality. She couldn't let the girl infect him, either. She still had plans for Mr. Sun Forrest.

"Who was that?" Sun's partner Milton asked eagerly when he returned from macking. "She's hot!"

"Who? Bryonna?" Sun laughed. He squinted at Bryonna walking away, trying to see the heat. Both she and Shyne both still wore loose fitting clothes to conceal their body parts and modesty.

"Yeah, she got a man?"

"Huh? No...um...but... That's my sister's partner, so..." Sun stammered as he struggled to explain what he couldn't understand.

"I'ma holla at her. Those the ones I like, good girls!" Milton exclaimed happily and tried to high five Sun.

"Nah, yo," he said, leaving him hanging. "Leave her alone!"

****

"Wow!" Shyne said, wide-eyed with shock when Bryonna confided April's HIV status. She risked her job and career but Sun and Shyne were like family.

"I know, right. I told Sun to stay away from her, but he still trying to mess with her!"

"No, I mean wow, I can't believe that you would go through all of that! I know you like my brother but DANG!" she laughed. Bryonna shut up her chuckle with a copy of her positive status. "Wow!"

"Wow is right! And I don't like your brother!" Bryonna shot back.

There was a brief moment of silence as the lie bounced around the room. Shyne twisted her lips like 'yeah right,' forcing her to come clean.

"Okay, so I do, but that ain't got nothing to do with this. Besides, that cute guy Milton asked me out."

"He did? You going? Where y'all going?" Shyne wanted to know.

"Yes, I might, and I don't know," she replied, answering all her questions at once. Then she drifted inside of her head to answer for herself. Should she keep waiting on Sun to grow up or explore other options? She was so deep in thought that she didn't notice Shyne get up and leave the apartment.

Shyne marched down the hall and banged on the men's condo door. She was too impatient to wait, so she tried the knob and it turned, so she barged in. Asad was doing push-ups in the living room and popped up to his feet when she entered.

"As salaamu alaykum," he greeted with a wide smile. Shyne didn't see the smile due to the muscles contorting the white wife beater.

"Um..." Shyne frowned, trying to remember the reply to the greeting. "Um..."

"Sup, Shyne?" Sun greeted as he came out and broke the spell.

"I need to talk to you!" she demanded, poking him in his chest until he backed into his room.

"What now?" he sighed, realizing it could be anything. Shyne had replaced their mother and he seemed to stay in trouble.

"I heard you messing with that nasty girl April!"

"Bryonna told you, huh? Look, I like Bryonna and if I was mature, she'd be perfect! But I'm not so I'ma hit all the hoochies and hoodrats I can get my paws on."

"And you gonna die. That girl is burning! Burning in the worst way!" Shyne said, sticking the paper to prove it in his face.

Sun waved it away and wouldn't even look at it. "Y'all bugging! Me and shorty hooking up next Saturday and that's that!" he huffed and stormed out of the unit.

"Sup with him?" Asad asked when Shyne came back up front.

"Nothing," she said, shaking her head. "And why didn't you greet me when I came in?"

Chapter 25

Shyne couldn't reach Sun so she decided to talk to April. She would've beat her up if not for her positive status. She definitely didn't want to get the girl's blood on her.

"Shit!" Shyne fussed when she arrived at April's apartment just in time to see her enter it with a guy. She let out a sigh and decided to wait it out. She pulled up the girl's social media to keep her busy while she waited. Every ratchet post and every twerk the girl had posted only made her madder.

April was with a different dude every day, even after getting her positive results. She bragged about bedding rappers and ballplayers. Her posts proved she had no remorse for her actions. That's why Shyne went and filled her gas cans. She was so focused on her mission that she neglected to fill her tank.

"Another one!" Shyne exclaimed when a man entered April's apartment right after the last one left. She would've waited for him to leave if she hadn't seen him take off his wedding band as he approached the apartment.

The light rain that had been falling increased just as Shyne made her move. She transferred the gas from the can into a bucket when she reached the front door. Her dad had taught them how to bypass most locks and security systems so she had no problem easing inside. The sounds of vigorous fucking reached her as soon as she entered.

"Whose...pussy...is...this?" the man demanded with each deep stroke. He had April's legs locked in his arms so he could pile drive the pussy. The sight froze Shyne in her tracks. She had never seen a live sex act and it amazed her.

"Yours!" she shot back. She couldn't give a name since she never got it.

Shyne cocked her head curiously at the copulating couple. The fuck faces, skin slapping and vagina squishing had her mesmerized. No telling how long she would have been stuck there if they hadn't changed positions and saw her. He pulled out and flipped on his back while she mounted him and began to ride him backwards.

"Who...are...you?" April asked the intruder as she continued riding.

"Huh?" Shyne asked in confusion. It came to her a second later when she felt the weight of the bucket of gas in her hand. "Oh yeah!"

"What the fuck!" the man shouted and shoved April off when he felt the cold gas hit his body.

Shyne got stuck again at the sight of his erection but quickly recovered her modesty. "Okay, bye-bye," she sang and waved with one hand and flicked a lighter with the other.

The couple screamed as they both went up in flames. Shyne cocked her head once more as she watched them run, jump and dance in an attempt to put the flames out. The man ran for the door and got outside. That was Shyne's cue to leave. The pouring rain put the man's fire out but he wouldn't survive the burns. Instead, he would die a slow, agonizing death. Still, it was better than letting him take AIDS home to his pregnant wife.

"What happened? Who me?" Shyne said, practicing for her brother. He'd told her to leave the girl alone but of course, she hadn't listened. She thought it was real funny until her truck sputtered and shut off. "Shit!"

"Where you going?" Sun asked when he saw Asad getting ready to leave. The fact that he had his car keys meant that he was leaving the building instead of just going down the hall to the girl's unit.

"Huh?" Asad asked since Shyne had specifically told him not to tell her brother he was coming to her rescue.

"Tell Shyne I said what's up," he laughed knowingly. He would've pressed for more information if he didn't have a date of his own.

Asad realized he should have taken an umbrella once he pulled out of the building's underground parking garage. It was too late now so he pushed on. He called Shyne and kept her company as he drove to her aide. She was on the opposite side of the highway so he drove to the next exit and came back around.

Asad pulled up behind Shyne and got out. He unwilling entered a wet t-shirt contest as he quickly got soaked. He won when the white fabric clung to the chocolate muscles underneath.

"Damn!" Shyne exclaimed when he reached her window.

"What's wrong?" Asad asked since she never explained what the problem was. She'd said, 'Come get me,' and he'd dropped everything to go get her.

"With what?" she asked. Seeing his shirt, face and braids had made her forget why she was stranded. "Oh! I ran out of gas!"

"You did?" Asad asked, frowning at the gas can in the back. He shrugged his shoulders and retrieved it. Instead of leaving her, he syphoned some gas from his own tank into the can.

Shyne felt a tingle through her whole body as she watched him through her mirrors. She squirmed uncomfortably as a puddle formed in her panties. As soon as he closed her gas cap, she started her vehicle and took off.

"What a strange girl," Asad chuckled as she pulled off. He put the gas can in his trunk and went home.

****

"Un huh, you got wet, huh?" Sun said when his sister got off the elevator.

"Ugh! You so nasty!" Shyne shouted in embarrassment, misunderstanding. He'd meant from the rain but she was soaking wet from being turned on by Asad.

"Huh?" he frowned at the crazy response. "Anyway, I'm out. 'Bout to go see April."

"She burning," Shyne laughed and walked away.

He'd get it once he got there.

Sun and Asad nodded 'what's up' as they passed each other in the parking garage. He then hopped into his vehicle and headed to his date with April. He raced across town, only to pull up to a crime scene.

"Shyne!" he shouted when he saw the fire trucks spraying water on the unit programmed into his GPS. This had her name written all over it. Her parting words popped into his head and he couldn't help but laugh.

'She burning.'

****

"Sup, yo?" Sun asked with a perplexed look when he walked into the lobby and saw Milton pressing the elevator's call button. They hung out every now and then but had no plans for the night.

"I'm taking Bryonna to the movies," he said, sticking his chin up defiantly.

"I thought I told you..." Sun began but paused when he realized he was whining. He cleared his throat and started over with a little more bass in his voice. "Yo, I know I told to leave her alone."

"Free country, my man," Milton shrugged. The elevator arrived and they both walked in. When it reached the tenth floor, only one got off. The other one was sleeping soundly in the corner with lumps all over his head.

"You right, it is a free country," Sun teased and turned down the hallway.

"Who?" Shyne barked, trying to sound tough. She knew Bryonna was expecting her date so she went on and pulled the door open. "Sun? What do you want?"

"Why I gotta want something?" he reeled as if insulted.

"Cuz err' time you come down here, you need milk, eggs, toilet tissue...something!" she reminded.

"Oh." Sun shrugged since it was all true. Bryonna broke up the banter when she came out looking cute. Her outfit was new and modest and the trace of lip gloss set off her pretty face.

"Did I hear the bell?" she sang as she fluttered in like *Gone With The Wind*. Milton would have been impressed if he wasn't riding up and down the elevator sleeping. "Where's Milton?"

"He, um...said he couldn't make it," Sun lied. He regretted it in an instant when he saw her lip poke out from being stood up. "But since you're already dressed, why don't we go to the movies?"

"We, as in, me and you?" Bryonna cheesed and looked to Shyne for approval. She didn't get it because Shyne was shaking her head no. "Sure!"

"Come on, let's leave this hater," Sun said as he escorted her out of the apartment. He remembered her date and suggested, "Let's take the stairs. You can lose a pound...or two."

Chapter 26

Christi had met a nice gentleman while the twins were juniors. By their senior year, he'd popped the question and she'd accepted. It was only then that she decided to introduce Daryl to her family. She had the ring now so he couldn't back out.

Killa decided to throw the cute couple a pre-wedding dinner party at a five-star restaurant. He had followed, spied on and checked out the man and approved. Wanting to make it a grand affair, he flew his grandmother along with Xavier and Rico down. They all met at the restaurant so Shyne wouldn't show out.

"So, grandson, have your finally declared a major?" Diedra asked.

"Huh?" Sun replied, not because he didn't hear the question but because he didn't have a major.

Sun was smart so he did well in his general education classes without much effort. He may have been a standout player in high school but was only in college so the NBA was out. He did like weed and pussy but those weren't really career choices. Luckily for him, his dad had plans for him.

"A-yo, you got a problem?" Rico finally asked, ending the staring contest.

Shyne had locked her eyes on his like a chicken hawk does a chicken. "Yup, you! Say one more word and I'ma come across this table and..."

"Shyne!" Grandma Diedra shrieked. She then turned to Killa and asked, "Aren't you going to say anything?"

"About what? Oh! Yeah, um, Shyne, chill," he said between bites of prime rib.

Shyne chilled but pouted about it. The boys had made a truce but not her. She needed someone to blame for her mother's death and they were it. She meant what she'd said, too.

"Tell them your good news, Asad!" Sun said to switch the subject. Asad had just opened the email on the way over so not even Shyne knew yet.

"Oh yeah! I got an offer to buy my game!" he said and cheesed proudly.

"You did? That's great!" Shyne squealed and kissed his cheek, causing him to cheese even harder.

"Two mil upfront and...eight percent royalties for life!" Sun added, just as proud. A win for one was a win for them all.

"Congratu-," Rico began but Shyne kept her word and came across the table. She stepped on the bread bowl and dove on her half-brother. Down they went, wrestling and throwing punches.

"So, anyway..." Killa said and continued the conversation. Poor Daryl had a look on his face like 'what have I gotten myself into?'

****

"Oh my God! You look so beautiful!" Shyne gushed when her big sister emerged in her wedding dress. Bryonna broke down crying from joy. This was the reward of being a good girl and guarding your chastity. Christi wasn't a jump off, side chick or baby mama. She was a bride.

"You guys look great, too!" Christi said of them in their bridesmaid's dresses with flowers in their afro puffs. She looked at Shyne's eye and shook her head. "Except for that."

"What, my shyner? Get it? Shyne, shyner...y'all wack!"

"You crazy! That was crazy!" Bryonna laughed at the fight. Her and Rico both missed dessert by rolling around on the floor.

"Oh! It's time!" Shyne shouted when she checked the clock. She and Bryonna joined the rest of the bridesmaids. She snarled at Rico standing next to Sun and the other groomsmen. He had a black eye, too, so they were even.

"If you hurt my sister, I'll kill you," Sun whispered through his smile.

It took Daryl a few seconds to process the threat because of the smile. "Trust me. She does," he replied.

That sealed it for Sun, who trusted his big sister's judgement. The smile became genuine as his father began marching the bride down the aisle.

"We're next," Shyne mouthed to Asad who nodded and cheesed. Graduation wasn't long off and they planned to marry shortly after. He had just purchased a five-bedroom house out in the suburbs to make sure Sun and Bryonna always had a place to call home as well.

"I'm so proud of you," Killa whispered as he presented the bride to her husband. He then fell into place and watched the nuptials.

****

Graduation rolled around so it was time for the family to come together once again. Shyne was anxious to hug her grandmother and fight her brothers, but she also had a bigger goal on her mind. Fuck graduation. She was ready to go on her honeymoon in a month.

"I'ma be like uh-uh-uh," Shyne said, humping the air in front of the mirror.

"Shyne, get help," Bryonna laughed.

Sun was still cock blocking dudes from getting close to her. In her mind, it meant they went together, but she accepted that their future was in the future.

"A-yo!" Sun called out as he entered the condo. "You heard from Pops?"

"As a matter of fact..." Shyne paused to check her phone. "No, I haven't."

"It's going straight to voicemail," he advised when she called. She found out for herself a second later when her father's deep voice gave the offer to leave a message.

"Um, Daddy, it's Shyne, your daughter. We're getting ready to graduate, college, in like...an hour and I was wondering where...the...hell...are you?" she fussed.

They fussed, cussed, called and waited until they couldn't wait any longer. The twins finally gave up on their father and grandmother attending the ceremony. They all piled into Sun's car and rode in silence to cross the stage once more. Bryonna was called first and then Asad. The Dean thought it was cute to have a set of twins graduate so he called them together.

"Shyne and Sun Forrest," he announced alphabetically.

"Come on, yo," Sun urged and stood.

Shyne let out a deep sigh and took to her feet. She scanned the audience one final time and there he was. "Daddy! He came!" she said with relief. It was short-lived when she noticed the stoic look on his face behind the dark glasses. Now she worried about him as she collected her prize.

They missed what followed by going to check on him.

"You okay, Pops?" Sun asked, putting a hand on his shoulder to comfort him.

"Is it Grandma?" Shyne asked, fearing the worse since she wasn't with him. She was old but only death would prevent her from seeing her babies graduate. Only death had prevented it but it wasn't hers.

"Xavier and Rico were shot last night," Killa croaked hoarsely. He had to clear his throat to get the rest out. "X died and Rico is critical. We need to go to New York."

"Say no more, Pops!" Sun agreed eagerly. He knew his father wanted get back and he planned to give it to him.

"We with you," Shyne cosigned. The lone tear that slipped from under the shades hurt her to her core. Somebody was going to die for it, very violently.

"Take your friends home and I'll be by later," Killa said and disappeared through the crowd.

"What we 'posed to tell Bryonna and Asad?" Sun wondered how to explain their sudden departure.

"Just say it's family business," Shyne replied.

Chapter 27

"Look, Pops, when we find out who did it, you just fall back and let me and Shyne handle it," Sun offered as they sped up 95 North.

"Shyne and I," Shyne corrected since they were college grads and all.

"You and Shyne? That don't make no sense!" Sun fussed and an argument started.

Killa just shook his head as they argued through the whole state of North Carolina. "You guys really have no idea who I am, do you?" Killa asked. "Me or your mom?"

"Sure we do. You're Killa," Sun said, using his fingers to make quotation marks at his name. "And mom was Yolo."

"You only live once!" Shyne added.

"Well, there's a reason that they call me Killa," he advised then began to fill them in. He started with *Chronicles of a Killa* when they reached Virginia and ended with *Yolo 3* at The Jersey Turnpike. "That's why."

Sun and Shyne sat there with their mouths wide open at the wild tales of murder and mayhem. If they were true, it made them both look like Girl Scouts. Sun turned to face his sister to get her take and then they broke out into laughter.

"Blew up a funeral home!" Shyne howled and cracked up. The young woman keeled over on her side holding her stomach. "You gonna make me pee!"

"Black Mob? Mommy?' Sun cackled and cracked up some more. Tears streamed from his eyes from laughing so hard.

Killa twisted his lips and changed directions once they hit the city. Instead of going straight to The Bronx, he took a detour to Long Island. The twins had residual chuckles as they reached the house in Wyandanch.

"Where we going?" Shyne asked when their father bypassed the front door and took them around to the cellar.

It was self-explanatory when Killa used a key to unlock the locks. Sun peered over his shoulder to see the code as he entered it.

"Sun and Shyne," Killa said, seeing him trying to get it.

"Why didn't I think of that!" he said, shaking his head. He had been trying to get down there from the second Yolo told him to stay out of it.

Killa led the way into the dark, dank cellar. He flicked on the lights and watched his children's faces light up.

"Oh my!" Sun exclaimed as his knees buckled. He leaned against a pillar to hold himself up as he scanned the room full of guns, knives and other killing apparatuses. He may have been trying to see it all but Shyne only had eyes for one thing.

"Is that...?" she asked and floated across the concrete floor. She reached the flame thrower and hugged it like a long lost friend. "Can I keep it, Daddy? Please!"

"Sure, you can, baby," Killa agreed, knowing she would put it to good use.

"What's this, Pops?" Sun asked, slipping a DC 2000 over his head.

"Don't move!" Killa shouted, freezing him in place. He came over and gingerly removed the deadly device from his neck. He sat it on a table and hit the switch.

"Damn!" Sun said, rubbing his neck where it had been seconds before.

"Can I have one of those two?" Shyne exclaimed, wide-eyed with delight.

"Sure you can, baby. You guys grab a gun so we can go to the city."

****

"You guys go in and check on your brother and grandma," Killa said when he pulled up in front of Lincoln Hospital. "I'm going to the projects to see what I can find out."

"Okay, Daddy," Shyne agreed and hopped out first. She led the way into the hospital with Sun on her heels. They were directed up to ICU where Grandma was sitting with Rico.

"Damn!" Sun said when he saw his half-brother stuffed with tubes and IVs.

"Hey, babies," Diedra sang and took them both into her arms. "I'm sorry I missed your big day. I..."

"It's okay, Grandma," Sun said with a squeeze.

"I need to go home and change. You stay here while Sun rides with me in a cab," Diedra directed.

Shyne twisted her lips but kept them closed. She sat in a chair across the room and tried to ignore Rico. The noise of the ventilator stole her attention so she got up, went over, and looked down at him.

"Wow, you look just like my fa- Daddy," she said, accepting for the first time that they were related. She felt a warm tear run down her face and angrily knocked it away. She got the first one but it was followed by so many more, she gave up and had a good cry. "It's not your fault," Shyne finally admitted. "We going to find the people who did this and kill them. All of them, and it'll be a beautiful death. Because they made dad cry and...cuz you're my brother."

Shyne left the room to grab a soda and missed the smile that spread on her brother's face.

****

"Sup, yo? What happened?" Killa sighed as he took a seat next to Villain in the project's courtyard.

"X and Rico were out here getting money. They had a nice little operation going. Just them, no extras. They didn't step on anyone's toes and they did good business," he explained.

Killa nodded along to what he already knew. "So, why wet 'em then?" he needed to know. "A robbery?"

"You ever heard of the Black Mob?" he asked.

"Yeah, they're extinct!" Killa said. He would know, too, since he and Yolo murdered them into the past tense.

"Nah, they back. They had sons, daughters, nephews and shit who started that shit back up! They all over the country and be on some get down or lay down type of shit."

"My sons wouldn't lay down for no one," Killa said truthfully which explained why they'd gotten laid down.

"Exactly, that's why they got hit up. Yo, you know they had love out here, so the streets are with you," Villain said just as Sun escorted Grandma from a cab and into her building.

"Nah, we got this. This is family business!"

Chapter 28

"Sun, Shyne, there are all kinds of people in the world. Some good, some bad and some in desperate need of being killed. A sad fact of life is that some people need dead. People like rapists, child molesters, boy bands, book publishers and the like. There's all kinds of fucked up people that the world can do without. There's pimps, pushers, robbers and crooked cops. They're all garbage that needs to be taken out. We can restore honor and dignity on the earth by removing foul people from the face of the planet. We..."

"But, Dad," Shyne interjected with her hand raised, "who are we to judge?"

"She's right. You and mom taught us that God was the only real judge," Sun added. Neither intended to question their father, but they sought clarity.

"That's right, only God can judge them. That's why we don't judge them, we just kill them!"

"The Black Mob was the worst of the worst. They turned dads into junkies and moms into prostitutes. They transformed family neighborhoods into slums. Ironically, it was started by a pasty white guy named Casper, who did his dirt in black face. And your mother was his best hitman."

"I still can't wrap my mind around mom being some ruthless kil-la," Shyne said, shaking his head.

"I don't know why not. You're just like her. You guys really think that I don't know what you've been up to? The principal. The five percenters. Christi's boyfriend..."

"Oh," Sun and Shyne gasped in union.

"Well, your mom and I killed them all, the entire Black Mob. We went state to state, city to city and murdered them all. Now they're trying to make a comeback. And if they get their numbers up, they'll be unstoppable. But we're not going to let that happen! We're going to kill them. All of them!"

"Starting with the ones who hurt our family!" Shyne growled.

"Of course! Then wherever they pop up, they'll get knocked off. Them and anyone else causing corruption in the land. This is who we are, what we do. It's our FAMILY BUSINESS!"

*****

"Mob shit!" Fresh shouted to his cronies as he held court in the courtyard of the Soundview Projects.

"Mob shit!" the crew shouted back like mindless minions.

Black people got lost somewhere along the way and felt a need to join groups, gangs and cliques, to be a part of something bigger than themselves. Dick riding had somehow become acceptable.

This was ground zero for the rebirth of The Black Mob. Fresh and his half-brother, Redd, had heard stories about how their shared father had once run The Bronx on behalf of The Black Mob and they wanted to follow in his footsteps. They wanted to get it popping once more. Once they took over the projects, they'd spread out through The Bronx like a cancer; aggressive and deadly. They'd give two choices when they came through; get down or lay down.

Xavier and Rico were seeing good figures wholesaling kilos of coke. The Mob got wind of it and wanted in. Hot headed Rico rudely declined by literally killing the messenger. He and X then sent him back Uptown in a body bag. They'd expected some retaliation but still got caught slipping.

Pussy was used to bait the brothers into an ambush.

Twin strippers, Fleek and Unique, had grown up in the Soundview, which made them Mob property. The two fucked and sucked on command from The Mob controlled T.H.O.T.S strip club. The acronym stood for Those Hoes on the Stage and it fit since dancers were forced to turn flips and tricks.

Killa was a bit of a trick himself. His father had been one as well, so it was only natural that his sons were tricks, too. Just like Sun was smashing in Wyandanch and Atlanta, his older brothers X and Rico slung dick and smashed throughout the city of New York.

The twin strippers used their plump breasts and fat asses to lure the brothers out into the open. Rico would've agreed to anything, including meeting her on the moon, when Fleek lolled out her tongue, showing off a lighted vibrating tongue ring. She opted for Co-op City instead. It was neutral ground so the brothers agreed.

As soon as X parked in the sprawling city within the city, gunmen came from every direction. Xavier pulled his brother down and fired back but was quickly overwhelmed and out gunned. He took out two and saved his brother's life, but it cost him his.

"Damn right, Mob shit! The world is mine!" Fresh shouted, barely able to prevent beating on his chest like King Kong. Power, the most dangerous drug to man, will do that.

"The world is ours!" Redd tossed in, feeling a little left out. The boys were the same age, being that they had different mothers, but Fresh was the more outspoken of the two. The meeting went on with them making plans for the future. Meanwhile, across town, another meeting was being held that would cut that future short.

****

"I suggest we just go up to Soundview and murder everything moving! Male, female, birds, rats, cats..." Shyne offered.

"Nah, cuz some gone get away," Sun said, shooting the idea out of the air.

Killa sat quietly as he listened to his kids toss ideas back and forth. Some were good, some were bad but all were violent.

"So how we gonna get 'em, Daddy?" Shyne whined. "I'm getting married in a week, so I ain't got time to be chasing nobody all over The Bronx!"

"Exactly. So we'll get them all together in one spot," he said and leaned back to see where they would take it.

"We kill one of them and get the rest of 'em at the funeral!" Sun cheered.

"And I can run up in the church with the flame thrower and..."

"A flame thrower, in a church, Shyne?" Killa said, twisting his lips.

"Why not? We never been to church," she countered.

"So, we still gotta respect people's place of worship," Sun answered, causing their father's head to nod in agreement.

"Now, a funeral home is a different story," Killa added. And he would know since he once blew up a funeral home full of his enemies.

"Well, can I at least set the strippers on fire?" Shyne asked hopefully. Poor thing, she wanted to use that flame thrower really bad.

"I don't see why not," her father said, sending her into her happy dance. She only got in a few moves before Sun shut her down.

"Nah, I got the strippers. You can get the funeral home."

"They don't call me Shyne for nothing!" the girl cheered with flames in her eyes. The revelry was short-lived when Grandma Diedra called out and reminded them of what day it was.

"Y'all come on. We can't be late to Xavier's funeral!"

****

Killa was on high alert as they reached the funeral home. He and his children had just made plans of mass destruction for another funeral so he was on point and heavily armed. He wore his black suit jacket two sizes too large to accommodate the two tech nine submachine guns he carried.

Killa nodded in appreciation at the large turnout at Xavier's funeral. The long faces proved that the mourners were genuine and not just gawkers who'd shown up just to gawk or haters who'd come just for the satisfaction of seeing him in a box.

Sun and Shyne flanked their grandmother on the front row. They each held a hand to comfort the angry old lady. Her only solace came from knowing that his funeral would lead to many, many more. And she was perfectly fine with that.

Killa played the back and scanned every face that entered for traces of guilt, satisfaction or gratitude. While doing so, he came across a couple of faces adorned with smug smirks and locked in on them. Villain saw who he was watching and came over with confirmation.

"That's them," he said out of the side of his mouth. "The one with the sandy brown hair is Redd and..."

"The fly guy is Fresh," Killa completed. He now had faces to go with the names. He turned his torso so the camera in his pocket would capture their images as well.

"Police outside," Villain tossed out when he heard a low growl emanating from his mentor. He was strapped too and would bust if Killa did. It would be an honor to ride or die with the legend.

"I'm good," Killa said calmly. He had no doubt that he would one day die in a blaze of gunfire, it just wouldn't be today.

The mourners filed out of the funeral home for the ride uptown to the cemetery. The twins followed the hearse while their father followed Fresh and Redd. He noticed that the police followed them as well, which killed any thoughts of killing them. Instead, he tracked their every move for the rest of the day.

****

"This some bullshit," Grandma mumbled under her breath at the gravesite. Sun and Shyne looked at each other to see if the other had heard her.

Both now realized that the grave next to their mother's belonged to Sincerity. There were two plots on each side and one in the middle. When Xavier was placed in the hole next to his mother's grave they guessed that the other one would be Rico's when his clock stopped. That meant that two on the side of Yolo's was theirs and that the space in the middle belonged to their father.

Xavier was a good dude, so the wails of sorrow when he was lowered into the ground were real. He and Rico gave back and treated people fairly so he would truly be missed. The only consolation was that he didn't leave any kids behind to grow up fatherless.

The twins simmered in silent rage until it was time to go. Once the dirt began to cover the casket, they led their great grandmother back to the car.

"I'll be watching the news," Diedra said offhandedly.

Sun and Shyne shot each other a curious glance wondering if she meant what they thought she meant. She did. She was expecting some get back.

Chapter 29

"No, I love you more," Shyne giggled into the phone. "Un uh, I love you more!"

"Damn shame," Sun protested, shaking his head as he walked in on his sister humping the air.

"I know you ain't talking, with yo-," Shyne cut the dis short when their father walked in behind him. "Asad, I gotta go. I'll be home in a couple of days...In sha Allah."

"M-m-muah!" Killa and Sun playfully blew kisses.

"Y'all some haters!" Shyne huffed once she hung up. "Pops, it's been awhile since mom...I mean, we wouldn't be mad if you found a woman. I wouldn't set her on fire or anything."

"That's, um...good to know," Killa replied. Truth be told, he could never love again. Broken hearts stay broken. A person can move on but they'd have to love with a limp.

"Speaking of vagina, I need some ones!" Sun announced and popped his collar. Shyne looked him up and down in the slacks, shoes and button shirt and twisted her face up. He knew that was her way of saying he looked nice and said "Thanks."

"Surveillance, Sun!" Killa reminded as he produced a thick roll of hundreds that made the twins wince.

"What, exactly do you do, Dad?" Shyne wondered. They had a great childhood filled with etceteras but neither parent went to work anywhere.

"Kill bad people," he reminded. "The family business pays well."

"I see!" Sun said as he forced the roll of bills into his pocket. He double checked his .9 for a third time and tucked it into the small of his back.

"Be careful!" Sun called to his back as she called her boo again.

****

"Call a spade a spade," Sun chuckled as he read the sign above the strip club. The name alone forced women to accept being a hoe to work there. Now they were That Hoe on The Stage and everything that went along with it.

Tonight was supposed to be strictly about surveillance, but Shyne had other plans. Plans to kill her enemies before her wedding next week. Nothing would stand in the way of her getting some.

Sun parked at the far end of the parking lot so he could watch before he went in. He pulled in backwards just in case he had to make a hasty retreat. The metal detector at the door beeped incessantly as goon after goon tried to bring a gun inside. He let out a sigh and tucked his pistol under the seat and went inside.

"Mmm," Sun said as he inhaled the smell of the women as he stepped inside. He looked around at all the ass and titties as far as the eye could see.

He spotted his targets by their trademark platinum wigs. Unique had her name tatted on the small of her back. The ink was slightly smudged from so many men skeeting on it. Fleek had her name tattooed on her neck in case the airhead forgot who she was.

The two tag team table danced for a baller who didn't seem very interested. He flicked bills in the air while talking on the phone.

"Sup, yo? You need a table?" hostess with the mostest big titties asked, stealing his attention.

"Huh?" he asked her breasts before raising his gaze to her pretty face.

"I...said...do...you...need...a...table?" she repeated, using her hands in mock Sign Language. Sun was fluent in American Sign Language so he knew that it wasn't real.

"Yes...I...do," he replied while signing 'can I fuck your face'. She giggled, which he took as a yes.

"Follow me," she said, putting a little extra in her walk since she knew he was watching. Both Sun's clothes and his swag suggested that he belonged in VIP, so that's where so took him.

"Thanks, ma," he said with a hundred-dollar tip. A glance at his phone proved that the loudmouths a few tables away were his main targets.

"Thank you! You need anything else just let...me...know," she cheered.

"Actually, I do. See those two, with the metal looking wigs?"

"Fleek and Unique? Yeah?"

"Send them my way when they're free," he ordered.

"Them hoes ain't never free. They cheap, but never free," the hostess laughed at her own joke before setting off on her task.

"Dom P," Sun said when a waitress approached to take his order. He didn't even look her way since he was locked in on his targets.

Killa was right, they were hard to get to. They barely ventured from their projects and had security when they did. This was the only place they went on a regular basis and he couldn't get a gun in.

"Thanks," he replied to the waitress as she returned and filled his glass. He gave her three hundreds for the two-hundred-dollar bottle and told her to keep the change.

"Thank you!" she sang as she fluttered her false lashes. She was about to flirt with him but Fleek and Unique arrived.

"Sup, yo?" Unique asked, placing her hands on her hips while sticking her pelvis forward to show off how fat her crotch was in her boy shorts. Fleek flicked out her tongue to turn him on but it had the opposite effect. He saw why they were able to lure his brothers into ambush and it pissed him off.

"You, dance for me," Sun ordered, managing to keep his cool and his eyes on Fresh and Redd. Both fondled a pretty young girl while she danced.

"It's fifty bucks a song up her, playa," Fleek replied.

"Each," Unique added and began to gyrate when he didn't flinch.

Sun couldn't tell if they were pretty or not under all the make-up. They were fine but barely held his attention as he scoped his prey. Fresh and Redd both suddenly stood and dragged the girl into a room.

"What's that over there?" he asked of the row of doors behind the VIP section.

"Private rooms. It's a buck an hour for the room and another buck for a girl."

"Each," Fleek threw in since she wanted to come, too. She showed off her tongue ring once more to seal the deal.

"Let's go," Sun said as he stood. He made sure to select a room next to where the targets went and paid the bouncer. He sized the huge man up and decided he didn't want to tangle with him without a gun.

Unique pushed Sun onto the sofa and dug into his slacks. She removed his flaccid dick while he checked his surroundings. It barely registered when she took him in her mouth as he scanned the room. The private rooms were thrown together with 2x4s and sheet rock. They were so flimsy he could clearly hear the gang rape in the next room.

"Um...," Unique said, wagging his soft penis in her hand.

"Oh yeah!" Sun laughed as he noticed the blowjob in progress. All three watched as he became erect. Fleek knelt down and got in on the act as well. "You guys share."

And share they did until the last drop. Once they returned to VIP, Fresh and Redd were gone. The night was still young so all was not lost.

"Let's get a room," Sun asked, making it sound like an order.

"That's gonna cost two grand," Unique shot back quickly.

"Each!" Fleek tried her luck. They usually did a 50/50 split but she saw the size of his bankroll and wanted in.

"We gon' fuck yo' brains out!" Unique bragged. She made sure to talk dirty to make up for her worn out vagina.

"Someone's brains is coming out for sure," Sun agreed as he drove. He pulled into a hotel parking lot, backing in so he could get away quickly. After all, it was about to become a crime scene.

"I see someone knew they was gonna bag something!" Unique laughed when Sun bypassed the office as he dug a key out of his pocket.

"Mmhm," he said as he unlocked the door and stepped aside. He locked it once they were all inside and hit the light.

"Who that?" the strippers demanded when they saw the girl sitting Indian style on the bed with a gun in her lap.

"That's Shyne, my sister," he replied, blocking the exit.

"Well, that's gonna be an extra grand!" Unique demanded. She had no problem sexing a brother and sister, it just cost more.

"Each!" Fleek said before showing Shyne her tongue ring.

"This bitch got a disco ball in her mouth," Shyne commented. "Is that what you used to lure our brothers?"

"Probably. Who's your brothers?" Unique responded. They had lured plenty of men into robberies or ambushes so she wasn't sure.

"Mmhmm, you know niggas can't resist some good head," Fleek giggled and stuck her tongue out again.

Shyne lifted the pistol and fired at the glowing tongue ring. Fleek's black soul left her body through the same large hole in her head as her brains.

"Told you," Sun said, seeing the brain matter on the floor before he swung on Unique. Her jaw broke with a loud crack that echoed throughout the room.

"Damn!" Shyne exclaimed excitedly as the girl was knocked down and out. She extended the pistol to him to end it. "Here."

"Un uh," Sun said as he stood over the girl. He lifted his foot and slammed it down on her face. The stomp woke the girl back up but the next one knocked her out once more.

Shyne watched as her brother stomped Unique into the afterlife. She was a mangled mess of foundation, mascara, lipstick and blood when he finished. He was covered in blood up to his knees, like he'd walked through a river of it.

"Come on, yo, let's bounce!" Shyne urged.

"What, you don't wanna burn 'em up?" Sun joked as they left the room.

"Ain't nobody got time for all that! I'm getting married in a week. I don't have time to be fooling around with..."

"Saving the gas for the funeral, huh?" Sun laughed knowingly.

"Yup!" she laughed as she got back into the vehicle she'd come in. Sun got into his rental and followed her back to the projects.

Chapter 30

"Surveillance...close observation, watch, scrutiny, reconnaissance!" Killa said, reading the definition straight from a dictionary. The news reports of the dead strippers told him what they hadn't. "You guys were supposed to watch them not kill them!"

"But, Dad, we had a shot and we took it! Now, when they announce which funeral home, they gon' use we gon' be ready," Sun explained. It was Shyne's idea but he took the heat for it.

"He's right, Daddy. We need to finish this so we can go back to Atlanta," Shyne pouted. Bryonna had been handling all the last minute wedding plans but they would need the bride to be finished.

"You two are something else!" Killa said, shaking his head. He did a lot that because of these two.

****

"Alright, the wake for Latrice and Patrice Johnson will be held at 2pm on Tuesday," Killa relayed once he'd heard the plans.

"Who?" Sun asked. "We tryna find out about Fleek and Unique, not Latrice and whoever else you said."

"Duh, that's their real names, crazy! Anyway, time for work," Shyne announced and left the apartment.

"You not going to help her?" Killa asked as his son turned back to the videos on TV.

"Nah, she got it," he shrugged nonchalantly. He was right, too, because she did have it. She had already secured a gas company truck and uniform. Now that she knew the when and where, she got to work on the what.

****

"Gas Company!" Shyne replied into the intercom. There was minimal security at the funeral home, which made her task easier. "I'm here about the leak."

"What leak?" the receptionist asked as she buzzed Shyne inside.

"The one I'm about to make," she mumbled to herself and got to work. Shyne finished shortly before two. Now it was her brother's turn to work.

"A-yo, no old people allowed. This some real nigga shit!" the security guard declared as he turned people away.

"Those are my nieces in there!" Fleek and Unique's aunt protested when she and her child were denied entry.

"Old folks and kids wake is tomorrow. Now, y'all beat it!" he barked. The woman cursed him up one side and down the other before storming off. He shrugged it off since he didn't care about getting cursed out. Sun did, however, care about killing kids and old people. So anyone who wasn't Black Mob affiliated got turned away.

"No sign of Redd and Fresh?" Shyne asked into her phone form where she watched and waited.

"Nah, and it's getting late. We may have to abort the mission," Sun said, sounding whiney from disappointment.

"Abort my ass! Not after all the work I did," Shyne fussed. "Go on, lock the doors and get as far away as possible."

Sun couldn't argue with the logic of killing the crew. They would catch their leaders later and they wouldn't have any soldiers to protect them. Sun wrapped heavy chains around the doors and secured them with even heavier padlocks. The hood preacher had just begun his song and dance when Shyne did what Shyne does.

"Fleek was on fleek and Unique...well, she was unique!" he preached.

Meanwhile, Shyne hit a button that started a fire. It was a small fire that produced just enough smoke to set the sprinklers off.

"The fuck!" a hoodrat shouted in horror of her hairdo getting wet. Everyone bitched and moaned until they realized that the sprinklers were spraying gas instead of water.

"Okay, bye-bye!" Shyne smiled and waved as she hit another button that started another fire.

The inside of the funeral home erupted when the flames met the gas. The thugs and thuggettes were quickly engulfed in flames. Their frantic screams could be heard down the block where Shyne watched with glee.

"Let's bounce," Sun called into his phone as he put his car in gear.

"Aww, man!" Shyne fussed but complied. She'd barely made it out of range when the building totally blew up. The entire block shook violently form the massive explosion. "Damn!"

"Eh, not bad," Killa said from where he watched. Almost seventy thugs, killers, prostitutes and pimps perished in the blaze. No, that wasn't bad at all.

****

"See, it's a good thing we didn't go to the funeral!" Redd exclaimed when they awoke to the news of the fire/explosion.

"Fuck them bitches! I wasn't going anyway," Fresh laughed. He didn't even mind losing so many of his team because it meant that he could recruit kids to sling his crack for half price.

"Yeah, fuck them bitches!" his brother agreed. "Let's hit THOTS and fuck one of those hoes!"

"We done fucked them all already," Fresh replied. Last night they'd taken a young girl to the back and raped her even though she was willing to give it up.

"Can't wait 'til they get some new bitches!" Redd sighed, wanting someone new to rape. He'd never heard the phrase 'be careful what you wished for'.

****

"What's Plan B?" Sun asked as they neared their destination.

"There ain't one," Shyne shot back. "But them niggas dying tonight! One way or another, they're both...dying...tonight!"

"Okay," he agreed.

The wedding was days away now and it was time to end this. That's why they'd both agreed to this risky plan without telling their father. It was literally do or die with no Killa waiting in the wings to swoop in and save the day.

"Hurry up," Shyne demanded as they pulled up to THOTS. She then stepped out the car, tossed her hair over her shoulder, stared at her brother and said, "I love you."

"Love you, too, Sis," Sun said before he drove off. He didn't go far, just around to the back of the building. Entering separately would make it easier to pull off their dangerous plan.

Shyne entered first and barely turned heads in the long wig and stunna shades covering her face. The six-inch heels under the floppy dress pushed her height to six feet tall. She rushed into a bathroom labeled Hoes like she had to pee really bad and ducked into a stall.

"Asad would lose...his...mind if he saw me wearing this!" Shyne fussed at herself as she pulled the big dress over her head. Underneath she wore a pair of yellow boy shorts that allowed her plump ass checks to hang out the bottom. Up top was the matching yelling bra that pushed mounds of her breasts out the top. Young Shyne was a woman now and quite fine. She gave a giggle at herself in the mirror and decided, "Asad is gonna lose his mind when he sees me in this."

Meanwhile, Sun made his approach to the club. He held his breath hopefully as he went through the metal detector. A sigh of relief came when the Plexiglas knives didn't beep. He paid the admission fee and swaggered inside. Sun paused to peep at a few booties as he entered. He locked eyes on a nice caramel set of ass cheeks until the girl turned around and he saw her face.

"Yuck!" he grimaced and spat when he realized he'd been looking at his sister's booty. "Pst, pst!"

Shyne stifled a laugh at the disgusted look on his face as she went into character. Actually getting a job in the club would require way more than she was capable of. Girls were required to fuck and suck their way onto the stage. It was, after all, called THOTS. She bypassed the application by entering as a customer and changing into a stripper in the bathroom.

"Hello again," the waitress who'd served Sun last time cheered when she saw him. Not only did she remember his face, she also remembered the big faced bills he'd tipped with.

"Sup, Ma, bring me a bottle of Dom, a stripper and two glasses," he ordered as he locked eyes on his prey. She was gone in a flash as Shyne approached.

"A-yo! What the, who the..." Fresh stammered as he saw Shyne for the first time. Shyne lifted her head and prepared to prance right by them but he grabbed her arm. "Hold up, Ma! Who you?"

"I'm Shyne and this...ain't no handle!" she said, snatching her arm away.

"Yo, dance for us!" Redd said, pulling out a thick roll of cash. Shyne responded by gyrating to the music.

"Here you go," the waitress sang as she returned with Sun's champagne, stripper, and glasses. Her eyes lit up at the hundred dollar tip he gave her. "You do whatever...he tell you to do! Understood?"

"Yes, ma'am," the girl said with a slight southern twang. Her calling the twenty something year old ma'am made Sun frown curiously.

"How old are you?" Sun barked a little harder than he intended.

"I'm not supposed to say," she said just above a whisper and looked around fearfully. She popped open her bra, revealing a pair of hard breasts that, from Sun's guess, made her about sixteen. They saved her life. When she turned to pop her ass, he only slipped half of the vial into her drink. The whole vial would've killed her; half was only enough to make her take a long nap.

"Hey!" Shyne shouted and reeled around when Fresh palmed her ass cheek. She swung her open palm and slapped the smirk clean off his face. It was followed by a tense few seconds as she waited for his reaction. If he popped up, she would pop it off and it would go down on the spot. They may not make it out but these two would die, too. Luckily, Fresh smiled slowly and rubbed the welts on his face.

"A shy hoe!" he laughed to his brother. "You ever seen a shy hoe befo'?"

"Nah! Bet she suck dick with her eyes closed," Redd said and keeled over laughing.

"I do not!" Shyne protested, stomping her feet. The brothers laughed even harder, giving her a chance to empty a vial in each of their drinks. She waited until they took a few sips before she invited them into a private room. "Come on, I'll show you."

"We gon' show you," Fresh said ominously as he led the way.

"Showtime!" Sun cheered when he saw the plan coming together.

"Huh?" the girl asked and yawned as he stood and steered her towards the private rooms. She let out a deep sigh when she saw where he was taking her. Fresh and Redd had raped her in their private room just a few nights ago.

He paid for the next room and pulled her inside.

"When you wake up, you go home to wherever you came from!" Sun growled into the girl's face while putting a wad of cash into her hand. "You hear me?"

"Ye-s-s-s!" she shouted in fear as she felt the effects of being drugged yet again. Last time, she woke up with semen in every orifice. The two nasty ass brothers had even skeeted in her ears and nostrils. She tried to fight off sleep with rapid blinks but lost the battle. She wasn't the only one.

"The fuck!" Redd fussed after a deep yawn. "I'm sleepy as hell!"

"Me too," Fresh complained as they got seated on the sofa in the VIP room.

"That's cuz I poisoned you," Shyne giggled. "Don't worry, it's not going to kill you."

"But I am," Sun announced as he kicked through the flimsy wall partition. He tossed one of the plastic knives to his sister and went in.

The drugs rendered both men helpless as the twins made pincushions out of them. Sun and Shyne stabbed Fresh and Redd up one side and down the other as if they were in a race.

"One hundred!" Shyne cheered when she won that race. They had a bet who could poke a hundred holes in their victim first. She did a victory dance covered in blood.

"I'm telling Asad!" Sun whined at her half-naked outfit.

"Sore loser," she said as she followed him through the hole in the wall. She saw the sleeping girl and raised her knife to finish her.

"Wait!" Sun shouted and deflected what would have been a deathblow. "That's a kid! I told her to take her ass home."

"Oh, okay. Oh!" Shyne shouted and went back through the wall. She dug wads of bloody money from the bloody men's bloody pockets and came back. The girl wasn't wearing much so she shoved the money into her panties.

"Let's bounce!" Sun said, helping his sister out of the window. They landed right in front of his parked car and made a clean getaway.

"Now what?" Sun asked once they were clear of the murder scene.

"Now, I get married!" Shyne said, lighting the night with her smile. "Yo, I'm getting married!"

Chapter 31

"Uh, uh, uh..." Shyne grunted as she humped the air in her wedding dress.

"Shyne, get help!" Christi urged when she came in and saw her.

"Oh, I'm about to!" she replied with one final thrust.

"I can't believe my girl is getting married!" Bryonna squealed as she came over to fuss over her hair once again.

"I don't know why not. I've been engaged since I was like seven years old!" Shyne laughed. In truth, she could hardly believe it herself.

"So, what about religion? He's a Muslim and you're a...what are you?" Bryonna wondered with a curious frown.

"I'm a...a...well, I believe there is only one God and like it says in Qur'an, 'To you be your way and to me be mine,'" she replied.

Sun and Shyne had never been to church because their parents didn't go to church. That's why a non-denominational wedding hall was selected for her and Asad's nuptials. It was both traditional and non-traditional at the same time. Shyne wore a long white gown and the Imam from Asad's masjid officiated. Sun served as best man, but still had jokes.

"Yo, my sister's going to need her gown," Sun teased Asad, who was wearing a long white robe of his own. His neat braids were covered by a sparkling white kufi.

"Huh?" Asad asked. He'd heard the words clearly but he was so nervous that his brain wasn't processing information quickly.

"Nothing, bruh," Sun sighed. He didn't need to threaten him to take care of his sister since he had been doing just that since they'd met.

"It's time," Killa said and went to collect his daughter to walk her down the aisle. It was the proudest moment of his life.

"It's time," Christi announced nervously when they heard a knock. A moment later, Killa stuck his head in and repeated the statement.

"Ready, baby?" he asked, amazed at how beautiful she looked.

"Um, yes, but um...Daddy," Shyne stammered, putting everyone on alert. Bryonna was ready to pounce if she tried to back out now.

"What's wrong, baby? Asad's a good man!" he demanded.

"I know! Second best man I know, after you. I was just wondering if, well, can my brother walk down the aisle with us?"

"I guess," Killa sighed. He knew how close Sun and Shyne were. After all, they had shared their mother's womb together. "I'll go get Sun."

"No, not that one. Rico!" she corrected to everyone's surprise. Rico had pulled through the shooting but still had a long road ahead to full recovery. Christi, Bryonna, Killa and Shyne had a brief contest to see who could smile the widest.

"Sure," her father agreed and went to retrieve him. A minute later, he wheeled Rico, who had a skeptical look on his face, in.

"A-yo, at least wait until I get out of this wheelchair before you jump on me again," Rico said.

"No beef, big bruh. I just need you to help our father walk me down the aisle," she assured him.

"Okay, bet!" Rico said, joining in the smile-fest already in progress. Killa got behind to push as they stepped out of the room. On cue, "The Wedding March" began as the three made their way up the aisle.

"Bimillahir-rahmanir Raheem..." the Imam began, praying for the couple in Arabic, which only Killa, Sun, Shyne and Asad understood. He repeated the prayer in English for everyone else.

The eclectic wedding ended with Shyne getting a ring but not Asad. She was thrilled with the diamond encrusted band and he with her. They fist bumped instead of kissing when the Imam pronounced them husband and wife. Bryonna was the only one who noticed Shyne humping ever so slightly as Asad led her back down the aisle.

"I'se married now! I said, I'se married now!" Shyne shouted like Shug Avery in *The Color Purple* as she walked. Poor thing just couldn't help herself. Who could blame her, though, since that was the best part of the movie?

The entire wedding party headed across town to the reception. It was more traditional with a cake and a DJ for the guests. There would be no showing off legs with the removal of Shyne's garter, but she did toss the bouquet.

"Nuh uh! Oh no you don't!" Bryonna shouted as the flowers sailed in the air. She shoved one girl out of the way, tripped another flat on her face then stepped on her back and launched herself in the air.

"Damn!" Sun exclaimed at her diving catch before she hit the ground. He lifted his arms like a football referee and announced, "Touchdown!"

"Look, Sun!" she shouted as she held up the flowers before breaking into Cam Newton's Dab dance. She was so into it that she didn't see Sun ease away until she looked up again. "Oh, you can run, Sun Forrest, but you can't hide!"

The reception was in full swing when Killa and Sun drove the bride and groom to the airport. They were off to Belize for a week long honeymoon. It was about to go down!

"Welp, I'm out," Sun announced once Shyne's plane lifted off. "I got a new chicken that needs to be plucked."

"Cancel it. Your flight leaves in a few minutes," his father informed.

"My flight? Where am I going?"

"Back to New York to take out some garbage," Killa said. He handed his son his phone with a video playing on the screen.

"Hey, that's Miss Rowland!" Sun shouted, seeing his sexy former teacher dancing naked. The smile on his face flipped when he saw a naked child on her bed. "What kinda fuck shit is this?"

"The worse kind of fuck shit! That's why you're going to New York to kill her!" Killa explained. He saw the murderous glee in his son's eye, but still instigated a little. "And don't forget all of your brothers and sisters that she swallowed!"

"Well, she swallowed plenty of your grandkids too, so..." Sun shot back. He turned the video off when she got into bed with the child.

"Do you, there are hundreds more pedophiles in the computer. I'm off to Miami to visit one myself."

"Say no more," Sun said, giving his dad a pound and a hug. They'd departed and went their separate ways so Killa didn't hear Sun say, "I'm still gonna fuck her first."

****

"Uh, uh, uh," Shyne whispered to herself as the plane began its descent into Belize.

"What are you doing?" Asad laughed when he saw her humping.

"Oh, nothing," she lied. He would find out soon enough. Shyne had been a good girl her whole life and had saved her virginity for her wedding night. Tonight was that night and she was ready to get her freak on.

"We need to see the Aztec Ruins! Oh, and Manatee Bay," Asad exclaimed as they walked through the airport and saw signs for those tourist activities.

"Mmhmm," Shyne grunted. She had no plans on leaving their room. "Look, who's that?"

"I don't know," Asad said of the elderly man holding a sign bearing both his and Shyne's names. He instinctively pulled ahead of Shyne to put himself between her and the man. Shyne smiled at the protective gesture and felt her panties get even wetter. The man had a callous prostration mark on the center of his head so Asad gave him the greeting, "As salaamu alaykum."

"Wa alaykum as salaam. You two must be Asad and Shyne. Yeah, you're definitely Shyne! You look just like your mom. I'm Malik, but everyone calls me Unc, so I guess you should, too. Your dad asked me to pick you up and take you to your hotel. If you need to go anywhere, you can give me a call and..." Malik rambled as he led the newlyweds out to his truck. He pointed out different sights as he drove them to their hotel. Once they arrived, he bid them supplication for a blessed marriage and As salaamu alaykum.

"Wa alaykum as salaam!" Shyne and her husband greeted back and waved as Malik pulled away. She snatched her man by the hand and dragged him into their room. Poor Asad wouldn't see daylight again until it was time to go home.

Chapter 32

"This some real Killa shit!" Sun chuckled as he found a car exactly where his father said it would be. It had a gun, clips and money in it just like his father said that it would. He finally realized they didn't call his father Killa for nothing.

A phone in the center console already had Miss Rowland's number and address programmed in it, but Sun remembered them both. He tried the number, which he hadn't used since high school, and found it had been changed. He made the drive out to Wyandanch and drove by her house.

"Must have company..." Sun said aloud when he saw another car parking in the driveway. He heard his father's voice in his head saying, 'be patient', which killed his wild cowboy idea of kicking the door open and murdering everything moving. "Gon' go get some pussy while I wait."

Sun had to stop by several of his old girlfriends' houses before he got lucky. One had four kids while another one had a live-in boyfriend. He passed another one on Straight Path flagging down cars to turn tricks with. Finally, he got lucky when he stopped by Shay's house. She let him inside and let him inside.

****

Miami, Florida had a bustling child sex market. Sick fucks from far and wide came to spend big bucks for small children. Most were smuggled in like dope from the Dominican Republic, Haiti or Cuba. However, they were far more valuable than the drugs that could only be smoked, snorted or shot up just once. These kids would be used over and over for the rest of their lives.

The lucrative market was run by a sixty-year-old woman called Grandmother. She had the child sex market on smash and was about to get smashed because of it. A killer had just landed in her city and was on his way to her gated estate.

The security was super tight to get into the subdivision by land but the waterfront was wide open. Killa arrived on a small boat loaded with big guns and crept across the backyard.

"Que es?" a security guard asked his partner of the tiny red dot that appeared on his head. He got an answer when the man's head practically exploded. The silencer prevented him from knowing which way the shot came from, so he took off running. A red dot on the back of his head made it a short run.

"Killa's here," Killa whispered as he stepped over the bodies and eased inside the spectacular house. "Damn!"

Killa quietly gunned down another security guard as he made his way through the house. He murdered a cook for cooking for the woman and the maid for cleaning up behind her. The driver got killed for driving her, along with the final guard for standing guard at her bedroom.

"What?" Grandmother called in reply to Killa's knock on the door. She hated being interrupted while reading bedtime stories to the children.

"It's me, Killa, I came to..." Killa stopped short of firing when he walked in and saw five or six five- and six-year-olds sitting on her bed. He got even angrier when he saw they were dressed in tiny little negligees. "OUT!"

"Who are you? Manuel! Jose! Carlos!" she shouted, calling for her security.

"You're going to have to yell louder than that for them to hear you!" Killa laughed. "Dead people don't hear well, you know."

"What do you want? Money? A child?" Grandmother demanded.

"I'll take some money," he shrugged, like why not. "I'm also taking the kids. Oh, and I need to know who made their little lingerie."

"Maria Lopez. She has a shop over on..." the woman snitched as she pulled stacks of money out of her nightstand.

"Thanks," Killa said as he accepted the money with a smile. She let out a sigh of relief when he put his gun away. It was as short lived as she was when he politely began to beat her to death.

Killa called the police from his boat as he left the scene. He reported the children as being left alone. He'd let them discover the bodies once they got here. He retreated to his hotel for a good night's sleep. The next morning, he headed back to the airport after making a quick stop at a seamstress's shop.

"Buenos días! Maria Lopez?" Killa greeted in fluent Spanish with a deceptive smile on his face. He looked jovial but was angry as fuck in reality.

"Buenos días, sí!" the woman replied and smiled because he did. She died with that same smile on her face when he whipped out his pistol and shot her through her black hear.

Now, his smile was genuine.

****

"Man, I gotta go," Sun whined as Shay bobbed her head below. Early morning head was the best and he hated to leave in the middle of it. Shay put her neck in another gear and increased her speed. A minute later, she swallowed in loud gulps.

"Okay," Shay sighed. She wanted to pack her clothes and go with him, but it wasn't an option. Sun saw the look of melancholy on her face as he dressed.

"I'll be in New York for a few days. Can you hang out with me?" he asked. He wasn't a user; it was just the best that he could offer her.

Her eyes lit up as her head began to nod. "Sure!" Shay shouted happily.

"Okay, I'll swing back by later," he said and set off on his mission.

The extra car was gone when Sun arrived. Little did he know, but that extra blow job had caused him to miss it by five minutes. That's why the teacher snatched her door open without looking out or asking who it was, assuming that it was the man who'd just left.

"Sun Forrest?" Miss Rowland gasped. "What are you doing here?"

"Huh?" Sun frowned in confusion. Her naked body made him totally forget why he was there. The large brown nipples on her plump breasts and the fat vagina hanging between her thighs erased his thoughts as thoroughly as shaking erased an Etch-a-Sketch.

"Well, come on in," she instructed as she stepped aside. She then closed the door behind them and led him upstairs. The freaky woman had spent the night freaking but was ready to go again.

"Oh yeah!" Sun exclaimed when he remembered why he was there. The teacher's lips on his dick jogged his memory. "Lay down, let me tie you up!"

"Okay," the woman giggled. "Oh, you brought your own straps!"

"Mmhmm," Sun hummed as he used a plastic tie to secure each of her wrists to her headboard. He then pulled her legs wide apart and fastened her ankles as well.

"The anal lube is in the top drawer!" Miss Rowland said, poking her ass in the air.

Sun was stuck for a second at the thought of trying dookie love for the first time. "Nah," he said, shaking his head with a repugnant grimace. Instead, he pulled out a small pocket knife from his pocket.

"Ouch! What the hell did you just do?" the woman demanded when she felt a sharp prick to her inner thigh. "I'm not into that freaky stuff!"

"I can't tell!" Sun laughed when he pulled open a nightstand drawer. It was filled with all kinds of freaky stuff, from anal lubes, balls, beads, plugs and, of course, pictures. Pictures of small boys engaged in all sorts of sex acts. Some were with her, somewhere with men while others were with other boys.

"I-I-I think you nicked an artery!" she squealed when she felt blood spurting from the small cut. It skeeted with every beat of her heart. "Let me up or I'll die!"

"I definitely nicked an artery but I won't be letting you up, so you'll definitely die!" Sun said as he put on gloves and went to work.

He made it look like a robbery gone wrong by ransacking the room. He collected all the cash and jewelry he found to take with him, while leaving all the child porn for the cops. He'd ignored her pleas so thoroughly that he didn't even realize when she'd left the building. He gave the corpse a sarcastic salute and departed.

****

Shay was face down, ass up with Sun grunting and sweating as he pounded her from behind. Her third orgasm barely registered from being so deep in thought. She and Sun had been cooped up in a hotel room for two days straight, but he was leaving tonight.

Not only had he wined and dined her, he'd also given her all the cash and jewelry he'd taken from the teacher's house. Besides the rough sex of the moment, he'd also made love to her a couple of times as well. It was the best treatment of her life.

"I'm...c-c-c-umming!" Sun announced, then kept his word.

It broke Shay's train of thought so she squeezed her vagina tight to aid the orgasm. They both collapsed face first on the bed. "Take me with you. Please!" Shay pleaded and squeezed some more hoping it would help.

"Huh?" Sun asked sure what she meant. "You mean to Atlanta?"

"Yeah! I can, I mean, I will be a good woman! Promise!"

Sun was moved by the appeal but knew he couldn't. "I would if I could, but I can't. I actually do have a good woman," Sun said thoughtfully. "I just gotta grow up so I can claim her."

Chapter 33

"Sup, yo?" Sun greeted when Bryonna opened the condo's door. Despite having their own rooms at Asad's house, they both chose to stay in the downtown condos.

Bryonna opted to stay to be near school since she would be attending medical school. Sun chose to be here so he could be close to the action. Neither would admit that the other also played a part in the decision but they both knew it.

"Sup," she said as he stepped inside and took a seat.

"You ready?" he asked when she joined him.

"Um...I mean...you know how I feel about you but I have to wait. I've waited this long so it would be crazy to do it now, before marriage. It's not like I don't think about it cuz I do. I just..."

"Bryonna, what the hell are you talking about?" Sun asked in total confusion. "Shyne and Asad's plane lands in an hour and we gotta pick them up. You ready?"

"Oh! Yeah, that's what I meant! What you thought I was talking about? You're crazy if you think somebody like you!" she fussed as she retreated to her room. Her booty had a captive audience as she stormed off.

"I don't mind waiting," Sun said low enough so she couldn't hear him.

She came out ten minutes later looking cute with her head held high despite being embarrassed.

Halfway to the airport, the awkward moment had finally passed and they were kicking it like they always did. A casual observer would think they were a couple by the way they interacted. Actually, they would be right because they were but they just didn't realize it yet.

"There they go!" Bryonna shouted and pointed when she spotted the newlyweds on the curb at the airport's concourse. They weren't hard to spot, with the huge grins they had on their faces.

"Sup, yo?" Sun said as he pulled up and hopped out to grab their bags.

Asad was smiling too hard for words so he just nodded his head. His braids were frayed from being tugged and pulled on all week.

"Hey, girl!" Bryonna cheered as she hugged Shyne. "How was the trip?"

"Great!" she said, walking with a slight limp. "I'm pretty sure I'm pregnant!"

"So, did you guys get to go scuba diving? To the beach?" Bryonna asked as they pulled away from the curb.

"Um...nah. They were closed, so we pretty much stayed in the room."

"The beach was closed!" Sun laughed. Asad still could only nod his head. Sun turned the radio on to provide background music as they rode out to the new house.

The mood was jovial until a breaking news report came on and fucked it up.

"*Nearly a hundred people overdosed at a Las Vegas rap concert. Thirty-five have already died while another fifty are in area hospitals where at least half of them are in critical condition.*

"*Critics are saying that controversial rapper Crack Cocaine and his performance of his hit song entitled 'Kill Yaself' is to blame. A rash of suicides and drug overdoses have followed his concert tour throughout the United States.*

"*When reached for comment, the rapper had this to say, 'So!' His lawyer has threatened to sue any venue that attempts to cancel a show. His next performance is in San Francisco followed by...*"

Sun and Shyne caught each other's eye and made a tacit agreement to murder the man. Like their father said, some people need dead. His last show would be just that; his last show because he wouldn't live long enough to make it to the next one.

"Ooh, whose car is that?" Bryonna shouted, referring to the Acura NSX in the driveway of Asad and Shyne's new home.

"Good question," Shyne said, turning to Asad hopefully.

"It's your dowry," he said proudly. The Islamic faith requires a husband to give his bride a gift in accordance to his means. He had some means thanks to the sale of one of his video programs. Shyne had told him to surprise her and he did.

"Wait 'til I get you inside!" Shyne vowed through clenched teeth. The looks on their faces told Sun and Bryonna that their company wasn't needed. The couple ran into the house without even saying goodbye.

"Well, it's early," Bryonna said once they got back on the road. "How does dinner and a movie sound?"

"Actually, it sounds great! Let me see who I'm gonna go with," Sun said, pulling out his phone. Bryonna calmly took it out of his hand and tossed it out the window.

"You're gonna stop playing with me, Sun Forrest!"

****

"So, what you tell Asad?" Sun asked as he and Shyne rode to the airport for their flight out to Cali.

"The truth; that I'm going to murder that rapper. He just laughed like I was joking and said okay," Shyne laughed.

"He probably needed a break! Poor fella got bags under his eyes!"

"That's cuz I been putting it on him! I been like, uh-uh-uh! Take that, take that!" Shyne shouted while humping in her seat.

"Chill, Shyne!" Sun shouted, causing the car to swerve. "I can't believe you turned my boy out."

"Whatever! Anyway, you think we should call Daddy and let him know where we're going? What we're doing?" she wondered thoughtfully.

Sun contemplated it for a few seconds before shaking his head. "Nah, we got this," he decided. This way he could be in charge instead of their father calling the shots. "Let him see it on the news."

Sun parked in long term parking, still hoping they that wouldn't have to be out west too long. They picked up their boarding passes and joined the long line to get through security. Shyne made her mean face when a fully covered Muslim woman and her child were pulled out of line for extra screening.

"You do this to me every time I fly," the woman grumbled, but remained patient. "I'm from the West End of Atlanta, not the West Bank."

"Damn shame, Islam has now become known by crap that is totally opposite of everything it is," Shyne lamented. "I read the Qur'an all the time and Allah never ordered corruption on Earth. In fact, He forbade it!

"Asad said he gets pulled out of line cuz of his beard," Sun added.

"That's only cuz he too sexy to fly," Shyne giggled. "You don't have to worry about that with that big ass head you got!"

"Big head? Girl, you look like a stick figure with your bony arms and big, round head! A female Charlie Brown!" Sun shot back. They cracked on each other to the entertainment of everyone in line. It was real funny until they started on them.

"Finally!" Shyne announced with her fussy face in place when they reached their gate. She looked at the row of seats and got a surprise.

"Is that..."

"Hey, guys! I been expecting you," Killa cheered and waved.

Sun sighed and twisted his lips at his instant demotion. Shyne, however, didn't mind at all. The daddy's girl rushed over to hug her beloved father. The killer kinfolk chopped it up until the announcement to board came over the P.A system.

"Fligh' five-fo'-fo- is finna bode at gate ni," a sexy southern belle announced with a sexy southern twang.

"We are definitely down south," Killa chuckled as they stood to board.

"Can I have a eh-ba fo' cri-ma?" Shyne pleaded.

Killa frowned in confusion and turned to his son for translation.

"She said can she have an X-box for Christmas!" he barely got out over his laughter.

"If your husband let you have a Christmas tree," Killa laughed.

"He ain't the boss of me!" Shyne whined and cracked her father and brother up. They all knew good and well that he was.

Chapter 34

The treacherous trio boarded the plane together, but wouldn't be sitting together. Sun and Shyne had purchased coach tickets while their father had first class tickets.

"I'll holla," he laughed as he hoisted his carry-on bag up to the overhead bin.

"Oh no, he didn't!" Shyne huffed as they made their way down the aisle. They found their seats over the wing. Sun put his bag up in the compartment and sat down. "Oh no, you didn't!"

"My bad," Sun chuckled and put her bag away. She thanked him by stealing his window seat. Now she had a nice view of the wing.

"Mmph!" Sun announced when a sexy stewardess stood to give her safety spiel. She went on about seatbelts, exits and oxygen masks, but Sun focused on the nipples pressing through her tight shirt. The top buttons were unbuttoned, showing off plump mounds of titty meat. It took two full minutes for Sun to make it up to her face. It was cute and colorful from all the make-up.

"No telling what she looks like under all that. Could be a man for all you know," Shyne warned when she saw her brother drooling over the woman. "Probably Caitlyn Jenner!"

"That ain't no man!" Sun assured her as he traced the curves of her hips. She saw him staring and cracked a smile. Sun hit her with the classic Forrest family smile and he had her.

She made a beeline to him once they were airborne. "Hello, can I bring you anything?" the woman purred. She then leaned forward so Sun could see her lacy bra straining to contain her heavy breasts.

"You already brought it," Sun said, licking his lips.

"Oh boy!" Shyne hated, with her cock-blocking self. "I'll take a... Oh no, she didn't!"

Yes, she did. She'd led her thirsty brother away to the staff's bathroom.

"We only have a few minutes," she urged once they were inside the tight space. She gave him a quick peck on his lips and turned around. She then rolled the tight skirt up over her ass and hips while Sun rolled a condom down his erection.

"It won't take that long," Sun said as he slipped inside of her tight space. He was right too, because the excitement proved to be too much for the youngster. A minute had barely passed before he grunted and filled the condom up.

"That's got to be a new record," the stewardess chuckled as Sun convulsed behind her.

"Thanks...I think," Sun replied, unsure if it was a compliment or complaint. He shrugged it off since it really didn't matter. Either way, he got a nut so that was all that mattered. He made sure to flush the condom in the blue water and put his wood away.

"You are so....so-so-so-so nasty!" Shyne fussed with her fussy face in place when he returned. "And you stink! Smell like...latex and thot."

"Don't hate cuz I'm officially in The Mile High Club!" Sun shot back.

"Uh, you late! Me and Asad..."

"Shyne, chill!" he shouted before she could finish. He let out a yawn, blinked and yawned again before falling asleep.

"Men!" Shyne laughed. An hour or so later, she saw the same stewardess leading Killa down the aisle. He didn't look at his kids as he rushed past. She also took him into the same bathroom and gave him the same thing. "Men!"

****

"So, what's the plan?" Killa asked as they walked through the airport in San Francisco. Sun and Shyne looked at each other but neither spoke. "You mean to tell me, you come all this way and don't even have a plan!"

"Yup, pretty much," the twins agreed, nodding their heads.

Killa shook his. Luckily, he had a plan. "Well, I got a plan. Some classic shit," Killa said, and nodded his head as he rapped a classic, "Who shot ya, separate the weak for the obsolete, Hard to creep on Brooklyn streets..."

"What's that, dad?" Sun butted in, smiling broadly at his father rapping.

"B.I.G!" Killa exclaimed in shock that they didn't know the song. When they looked at each other and shrugged, he realized that they didn't even know who he was. "Really? The Notorious! Brooklyn's finest? *It was all a dream, use to read* Word Up *magazine*?"

"Still nothing," Sun shrugged again.

Meanwhile, Shyne googled him on her phone. "The Notorious B.I.G, a Brooklyn rapper, circa 1994. He was killed in a drive-by shooting... Oh! I get it!" Shyne announced triumphantly.

"Well, I don't," Sun admitted.

"You will!" his father assured him. He then filled his kids in on the plan as they left.

Sun and Shyne gave each other a 'will you look at this shit' look as he moved fluidly when they arrived. A rental car was on stand-by when they landed. Killa drove it to another car loaded with guns, vests, phones and all the other etceteras needed for a hit. Like B.I.G said, "Bad boys move in silence and violence."

"You guys sleep off the time difference to be ready to go. That...that..." Killa said searching for words.

"Piece of shit," Shyne tossed out helpfully.

"Piece of shit," Killa agreed, "has a show tomorrow night and more kids will die. So, he's not doing that show!"

****

Sun and Shyne took their father's advice and crashed out as soon as they got into their shared room. However, Killa didn't. Instead, he headed to his separate room where he had a friend waiting with open arms. Once he arrived, she opened her legs as well.

Shyne woke up first and hopped into the shower. Afterwards, she changed into her outfit and admired the results. The tiny skirt and wig made her look like the same girls she talked about.

"Cute, though," she giggled and blew herself a kiss in the mirror.

"Homo," Sun said, shaking his head when he woke up and saw his sister.

"Shut up and get dressed. You got the fun part," Shyne spat with envy dripping from her words. Sun got to be the shooter while she had to be a prop.

Sun rolled out of bed and complied. By the time he got out of the shower, his sister was gone. She had to get to the party early enough to get in so she could do her thing.

"Westside!" Sun shouted and threw up a 'W' with his fingers as he admired himself in the mirror. He looked like a West coast gangbanger in the black khaki suit, black shades and bandana. He grabbed a black plastic pistol and left the room.

"Final call, my brother?" Killa greeted in a suit and Nation of Islam like bowtie.

"Not! And I don't want no bean pie either!" Sun laughed. Why wouldn't he laugh at people standing around in suits selling bean pies in hundred-degree heat? That's some funny shit that has nothing to do with Islam. "Anyway, Pops, you sure that this is going to work?"

"It's worked before," he assured him.

****

"What's up with you, cutie pie?" a man asked, invading Shyne's space as he confronted her at the bar. Not only was his presence unwanted, he also blocked her view of her target.

Crack and his crew were holding court in the VIP section. They popped bottles and groped groupies vying for attention, each hoping for the privilege of being taken back to his hotel and taken advantage of.

"What!" Shyne fussed at the distraction. She thought about sticking the candle on the bar up to his greasy Jheri Curl and setting it on fire.

"Can I buy you a drink?" he offered graciously since every playa assumed he was entitled to some ass if a woman accepted a drink.

"The doctor said I can't drink with my HIV meds," Shyne said, figuring that would run him off. She figured wrong.

"So, you wanna smoke some weed then? We can go to my place."

"Beat it!" she finally barked. She almost felt bad when a look of sorrow spread on his shiny face.

"Must be a dyke!" he spat and stormed off. Every playa also assumed that a woman must be a gay if she turned down their corny come-ons.

"Me and yo mama!" Shyne shot back and laughed. Once he was gone, she resumed her surveillance. She couldn't help but notice that there were male groupies there, too. Grown ass men who co-signed Crack's every word and laughed at his every joke.

Shyne moved closer to get a closer look and noticed he looked to be around her father's age. She was right because the man was in his mid-fifties and still rapping. He dyed his hair and wore the same fashions as his grandkids.

"We ready," her phone read after vibrating. Shyne got up and entered the ladies room. The stall with the vent was occupied so she had to wait a couple of minutes.

"Eww! Who shits at the club?" she fussed upon entering the smelly stall. She retrieved a lighter and smoke bomb from her bra and climbed on the toilet. She opened the grate in the ceiling, lit the device and walked out. Smoke quickly began seeping from all the vents.

"No problem! Nothing to worry about!" the club manager pleaded. The last thing he needed was a fire. The night was young and he couldn't stand to lose out on a full night's revenue. Unfortunately, police assigned to watch the rapper were eager for the detail to end. They wanted to kill him themselves instead of protecting him.

"Please evacuate! Everyone, please remain calm and evacuate!" one of the officers announced. The crowd let out a collective groan over the party breaking up.

"After party in my suite!" Crack announced and started an exodus form the club.

Once outside, Crack and his entourage piled in SUVs leading the pussy parade headed for his hotel. They approached the light and Killa made his move.

"What the fuck?" the driver of Crack's truck cursed as he slammed on the brakes to avoid hitting the man in the bowtie. The light turned red, trapping them in place.

"Bean pie, my brother?" Killa asked as he came around to Crack's window. The window lowered as Sun eased up beside them.

"Hell yeah! I love them shits!" Crack proclaimed. Those would be his last words. Sun whipped up in a growling '96 Impala and hopped out.

It was supposed to be a drive-by but a walk up is so much more fun. Sun snatched the SUV door open and began firing. The first shot entered Crack's nostril and came out his ear. Sun continued firing, emptying the clip into his face, making his head nod like he agreed with getting murdered.

"Do you see this shit?" the stunned cop asked his nonchalant partner.

"Nope!" he replied and turned his head. Meanwhile, Killa beamed with pride as his son pulled off.

"That was so gangsta!" he said to himself as he made his way to where his vehicle was parked. Sun and Shyne were back in the room when he arrived.

"Huh? Did we rock or what?" Sun bragged. He and Shyne shared a high-five at the mission accomplished.

"Yeah, that was dope!" their father admitted.

"Next time I get to pull the trigger! The world is better already with that dude gone!" Shyne celebrated.

"There's plenty more people who need dead," Killa advised. "Remember the old saying, the family that kills together...um...?"

"Chills together?" Sun tried.

"Builds together?" Shyne tossed.

"Something! Anyway, there's plenty more where that came from."

Chapter 35

Shyne may or may not have gotten pregnant on her honeymoon or on the flight back but her first post wedding period was a no show. She let another month pass before building up the nerve to take a test. Shyne bought one of every type of pregnancy test on the shelf and lined them up. She locked the bathroom door and peed on them all.

"I love it when you call me Big Poppa!" Shyne rapped as she entered Asad's home office. She and Sun had both become addicted to the late rapper's music since they discovered him.

"I'm sure you mean something by that?" Asad said knowingly. He and the twins had known each other almost their whole lives. Sometimes they could talk without saying a word. He had a certain smile that said 'I love you' and she could return it just by batting her lashes.

Being married to your best friend is proof of God's love for humanity. They loved each other for the sake of God first and then their own reasons. The two peas in the pod were about to become three.

"This..." Shyne paused to climb on his lap and hand him test results, "means that we're having a baby!"

"Allahu Akbar!" Asad shouted and jumped to his feet. The leap sent Shyne sprawling on the floor.

"God is the Greatest!" she agreed as he helped her up. He picked up the pregnancy test and smiled proudly.

"Why is it wet?" he wondered.

"It's pee," she cheered happily like it was no big deal. Obviously, it wasn't since her husband didn't flinch.

"Cool. You better call your dad, Sun, Christi, Bryonna and Rico."

"Um...I think I'll wait a little while before I tell them," Shyne said. She nodded her head, hoping to get him to nod his as well, but it didn't work.

"Why?" Asad asked curiously. He was ready to call his own mom and dad to share the news.

"Huh? Um... Damn, you're sexy!" she said and moved on him. He twisted his lips as she planted kisses all over his face.

Shyne wouldn't like to tell her husband but the truth was she were having too much fun killing Black Mob members and didn't want it to stop. They had made a mess in Memphis, slaughtered in Sacramento, killed in Kansas City and had a hanging scheduled for Houston. She knew that her father would clip her wings when he found out that she was pregnant.

"Oh, okay," Asad gave in to her seduction as she led him to their bedroom. "You can tell me why later."

****

"Houston, Texas, home of Black Mob Records," Sun read out loud as the family walked through the airport.

"Time to put those fuckers in the past tense," Shyne said with a snarl on her face.

"Did I turn invisible? Can you see me?" Killa asked, waving his hands.

"I'm sorry, Daddy, but I hate those...fuckers! I don't know if they are affiliated with the Mob Movement or not, but them songs they put out... Sheesh, Daddy!" Shyne griped.

She was right, too, because Black Mob Records put out songs that dumbed down the nation. Impressionable young girls tried to imitate their nasty R&B Diva called Kitty-Cat. Her hit song "No Names" was an ode to one nightstands. Her other titles included "Drink the Babies" and "Ode to Swallowing". "My Lips on Your Lips" encouraged girls to eat pussy and "Fuck Me, Pay Me" needed no explanation. The shit was just as ridiculous as some urban book titles. What the fuck is a *Yung Pimpin*?

Kitty-Cat had recently leaked a sex tape to boost the sales of her upcoming album.

They also had a rapper called Brain Dead. His hit record 'Just Sippin' made it cool to sip codeine laced cough syrup. Kids were putting themselves to sleep forever trying to use his so-called formula. He just released a remake of a MC Hammer song "Hammer Time", it was blowing up.

"Well, I'll take this Kitty-Cat," Sun suggested. Shyne saw right through his shit and twisted her lips.

"You seen that tape, huh?" she asked, referring to Kitty-Cat gagging herself while giving head.

"Tape? What tape?" he lied. He had no problem killing the bad influence, but he did want a little head first. And who could really blame him?

"I'll take the girl. You two go..."

"Daddy, really? Seriously?" Shyne demanded with her hand on her spreading hips. The baggy shirt she wore concealed her slight baby bump. "I'll kill the chick, you two make ol' Brain Dead live up to his name!"

****

As usual, the well liked, well-respected and connected Killa had people in Houston. He had cars, guns, hotels and everything already at his disposal, but that was all he had. This time it was up to Sun and Shyne to provide intel on their victims. They didn't disappoint.

"Okay," Shyne began and paused dramatically to ensure she had her father and brother's full attention, "Kitty-Cat, AKA Catherine Dalton, is a real hoe! She's not fronting for the industry. She had sex with three men in one day!"

"And?" Killa asked when his disgusted daughter got stuck on that part. She'd followed her for two days and all she'd done was eat, smoke weed, have sex and switch weaves.

"She gets her hair 'did' at LaQuisha's over in the 5th Ward. LaQuisha likes dead white men so I gave her ten thousand of them to get inside.

"Not bad. Now what about this Brain Dead fellow?" Killa asked turning to Sun.

"He has a studio session Saturday night. A gas leak will get us inside where we can kill him and destroy all his masters," Sun advised.

"Why not just use the gas leak and blow up the building? That would kill him and destroy the masters," Killa replied even though he already knew the answer.

"Yeah, I guess...but, what fun is that? It's 'Hammer Time'!" Sun cheered. His father didn't know what he meant by 'Hammer Time' but was he was about to find out.

"Can we eat now?" a greedy Shyne moaned. She was eating for two every two hours.

"Hell yeah!" her brother agreed and picked up the menus. He made the decision for all of them and called a Chinese restaurant. Thirty minutes later their food arrived.

"Why don't I fix the plates?" Shyne asked sarcastically when neither her father nor brother budged.

"Great idea. Thanks!" Killa and Sun called out from in front of the TV. They missed the sarcasm as they focused on the basketball game.

"Shri-fri-ri, Moo Goo...uh oh," Shyne said while plating the food. The smells overwhelmed her and turned her face green. She took off to the bathroom where she upchucked her lunch.

"Dang, she couldn't finish fixing the plates first?!" Sun griped.

Killa shook his head at him as he went to check on Shyne. He waited until her heaves turned dry before asking if she was okay. From the doorway, of course, since he didn't want any throw up to get on his new shoes.

"Huh? Who? Me? Yeah! I'm fine! I'm good. Nothing wrong me!" Shyne said emphatically. She stood up and put a crooked smile on her green face as proof.

"Um, okay," Killa said skeptically. The wise man assumed she was pregnant but had no choice but to believe her. He was sure that she would tell him if she were. She was a grown married woman, so a pregnancy was to be expected.

When they returned, Sun had eaten half of the food.

Chapter 36

"That new shampoo girl ain't worth a damn!" a customer complained as she returned to her stylist's chair after a near drowning with shampoo still in her hair.

"She's trying," LaQuisha said in defense of the ten grand she'd been paid. "I'll finish you up."

Several hours later, Kitty-Cat arrived with her small entourage. Shyne thought about just shooting her in her face but wasn't sure if a bullet would penetrate all the make-up. Besides, she didn't have enough bullets to kill all the hangers-on surrounding her.

"Heeey, Kitty-Cat in this bitch!" the diva announced as she began to twerk. For some reason, she flipped her skirt up and flashed the salon full of women.

"Eww," Shyne grimaced at the tampon string hanging from her thong. There were several men's names tattooed on her ass as well as a bull's eye with the caption 'skeet here'. It was a form of birth control to the famous thot. Another one was swallowing.

"Gurl, you too much!" LaQuisha cheered, laughed and clapped.

"I'm is!" the ghetto girl agreed. "I got a show tomorrow so you know I needs my shit tight!"

"You know we got you. Gon' on back and get shampooed wo we can get started."

"Okay."

LaQuisha removed her large weave that looked like an Indian head piece before she twerked her way on to the back to get killed.

"Right this way," Shyne smiled and invited her to sit down. "Lean back."

"You must be new," Kitty-Cat frowned at the unfamiliar face.

"Mmhm," Shyne agreed as she sprayed the girl's short fro. She lathered it up really good and then made her move.

"Turn around."

"'Kay," the diva agreed so that the shampoo could be rinsed away. However, instead, Shyne grabbed the expensive scarf around her neck and pulled tightly. At the same time, she forced her head under the standing water. The loud music up front helped drown out the sounds of struggle as Shyne drowned the girl.

"Die already!" Shyne fussed at Kitty-Cat's struggle to live. Finally, the lack of oxygen proved to be too much and she stopped squirming and blowing bubbles. Shyne held her down for another full minute before letting up. She then eased out the backdoor to her borrowed car. Once she pulled away safely, she texted her dad.

"One down"

****

"Man, that's fucked up," Brain Dead sighed over the death of Kitty-Cat as they reminisced in the smoke filled studio. "She had some good, good pussy." His engineer and the security guard both nodded in agreement as well. All three swerved as proof of just how generous she was with her vagina.

"Don't forget that dome!"

"Man, could she suck a dick!" Brain Dead replied and shed a tear for her head game. Everyone will be remembered for something, good or bad. "I should write a song 'bout that bitch."

"You should, you shall should!" his manager exclaimed. "I miss my bitch!"

"The best bitches die young," the manager tossed in. "You never miss yo' bitch until the bitch is dead."

"Who?" the security guard barked at the knock on the door. The big burly man was just as high and drunk as everyone else. He picked up his pump shotgun and went to the door. He turned to relay the reply from the other side of the door. "Gas Company?"

"I thought I smelled gas," the manager announced. He did thanks to the slow leak that Killa had just made. It was just slow enough to let them handle their business and get away safely.

"Gas leak," Killa said as he and Sun entered. Each had a tool box in one hand and a heavy sledgehammer over their shoulder.

"I wouldn't do that," Sun advised when Brain Dead lifted a blunt to his black lips.

"You right! You shole right!" he agreed, nodding his head.

"Can you put on your song 'Hammer Time'?" Sun asked happily since it was now hammer time.

"Oops!" Killa said as his tool box slipped from his hand. All heads turned towards the distraction just like he knew they would.

Sammy Sosa would have been proud of Sun's major league swing. He hit the security guard so hard that it literally knocked his brains out. His neck was broken so severely that his head lay flat on his shoulder.

"Stop...it's hammer time!" Killa cheered to the throwback beat. He tried, but he couldn't stop himself form doing the hammer dance.

"Pops!" Sun yelled, embarrassed at his father's dancing. "We're kinda busy here!"

"Oh yeah!" Killa laughed a brief chuckle before swinging his own hammer. The heavy blow broke several of the manger's ribs and dropped him.

Sun dropped the engineer with a savage blow to his collarbone. He raised his good arm to deflect the next blow but it proved as futile as trying to block a sledgehammer with a forearm.

Brain Dead was frozen with fear as he watched the gas company men beat his friends to death. He actually thought that it was because they didn't pay the bill. "I'll pay! I'll pay! Here! Here!" the rapper pleaded as he emptied his pockets. Killa frown at the stacks but Sun scooped them up.

"What?" he asked, seeing his father's reaction. "He ain't gonna need it!"

"Drink it!" Killa demanded as he poured the entire bottle of cough syrup into the cup that the rapper had been sipping from.

"That's too much!" Brain Dead pleaded. He was stupid but not crazy. "It's gon' kill me!"

"No, it's not. Promise," Sun assured him as he raised his hammer to strike.

"Wait! Wait! I'll drink it!" Brain Dead pleaded. Sun used the man's phone to record his final drink and uploaded it to all his social media accounts.

"Let's bounce!" Killa announced, noticing how thick the smell of gas had gotten as it filled the room. Brain Dead couldn't believe his luck when they left him alive.

"Suckas!" the rapper laughed as he called 9-1-1. He had consumed too much codeine laced cough syrup but emergency rooms in the area dealt with those types of overdoses on a daily basis.

"Help is on the way. Stay on the line," the operator instructed.

"'Kay," he agreed and decided to smoke a blunt while he waited.

"What a dummy!" Sun sighed when the explosion lit up the night sky and shook the ground.

"They didn't call him Brain Dead for nothing," his father laughed. "Your mom taught me how to do that."

"She did?!" Sun exclaimed wide eyed with excitement. The thought of his mom being a ruthless killer amazed him. "What else she teach you?"

"I'll show you tomorrow!"

****

The next day, Killa kept his word and showed his children a lesson that Yolo had taught him. They decided that the radio station's program manager was just as much to blame as the rappers and singers.

No, they didn't make the destructive music, but they pushed it. The music he pushed corrupted the youth and destroyed the hood while he was safe and sound in the suburbs. Safe and sound until along came a Killa.

"Package," Killa smiled a deceptive smile as the door opened. He was still smiling when he fired a silent round into the man's forehead. Sun and Shyne quickly joined him inside with Yolo's black bag of tricks. They dragged the dead man into the bathroom and got to work.

"It's just like chicken!" Shyne cheered as they clipped off his wings. It dawned on her that her mother was actually teaching her how to dismember a body. "Hey!"

"I know!" Sun shouted when he caught on as well. Their revelry was short lived when Shyne turned green and turned to the toilet. Killa and Sun both looked at her, looked at each other and then back at her.

"I'm good. Y'all go 'head. Must be a bug or something I ate!"

Chapter 37

"What's wrong, Bae?" Shyne whined when she saw the distress on her husband's face. He was usually happy and content when he came in from Friday's prayers, but lately he was dark and moody.

"The new Imam is a liar!" Asad proclaimed. A new prayer leader from the Middle East had taken over about a month back. He'd started off fine but got a little more radical each week.

"Why? What he say?" Shyne wanted to know. Her husband usually filled her in on the sermons, until he'd started.

"He said that Jihad is holy war. That we have to fight all non-Muslims!"

"Even I know that's not true! How can war ever be holy? Besides, that's not even what Jihad means!" Shyne protested since she knew enough about Islam to know better.

What most laypeople don't know is that Jihad means to strive and struggle against evil. That battle begins with self, with one struggling to be upright. Everyone, no matter what religion they follow, can relate to that.

"I don't like him. He's radical," Asad decided. He knew something had to be done but hadn't decided just what.

"Well, I need to go to Tulsa with my dad and Sun. Family business," she said hopefully. She knew Asad trusted her and didn't question her. Good thing, too, because she would have told the truth had he asked.

The truth was that The Black Mob had taken over the city. A guy named Shelby ran all operations from dope and pussy to gambling and extortion. The Black Mob had sent their goons to spread their gospel of get down or lay down. The sissy chose to get down and was about to get laid down for it.

"Okay. Hey, have you told them yet?" he wondered as he rubbed her belly.

"Um... Oh, can I get a little before I go?" Shyne purred.

"I love the way you change a subject," Asad laughed and agreed to being seduced.

****

"Where's your sister?" Killa asked as he enter Sun's condo.

"Don't know. I haven't seen her since we got back from Houston," Sun frowned. A text from Shyne came in as they were speaking and he relayed its contents to his father. "She's here. Down the hall with Bryonna."

"Speaking of Bryonna, what's up with you guys?" Killa inquired nosily.

"Huh? I mean... You know... We... I'm saying, though. Time to go."

"I see," he laughed as he followed him down the hall to the girl's condo. They rang the bell and Shyne pulled open the door.

"You guys ready? Let's bounce!" she said loudly, hoping to keep the attention on her face. It didn't work and her father and brother both lowered their gaze to her stomach. The large shirt couldn't conceal her four-month pregnant stomach.

"Anything you wanna tell me?" Killa asked curiously, cocking his head.

"Me? No, nothing. Everything is good, nothing to report. You guys ready? I'm ready! Let's go handle this business!"

"But..." Sun said, pointing at her protruding stomach.

"But what, my nigga? What, what?" Shyne spat like she was ready to fight. He stepped behind their father for protection.

"Shyne, are you pregnant?" Killa asked plainly.

"Technically, yes, but I can still handle mine. I'm good!"

"No, you're not. Go home. Rest up so I can have a healthy grandchild," he ordered. He'd never told them about the same type of stress leading to them being born prematurely.

"If you guys need a hand, I can go help out with whatever it is that you guys do," Bryonna offered. She had no clue what they actually did beyond it being a family business. She and Sun spent a lot of time to together but there was no romance. Sun still smashed a variety of Georgia peaches but never brought anyone to the condo.

Shyne and Killa turned to Sun to handle the question.

"No, you stay here. I'll see you when I get back," he replied in that tone that men used when they spoke to their woman.

"Ok-a-a-y," Bryonna sang, making Shyne giggle girlishly. She loved their tacit relationship and just knew they were right for each other. Now if only Sun would figure it out.

"Mmhm," Shyne hummed when her brother and father left the condo.

"Mmhm, what?" Bryonna giggled like she had no idea what she meant.

"You and my brother is what! You two are in love."

"Maybe, maybe not. I'm not waiting forever, though. I told him once I finish grad school, I'm getting married, with or without him."

"What he say?" Shyne inquired wide eyed with excitement.

"He said okay. Whatever that means."

****

"So, anyway, the girl's sister went into her phone and saw the wood and wanted some for herself. Who am I to say no?" Sun relayed to his father as they rode.

"Yeah, but what's up with Bryonna? I mean, I know the thots are fun but what about your future?" Killa urged in a tone that made Sun take his eyes off the road. "Don't waste your life like me."

"She's probably the one, but I don't want to do her wrong. I'm too immature," he admitted. The car went silent as Sun reflected on his life and future. That's exactly what his father wanted to do.

"Look at me, forty-something and still single. Maybe things would have turned out different if...," Killa said but got cut off.

"'If' is from the devil. What happens is what is already written to happen," Sun said, imparting some wisdom from Asad. "Besides, you're in your fifties not forties!"

"Anyway, give her this, maybe it will hold your place," his dad said, removing the diamond solitaire from a chain that he wore around his neck. "It was your moms."

"It was!" Sun exclaimed and inspected it. "I never saw her wearing this."

"That's because I never got the chance to give it to her. She died before I could," Killa said, sending the car back into total silence. They didn't speak again until they landed in Oklahoma.

****

"So, I know you got the scoop on this Shelby dude," Sun said when they rode away from the airport in a rental. As usual, his well-connected father had everything mapped out.

"Old school cat, 'bout my age. Hangs out in his club called Man on Man. He..."

"Man on Man?" Sun cracked up, "Yo, you gotta say no homo when you say a name like that!"

Killa pressed his lips together trying not to laugh but ended up wearing a smirk instead. Sun smiled at his father's smile until he got it.

"Dad! Say no homo! Say it!" he pleaded.

"I wish I could. It's a gay club because he's a gay man. That's the only chink in his armor. It's the only way we can get close to him," Killa replied.

"Well, you gotta do what you gotta do. I understand, Pops."

"I'm glad you do because he likes young boys. Let him take you home and knock his head off. I'll take care of his crew. Shyne would be so proud!"

Chapter 38

"Mannn!" Sun whined at his reflection in the mirror. He looked the part of a fuck boy with his little goatee and mustache shaved off. "I may as well wear a skirt, too."

"If you think it'll help," his father said, trying and failing to keep a straight face. "I do love your earring, though."

"Yeah, it is kinda cool," Sun cheered at the large wire hoop in his ear. It was the only weapon he would be able to get into the club.

"It may be cool but his team is about to be hot!" The men bumped fists and went their separate ways.

Killa arrived at his destination first. He parked outside of the crew's hangout and waited for the call. Meanwhile, Sun reached the club and parked.

"Man oh man, kinda fuck shit is that?" Sun griped as he read the pink neon sign. He watched all kinds of gay men enter the club. Most looked like regular everyday guys, with a few effeminate types mixed. He swallowed his pride, let out a deep sigh and went inside.

"Uh, uh, uh, go, lil mama! Uh, uh, uh," Shelby sang and tossed money to the fuck boy dancing in front of him. The skinny teen wore skinny jeans and a fresh Mohawk. His big, collagen-injected lips made him very popular.

"Really?" Sun asked himself as he walked in and saw a thugged out rapper performing on stage. "Homo thugs."

"Uh, uh, uh, huh?" Shelby said when he saw the new meat walk by. He stood up and left the sissy and made a beeline to where Sun was. "Who...are...you?"

"What?" Sun barked then caught himself. He softened his tone and got into character. "I mean, what?"

"I ain't never seent you 'round her befo'," Shelby flirted. He reached to touch his unusual earring but Sun moved his head.

"That's cuz I'm new in town," Sun said, deflecting his hand.

"Well, I'm Shelby and Tulsa is my city. I run err'thang 'round here," he bragged.

"I heard Black Mob run this town," Sun shot back sassily like Shyne would speak.

"Fuck a Black Mob! Trust me, once I get my team right, that Lil' Rock gonna be paying!" Shelby snapped.

"Little Rock, huh?" Sun misunderstood.

"Anyway, let's get up out of here. Go get our smoke, drink and whatever else on," Shelby suggested.

"Just me and you?" Sun asked to make sure he could get him alone. "I'm not into groups."

"Say no mo'," he said, waving his bodyguard away. "Let's get up out of here!"

Shelby rushed his latest catch from the club and into his Shelby Mustang. He just knew he was about to fuck something but little did he know, he was about to get fucked up. He rambled on and on to impress the kid as they rode. In his bragging, he gave up vital information.

"Here we are," he sang when they reached his house. The high ranch home was fifty years old but had undergone extensive renovation. Shelby let Sun enter first so he could get a look at his booty. He liked what he saw and gave it a pinch. Any man who wears skinny jeans is just asking to get their butt pinched.

"Chill, yo. I mean, ki-ki-ki," Sun said as he slapped his hand away. He fought off the urge to attack, not knowing if anyone else was inside. "I thought you said something about smoking?"

"Come on! I got the best weed in town!" Shelby bragged as he led him into the den. A large, ornate bowl full of light green weed sat on the coffee table.

"Ooh, popcorn!" Sun cheered, rushed over and began to roll up a blunt. "This is some gas!"

"Best in town!" he repeated, then added, "Oh, and I give some good head, too!"

"We better smoke our own blunts," Sun grimaced at the thought of smoking after the cocksucker. Never mind the thots he smoked with on a regular at home.

Sun rolled another blunt and listened to the man brag like men do when they're trying to hit something. The weed burned out and it was time to get down to business.

"So let me see what you working with," Sun dared as he carefully removed the large hoop from his ear. He fiddled with it while the punk proudly produced his penis.

"This guy so nice, I wish I could suck it myself!" Shelby bragged once he got his dick out. Sun frowned up at the sight of the man's dick as Shelby stroked himself erect. Never mind how many dicks he saw watching porn all day.

****

"'Bout time!" Killa fussed when the text finally came. Sun had just sent Shelby to the afterlife so it was time for his crew to join him. A couple members of the crew left early and would live to die another day.

Killa padlocked the back, side and finally front doors. The building didn't have gas lines, so he had to go old school. He lit the cocktails of gas and laundry powder. The latter made the gas stick to flesh.

"Okay, we'll holla!" he chuckled as he began tossing them through the windows. The men inside did indeed holla when they caught on fire. A few managed to get out but got gunned down.

Killa drove away smiling when first responders began to arrive. When he made it back to the hotel, it looked like there had been a fire there as well.

"Damn, Sun!" he fussed as he entered the smoke filled room.

"Hey, Pops!" Sun said with a happy smile pasted on his face from the good weed. He extended a smoldering blunt to his father.

"Why not?" Killa shrugged and took a toke. "The family that gets high together..."

"Causes people to die together!"

Chapter 39

"A deadly night in Tulsa Oklahoma..." the news reporter announced with the same smile she had when she gave the weather report.

"This ain't no fuckin' co-in...um, what you call them things that be happening?" Little Rock asked his woman.

"A coincidence," India replied, flipping her long Indian hair.

"Yeah! Hell naw, it ain't! Something up and I'ma find out what!"

Little Rock was the son of B-more's infamous Big Rock. His father once ran the entire city on behalf of The Black Mob. He took it in a violent coup. He was sold out by his best friend and bodyguard Bull. He'd fed him to Yolo and took over the city.

The son had grown up hearing tales about his dad and wanted to be just like him. What he didn't hear was how Bull had betrayed him and took his mom. He'd never heard that his dad went out like a bitch and jumped out of a window rather than face the woman.

"I know, baby," his woman purred. They had a comfortable life but wanted more. They wanted it all.

****

Little Rock wasn't the only one hot about the Tulsa murders. Shyne watched the same news reports and turned green with envy. She hated being left out from all the fun; especially when she heard about the fire.

"Dang biter!" Shyne fussed about the blaze. "Bit my style!"

"Chill, Shyne," Asad said, rubbing her belly. She got a reminder of why she had to stay when the child inside of her began to stir. Asad leaned in and began to recite some Qur'an in melodious tone.

"Bismil-lahir Rahmanir-Raheem, Alhamdulillahir-Rabbil Alameen..."

Shyne's phone began to vibrate on the table but would have to wait. She smiled softly and listened to her husband. Both she and their baby basked in tranquility.

"It's my dad," Shyne said, checking her phone once he finished his recital. The daddy's girl twisted her lips like 'yeah right' but still returned the call. "Mmhm."

"Aww, baby girl, don't be salty," Killa laughed.

"It's not funny! I had to miss out on all the fun," she whined. Asad kissed her belly and cheek, then got up so that she could talk to her father in private.

"Daddy, I need you to go to the Masjid with Asad. Something's up with the new Imam."

"Say no more," her father replied.

They spent a few more minutes going over the details of the Oklahoma trip before hanging up. Shyne was still frustrated about not being able to go. A frustrated Shyne is a dangerous Shyne. It wouldn't be long until she went looking for trouble.

****

"What?" Killa asked as he saw Asad staring at him from his peripheral.

"I'm saying, though," he asked, wondering why his father-in-law had popped up on Friday to offer Friday prayer with him.

"Son, it's been a while since I've had the chance to chill with you and even longer since I've been to Jumu'ah prayer, so I figured I'd kill two birds with one stone," he replied. It was mostly true but he also wanted to hear this radical preacher who was preaching. If he was a terrorist, he was going to make it three birds with one stone.

Asad watched as his father-in-law made proper ablution and then prayed the customary two cycles of prayer required upon entering the Masjid. He did the same and they sat on the carpeted floor to listen to the sermon.

Imam Jamal Alaki hailed from Yemen. He'd studied under renowned Sheikhs and scholars. He'd memorized the entire Qur'an by age ten. He'd attended college in England and graduated with honors. Somehow, somewhere along the way, he'd gotten radicalized. He began to twist Qur'an and misquote the Prophet, Peace and Blessings be upon him, for his own gain.

"Lies," Killa mumbled under his breath as the liar told lies. Most of the congregation looked shocked, but a couple of impressionable young men smiled with glee.

"I can't!" Asad said and got up. He walked out shaking his head and offered his prayer in the parking lot. Killa managed to stick it out until the end. He then joined the ranks and prayed along with the other men. He waited on the Imam to have a word with him.

"As salaamu alaykum. I think I read between the lines and would like to pick your brain," Killa greeted and stated.

"Wa alaykum as salaam. It's about time someone heard the message. It's time to act. I will gladly allow you to pick my brain."

"And pick it I shall," Killa said with a smile. They made an appointment for the next day and departed.

"Afwan, Pops, I can't listen to that guy," Asad apologized.

"I understand. You guys need a new Imam," his father-in-law stated.

"Tell me about it," he replied, not fully catching the statement. Killa made an abrupt turn into a hardware store. "What you need from here?"

"An ice pick?"

****

"I read that babies need to interact with other babies at an early age. It's good when they have siblings but if not, then a good daycare," Bryonna said flailing her hand. The exaggerated hand movement made Shyne take notice.

"Let me see!" she said, grabbing her hand. She blinked rapidly at the diamond solitaire. "Where did you get this from?"

"This?" she asked, sticking it under Shyne's nose. "Oh, your brother gave it to me."

"He did? Girl, this is an engagement ring! He asked you to marry him? What you say? Why you ain't tell me?" Shyne fussed.

"Well... Actually, he didn't quite...exactly ask me," she admitted.

"He didn't? So what he say? Just tossed it at you?"

"No. He said, 'Here,' and put it on my finger, then walked away."

"Same thing. He asked and you said yes!" Shyne clapped happily. "I guess I'll look into this daycare thing."

"You should cuz you'll be a mom soon. I can't believe it, Shyne, you're having a baby! You're getting so big!"

"I know, right!" Shyne agreed. "I still be throwing it back, though! I be like uh, uh, uh!"

****

"So, are you ready for Jihad? Ready to strike fear into the hearts of the disbelievers?" Imam Alaki asked once Killa was seated in his apartment.

"How, exactly?" Killa asked. He wanted to see just how far the man was trying to go. Playing dumb is an excellent tool to get information out of people.

The liar began his spiel on so-called Holy War, unaware that Killa knew better. Every person from every faith must strive against his or her own desires. They must strive against the devil and his whispers. They must strive to be upright at all times, even in the face of corruption. Now *that* is Jihad.

"Jihad is the duty of every Muslim!" he began truthfully. One ploy of the devil and his soldiers is to tell a truth and then add 99 lies to it. "It's okay to kill yourself. Allah commands it!"

"He does?" Killa asked, as chapter 17, verse 33 clearly states, *"And do not kill anyone..."* and chapter 4, verse 135 commands Muslims to, *"Stand firmly for justice..."*

Killa had heard enough so out came the ice pick. He went over to the table and thrust it into the man's sinful, lying frontal lobe. His eyes fluttered to go with the curious look on his face. Killa watch him struggle in vain to remove the tool from his brain. He almost had it but the angel of death swooped in to collect what he was sent for.

"May Allah have mercy on you," Killa said on his way out. He chucked deuces and left the same way he came. In peace.

Prints linked the dead Imam to a bombing in Yemen and another one in England. His phone gave up information on other like-minded people who were arrested or deported. Killa had saved the day.

Chapter 40

"Relax, breathe and push," Asad coached just as he'd learned to do in the birthing classes he'd attended with Shyne during her last trimester. He'd learned about everything needed to deliver a baby, except about getting cursed out.

"Relax? Did you just tell me to relax with a whole person trying to come out my vagina? Shut the hell up!" she fussed.

"Relax, breathe and push," her unflappable husband repeated. As he'd insisted, he was the only man in the room.

"I see the head! She's got a head full of hair!" the doctor said as the new person emerged from the womb.

"Pay up, my nigga!" Shyne yelled and cackled upon hearing the word 'she'.

"We didn't bet, you did," Asad reminded. He'd hoped that their first child would be born a boy, but she'd bet that it wouldn't. She claimed that the way she threw it back ensured that it would be a girl.

"Whatever, here comes Shyne Junior!" she giggled and grunted through the pain.

"Your daughter has a penis," Asad announced when their baby boy was pulled free.

"See, I should whoop your ass!" she growled at the doctor. However, a glimpse of her son drove all the malice away. The room went quiet as Asad softly chanted the call to prayer in Arabic in his son's ear. He'd heard it in the womb and it was only right that it be the first thing that he heard in the world.

"That was beautiful," a nurse gushed. "What does it mean?"

"He said, 'God is The Greatest. I bear witness that nothing deserves to be worshipped except God. Come to pray, come to success. Nothing is worthy of worship but God," Shyne relayed. "Now stop flirting with my husband before I come off this table and..."

"At least let me stitch you up before you do," the doctor laughed.

"Yeah, put it back like it was," Asad insisted. He was deadpan and serious so he didn't get any chuckles. "What?"

"Welcome to the world, Malik," Shyne greeted her newly born son. "He looks like *The Fly*. 'Member that movie?"

"She is sedated," the doctor said in response to the look on Asad's face. One would think that he was used to Shyne's antics by now but she never ceased to amaze him.

"Malik is a good name," he agreed. The baby did look a little like *The Fly* but he'd never admit it.

"Well, what is it?" Bryonna pounced when Asad stepped into the waiting room.

"It is a he. Malik Abdus-Salaam," the proud father proclaimed.

"Congrats, bruh!" Sun said and gave his brother-in-law a pound and a hug.

"Thanks, bruh. Now when are you two gonna give him some cousins?"

"I'm ready! Tell your friend..." Bryonna began as Sun fled the room. "Sun! You can run, but you can't hide!"

****

"Nice job," Killa congratulated after inspecting his grandson. He'd turned the baby over and upside down as he did.

"Uh, thanks? We had help, though," Asad replied. As usual, he gave God the glory for everything.

"Not just him, for everything. I'm very, very proud of you, son," he replied. He was, too, because Asad provided a stable house and family to his daughter. He was at complete ease and satisfied knowing that she was in good hands. Shyne blushed proudly at two of the men in her life.

The doorbell rang, announcing the arrival of two more.

"Look who can walk!" Sun announced as Rico walked in at his own speed. He had finally made a full recovery from the brutal shooting that had left his brother dead.

"Hey, big bruh!" Shyne cheered and rushed over to give him a hug. "You remember my friend Bryonna."

"Yup. Sup, Bryonna," Rico said a little too flirtatiously for Sun. Shyne giggled at the perturbed look on her twin's face. "Sup, Pops."

"Looking good," Killa greeted and hugged his oldest son. He threw a few playful jabs for him to duck and block to make sure he still had it.

"Well, the gang is all here, so let's go eat!' Shyne cheered. "I'ma ride with my brothers!"

"Um, I got a gas leak in my whip," Sun warned.

Shyne shrugged and followed him and Rico out to his car. A cloud of weed smoke rolled out when she pulled the door open. "Ugh!" she complained, waving the smoke out of her face.

"Told you," Sun laughed and got in. Rico rode shotgun with Shyne in the backseat. Small talk and laughter filled in the space between the suburban home and downtown restaurant. Asad made sure to go to a halal soul food spot so he could eat anything on the menu.

****

"Hey, Sun," the pretty hostess sang when the dinner party arrived. Bryonna sucked her teeth so loudly everyone turned in her direction.

"Hey, um..." Sun greeted as much as he could since he didn't remember her name. Although her name escaped him, he did, however, remember that she liked to ride backwards.

"LaDonna...Monae...Antonique," she giggled, pointing at her big ass name tag.

"That explains it," Sun mumbled. No wonder he couldn't remember, it had eight syllables and three hyphens. Shyne shook her head as they followed her to their table. Meanwhile, Bryonna had silently reached the end of her rope.

"What can I get... Hey, Sun!" the pretty waitress gushed upon seeing him in her station.

"Hey, umm..." Sun uttered, forgetting her name as well. In his defense, he did smoke a lot of weed. He'd had a lot of women, too. A glance at her name tag gave up the good. "Cynt."

"No, I'm Autumn, this is just Cynt's smock," she explained. She took their order and rushed off to fill it.

Sun sensed the heat coming from Bryonna and made a mental note to take her out soon. Spending quality time with her usually appeased her when he got in trouble. What he'didn't know was that usually came with an expiration date and it had just expired.

"So, Rico, how long you in town for?" Asad asked. He hoped to get to know him a little better.

"Not long. Me, Sun and Pops 'bout to head down to New Orleans in a couple of days. Do a little Gator hunting," he replied casually.

Asad nodded at the answer while Shyne caught its meaning. She knew that the New Orleans chapter of The Black Mob was run by a gold toothed dread called Gator. The Killa clan was headed down to make some shoes and belts out of his ass and she wanted in.

"Nope!" Killa tossed across the table as soon as she opened her mouth to speak. "Get you some rest, young lady."

"The doctor said I'll be ready for action in six weeks!" she said, causing her husband to blush and everyone else to shake their heads.

"Shyne, chill," Sun said without looking up from his meal.

Bryonna only managed to eat half of her thanks to pouting so much. Killa paid the large tab from a large bankroll when it was time to go.

"A-yo, B," Sun called out once they got outside. He and Rico were about to hit the streets so he wanted to say bye. "Sup for tomorrow?"

"Nothing. Here," she replied and returned the ring he'd given her with the same words she gotten it with. Sun opened his mouth to speak but she was gone. Once a good girl is gone, she's gone for good.

****

"Uh-uh, make it clap! Make it clap!" Rico cheered and clapped at the big ATL booty clapping in front of him. The high yellow girl had a hand tattooed on each butt cheek that added to the spectacle of her ass clap routine. "You see this shit, bruh? Bruh?"

"Huh?" Sun asked when his brother snatched him from his thoughts. Sun was foolish but he was no fool. He'd fucked up and he knew it.

"Shorty got you fucked up, huh?" Rico asked, ignoring the big booty. The girl got paid whether they watched or not so she kept right on shaking what her mama gave her. She could prove it, too, since her mama was a couple tables over giving a table dance of her own.

"Yeah, bruh. She done, too. I know her and she sticks to her decisions," he replied correctly. Bryonna was the female version of a man of his word. She vowed to never set foot back in Wyandanch when they left and she hadn't. She hadn't even seen her mother in years.

"Bruh, Pops ain't raise us to fail. Get yo' woman!" Rico said.

"True, but how? What do I do?" Sun whined.

"That's easy, whatever you have to. Handle yo' business!"

Chapter 41

Killa and sons slid quietly into New Orleans and set up shop. They wisely watched and waited before striking at Gator and his crew. Sun and Rico added a slight twist to dad's usual kill the bad guys plan. They intended to take all their money as well.

Pops partook in some good Cajun food when they weren't busy while Rico explored some southern vaginas. Hot sauce and spicy spices added a little extra heat. Meanwhile, Sun moped and nursed his broken heart. After two weeks, he finally called his sister for guidance.

"Sorry about your car," Shyne said, immediately upon taking his call.

"My car? What happened to my car?" he asked. He had just recently upgraded to a new Benz that he adored.

"It burned up. I accidently spilled a five-gallon gas can inside and lit a match. My bad. Sorry," she explained dryly.

"Oh, okay. Sup with B? I can't get her on the phone."

"Oh, cuz she ain't fucking with you no more," she explained cheerfully. "Matter of fact, some guy at the hospital been cracking at her. A doctor."

"He gon' need a doctor... I mean, oh, okay," Sun growled then caught himself. "That's um, nice."

"Yeah, right! Nigga, you better step up and get yo' woman! I swear I'ma fuck you up! I got more gas! I...,"

"A'right, a'right! Check it, here's what I need you to do..." he said and filled her in on his harebrained plan.

"That just might work!" Shyne agreed. "I'm on it!"

****

"Yo, Sun, I can feel her heartbeat!" Rico said of the girl under the table at the raunchy club. He was so far down her throat that he could feel her internal organs functioning.

"I bet," Sun sighed. He hadn't been with a woman since Bryonna had given him his ring back. Part of it was out of respect and part of it was out of disgust. He'd suddenly thought better of himself than to offer himself to every pretty girl who passed by. Morals are like that once they take hold.

Gator liked to frequent the off the books strip club for the same reason Rico was enjoying it. The strippers here turned more tricks than flips. That's why the joint smelled like sweat and cum. He was in the middle of making his pick-ups from various trap houses when he decided to pop in and get his rocks off.

"Yeah, lil bih, suck dat dih," he demanded, still refusing to say a complete word. It's unknown what beef he had with the last few letters of words but he wasn't fucking with them. "I'm finna...ugh!"

Shaquita-Nita didn't need to hear the end of those words to know what he meant. A gush of salty slime filled her mouth to complete the sentence. The professional cum guzzler could easily identify everything he'd eaten and drank for the day. Gator had also snorted a lot of coke and she got a buzz from that as well. It could be called a tip, perhaps.

"You sho' got sum fi' hea', you hear," Gator congratulated as he put his clean, shiny dick back in his pants.

"Thank ya," she smiled at the compliment she heard all day, every day. She batted her lashes in hopes of a tip but the coke laced cum was all she had coming.

Gator walked away scanning the club to make sure he wasn't being watched. He had several hundred grand in his car and wanted to make sure he wasn't followed. Sun locked eyes with him for a second before turning away. He then knocked on the table to alert his brother.

"A-yo, let's bounce," he said once Gator had left the building.

"Damn it, man!" Rico complained as he extracted himself from the hot mouth. The pretty girl popped up with a confused look on her face. Blowjobs always ended in gulps and swallows so his sudden departure was a first.

"I did something wrong?" she pouted with a sweet charm. The girl was eager to please and probably would have made a great wife. Unfortunately, the wrong man had gotten a hold of her and turned her life in another direction.

"Nah, you good, ma," he said and peeled off another hundred from his bankroll. He had to rush to catch up with his brother.

"He better slow down. These cops round here don't play," Sun quipped as they loosely trailed their prey. They were in no rush since he wasn't going anywhere.

"Wha' the fuh," Gator fussed when the cop car lit him up. "He mu' na kno' who I'm is!"

The police car pulled to a stop behind Gator and paused. The door opened and he approached with his hand on his pistol. Gator strained to recall the face but realized he didn't know this cop.

"Say, Woady, you know who I'm is?" Gator asked, sticking his head out the window.

"Yup," Killa replied and pulled the cannon off his hip. He fired a round into his face that nearly took the man's whole head off. He tipped his hat to his sons as they pulled up.

"Damn, Pops!" Rico laughed when he saw the mangled man.

Dude actually had two of his gold teeth hanging from a dred on the back of his head. Sun was used to their dad's handwork. He snatched the bag of money and made it back to the car. Gator paid for his own hit.

＊＊＊＊

"Again! A-mother-fucking-gain!" Lil' Rock shouted at the news report of yet another Black Mob rub out. He happened to be visiting his mom when he caught the story.

"Just like old times," his tipsy mother said between sips. The woman had a tendency to talk too much when drunk. Bull had used it to double-cross her late husband and take his spot and his woman. He'd raised Little Rock since he was a child. "That damn Killa..."

"Is nothing but a myth!" Bull said, coming in and cutting her off just in time. Little Rock glared at him glaring at his mother with a 'shut the fuck up' look on his face.

"Pssh!" the woman hissed and went back to sipping. Her son made a vow to himself to get to the bottom of this.

****

"Your Paw-paw and uncles made alligator-soufflé," Shyne said to little Malik once the gruesome newscast ended. As much as she wanted to hang out with them, her baby boy took precedence over everything. Malik means king and he ruled her heart. She was perfectly content with staying home with her family. That's why she was happy the next story was local.

"Drug Company CEO Charles Siebert was acquitted on all charges today. He made headlines a few years back when he raised the prices of life saving drugs by five thousand percent. He was indicted on the tax charges but today a jury cleared him of the charges. As of today, Charles Siebert is a free man."

"Charles Siebert is a dead man," Shyne corrected. He lived in Atlanta so she could knock him off at naptime.

Chapter 42

"Who? Who? Who?" Bryonna shouted as she approached the condo door. The incessant ringing of the doorbell forced her out of bed where she'd planned to stay all day. The person on the other side refused to reply so she took a peek through the peephole. "Shyne!"

"Hey, ma, get your shoes on. I need you!" Shyne said urgently as she rushed inside.

Bryonna rushed to get a pair of sneakers on before asking what was wrong. "Let me change out these!" she urged. She was halfway down the hallway when she saw she had on her around the house sweatpants and t-shirt.

"You good for where we going," Shyne assured her as they entered the elevator.

"Uh oh, who you beefing with?" Bryonna demanded. Shyne was actually cute in her white summer dress and sandals but she didn't have her baby with her. "Where's my nephew?"

"I'm not beefing with nobody and Malik is with his daddy," Shyne said proudly. Her face lit up anytime she spoke of her husband and child.

"Shyne, where are we going?" Bryonna insisted again as Shyne sped through the city.

"Chill, B, you'll see when we get there. Don't you trust me?"

"Umm...for the most part...I...um...I guess," she chuckled. Shyne was shot out but she trusted her with her life.

"Oh wow!" Shyne laughed along with her. They yucked it up until Shyne pulled up to the same wedding chapel that she and Asad had gotten hitched at.

"Why are we here?" Bryonna asked, looking confused. It was an early Saturday morning so there was no way a wedding could be in session.

"Will you just come on?!" Shyne fussed like Bryonna was getting on her nerves. She stomped inside with her close on her heels. Once they were in, she stepped aside so Bryonna could see.

"Ma?" Bryonna asked when she saw her mother standing by the door.

"Hey, baby!" the woman squealed and embraced her. "I'm so proud of you!"

"Uh, thanks," she said, noticing the rest of her extended family. Killa, Asad-holding baby Malik, Christi and her husband and Rico all smiled happily at her. "What's going on?"

"This..." Sun replied as he stepped from a room. He presented her with the ring again, but this time he sank to his knee and did it right. "Bryonna, will you do me the honor of becoming my wife?"

"Uh, no!" she spat and turned towards the door. She didn't make it two steps before she turned back around with a huge grin on her face. "Okay!"

"Yay!!!" Shyne clapped and cheered. "Come on!"

Shyne pulled her friend and future sister-in-law into a dressing room. Christi quickly followed and closed the door behind them.

"Wow!" Bryonna marveled at the wedding dress on the hanger in front of her. It was the same one she'd picked out hypothetically when Shyne had gotten hers.

The girls all giggled and cackled as they helped the bride get dressed. Christi fussed over her hair and folded it into a cute style. Shyne's phone began to chime when an alarm went off.

"Yessss!!!" Shyne shouted and threw her hands up triumphantly. "Today is six weeks! I'm getting some tonight!" she replied and started humping the air. She got into it and raised one foot. "I'ma be like, uh-uh-uh!"

"Wait!" Bryonna said suddenly looking sad. "Who's going to walk me down the aisle?"

"Who else?" Shyne frowned like it was a dumb question. She opened the door and stuck her head out. "We're ready."

"Congratulations," Killa said and kissed his soon-to-be daughter-in-law on her cheek. He extended his arm to be her escort.

"Thank you," she smiled despite her tears. Her face and neck were completely wet by the time she reached the altar.

"Bismil-lahir Rahmanir-Raheem...," the Imam who married Asad and Shyne began. The bride and groom looked into each other's eyes until he pronounced them husband and wife. They exchanged rings and shared their first kiss.

"What do we do now?" Bryonna asked unsurely. She'd began her day with plans to read and watch Netflix but now she was married.

"Now we go eat cake and dance. Then we fly down to Belize," Sun said softly.

"But I...I don't have any clothes! I don't have my passport! I don't hav-..."

"Chill, ma! I got you!" Shyne said, holding up her passport. "You ain't gone need no clothes!"

****

Five days later, it was Asad and Shyne's turn to pick the newlyweds up from the airport. Paw-paw Killa had his grandson for the day so they could hang out a little. Just a little, though, because Shyne couldn't go too long without her baby.

"There they are," Asad said as he pulled into the concourse. Shyne followed his finger and spotted them as well. He flipped his blinker on and pulled over.

"Sup, yo?" Bryonna cheesed and high-fived her sister-in-law.

"Un huh, and how was Belize?" Shyne asked.

"I'on know," she shrugged. "I'm pretty sure I'm pregnant, though."

"Girl, me too!" Shyne cackled. The two women huddled in the backseat and snickered while Sun slid into the passenger's seat.

"As salaam alaykum," Asad greeted, extending a fist to be bumped.

"Wa alaykum as salaam," Sun replied, bumping it.

The foursome was as close as any people could ever be. Family by blood, marriage and friendship. They didn't know it yet, but both of those chicks in the backseat were actually pregnant. Life was good.

Chapter 43

The Killa clan maintained the Long Island home. They would never live there again but it would always be home. Since Atlanta was now their home base, they moved their arsenal from the basement to a stash house in the suburbs. All they needed now were some pigs.

"Sorry, you can't come with," Killa said when they planned their next trip. A Black Mob faction had popped up in Philly and was about to get knocked off.

"No prob," Shyne said so easily everyone frowned up in curiously. Even she realized she gave up too quickly but still asked, "What?"

"What are you up to?" Killa asked, squinting at his daughter so he could see through her bullshit.

"Mio?" Shyne asked, batting her lashes coyly. "I'm not up to anything. In fact, I resent that remark!"

"You resemble that remark," Sun chuckled as he selected weapons for their trip. Overkill is better than under kill so he picked out the heavy artillery.

"Where's Rico?" Shyne asked because she wanted to know as well as switch the attention from herself. She was quite fond of her new big brother and tried her best to make up for the time they'd lost beefing.

"Up top. He gone meet us in Germantown," Sun replied to her but filled in their father at the same time.

"I still can't believe those goons had the audacity to set up shop in Germantown with all those Muslims," Killa said, shaking his head in disbelief.

Law enforcement watched the Muslims so hard that it allowed criminals to flourish. They openly sold drugs on the same streets kids once played. Those same streets became hoe strolls once the sun set. This normally would have gotten a heavy handed response from the Muslims but police and feds watched their every move. No worry because along came a killa and his sons.

"Well, be safe. Have fun killing bad guys!" Shyne cheered and waved, getting more suspicious looks form her dad and brother. "Okay, bye-bye."

"Somebody's in trouble," Sun said once they were seated in the car.

"Definitely. Someone is about to get fucked up," Killa co-signed. They were right, too, because Shyne shopped for a weapon the second they left.

"Okay, let's see..." Shyne sang as she perused the weapons as if she were in the produce section. The clouds opened up, allowing the sun's rays to beam brightly when she saw it. "This...is it! It's getting hot in here..."

****

Killa and sons landed in Philadelphia and took a cab to Germantown. Rico and Sun hopped out, leaving their dad to pay the fare. Proof that no matter how old they get, children expect their parents to pick up the tab. He did before leading the way inside the Masjid.

"As salaamu alaykum! What's good, homie?" Imam Mezan greeted with a wide smile, pound and man hug.

"Wa alaykum as salaam," Killa said as they embraced. It was crystal clear that the two men had genuine love for one another. His sons could tell that they were close but what couldn't be seen was that Mezan was once a thug himself. That is, until God redirected him to something else and changed his life. After all, men and jinn were only created to worship God, alone with no partners in worship, Lordship or names and attributes. *That* is Islam.

"Say, um...Dad?" Sun said, raising his hand. The two old friends chopped it up as if he and his brother weren't even there.

"Oh yeah! My bad. These are my sons, Rico and Sun," Killa finally introduced.

"Sup, yo?" the Imam greeted with a pound and a hug.

"So anyway..." Killa cut back in, "we heard about your infestation and we're here to help."

"Thanks, because we need it. It's getting crazy around here, bruh. Last week, a sister got her purse snatched on the corner. Feds everywhere but they so busy watching me that they didn't even help her. Some brothers chased him down and took the purse back, and Philly PD charged them with robbing him!"

"Y'all may not eat swine but I do," Rico growled. He had a healthy hate for crooked cops and didn't mind putting them on a plate.

"Maybe next time," Killa said to remind him of their mission to kill the Mob. Still, he asked, "Where is this purse snatcher now?"

"Lurking about. Probably out there now. Do you know how frustrating it is to have that little bastard thumbing his nose at me? Like he can't be touched," Imam Mezan fumed.

"Oh, he can be touched," Killa said with a slight nod to his sons.

"A-yo, we 'bout to grab a slice," Rico announced as he and Sun stood.

The old friends got back to the issue at hand. "So anyway, The Black Mob is run by this clown called Igloo. He's a local thug who got his numbers up and spread out. All the coke and heroin in the city flows through him. His...departure would be a benefit to all!"

"Well, his departure is imminent. Once he's gone, someone will step up to take his place. He'll get the same and so on and so on," Killa sighed.

"Unless it's so violent no one will want the job," Mezan suggested with a shrug.

"Violence is my specialty!"

****

"That's him," Sun said of the shifty eyed little fellow on the corner. His nose ran from the onset of withdrawals while his eyes darted in every direction looking for something to steal.

"Feds out here. There and there," Rico said, pointing them out with his eyes. The tinted out vans with satellite antennas were a dead giveaway.

"Yo, go to the alley. I got a plan," Sun smiled deviously.

Rico rushed around to lay in wait. Sun took a lap around the block before approaching the thug. "Sup, yo, who got that shit?"

"Ant got that diesel! I'm 'bout to catch a lick and get me a sack!"

"A lick? In front of a place of worship?"

"Hell yeah! Po-po letting us eat off them Muslims. I'm snatching chains, purses even breaking in cars! All right in front of the po-lice!"

"Word, word. I just seen an old lady in the alley with a big ass roll of cash!" Sun said, putting cheese on the rat trap.

"How old?" the thug asked in trepidation. A sixty-five-year-old woman had whooped his ass just a few days ago about her purse.

"'Bout...ninety, a hun'ned maybe," he replied. Sun saw his eyes light up with greed and had to restrain himself.

"Round here?" the addict asked, heading around to the alley. He rushed away to catch the lick with Sun right behind him. He lagged back to cut off any chance of escape. Rico ducked into the shadows when he heard him approaching. Then he coiled like a snake ready to strike.

"Ugh!" Rico grunted as he swung a haymaker. The man's jaw cracked so loud it echoed between the buildings. He then stumbled, caught his balance and took off.

"Un uh," Sun said, lifting him off his feet with an uppercut. The man curled into a fetal positon as his attackers attacked. They kicked and stomped him in submission.

"Hold his arm out!" Rico demanded. Sun complied and his brother savagely stomped it. Bones crunched loudly under his boots.

"A-yo, on my momma, if you ever step foot around here again, I'ma murder you!" Sun vowed. The malice in his words reverberated through the alley.

"A'right, a'right!" the man managed through his broken jaw. As soon as Rico and Sun turned to leave, he used his good hand to pull a gun.

"Watch out," Sun said and dived on the thug. He wrestled the gun away and shoved it so far down the man's throat that his hand was in his mouth.

"Wait!" Imam Mezan shouted a split second before Sun put death into his life. He only paused, trying to decide if he should shoot or not until he heard his father speak up.

"Chill, Sun," was all that needed to be said for Sun to chill.

"Come on, young man," the Imam said, helping the man to his feet. He looked totally confused at his enemy helping him.

"Thank you sir," he grunted, clenching his broken jaws shut.

"Thank God, not me," Mezan replied and helped him to his car so that he could take him to the hospital. *That* is Islam.

Chapter 44

"Bitch! Slut! Dick sucking bitch slut!" Charles Siebert grunted as he slammed in and out of the rented vagina. For all his wealth, he couldn't keep a woman, mainly due to his foul mouth and fucked up attitude. He had zero respect for women and viewed them as second class citizens. Blame his mother for not hugging him as a child.

"You...know...what! Get off me!" the high price escort demanded. She may not have any morals, but the shred of dignity that remained couldn't take another second of his verbal abuse.

"Bitch, you have...been...bought...and...paid...for," Siebert insisted and kept on stroking. It became rape at that point, but who could she tell? He kept right on humping until he got a nut. "Now, get your ass out of my house!"

"Bastard!" the prostitute spat as she scrambled to get dressed.

"You sure have a thin skin for a whore," he laughed and produced some cash. The visit had been paid for by credit card but he flicked a tip at her. "Pick that up on your way out."

"You pick it up and shove it up your ass!" she said as she stepped over the money.

"So, same time next week?" Siebert called out after her and cracked up.

"He's a sick fuck!" the prostitute warned the woman in uniform she passed on his steps. The woman watched in curiosity as she jumped into her coupe and sped away. She shrugged as best as she could with the bulky apparatus on her back and rang the bell.

"Ah, knew you'd come back for your money," the man laughed, assuming the escort had returned. He snatched the door open and saw an employee from pest control.

"Exterminator," she informed when he did.

"Here? I assure you, we ..." Siebert began, then noticed the light brown woman was cute. He decided to let her in and have a little fun. "Yeah, yeah, come on in."

"Thank you," Shyne smiled as she stepped inside. She planned to have a little fun as well.

"What the heck is that?" Siebert chuckled at the strange equipment on her back. "It looks like a flame thrower!"

"It is!" she laughed and lit it up. She was the only one who found it amusing.

"W-w-w-what are y-y-you d-d-doing?" he asked, backing away from the flames.

"About to b-b-burn yo' b-b-b-bitch ass up!" she cackled and did just that. She sprayed his feet and shins, setting him on fire.

"Yeow!" Siebert screamed as he danced, trying to put out the fire.

"Hey! Do that dance, do that dance!" Shyne cheered. She saw the bills on the ground and tossed them at him, "Make it rain, make it rain!"

Siebert took off but Shyne was right on his ass. She sprayed him with more flames all the way up to his waist. The man howled as he stopped, dropped and rolled. Finally, Shyne hit him with a full dose. Death was a welcome relief from the heat of the flames. Shyne made a quick tour of the swank house before setting it on fire as she went.

"Mm-mm-mm!" the real exterminator said from beneath his gag when Shyne returned to the borrowed van.

"I don't speak that!" she said indignantly. She had attempted to bribe the man to use the van but he insisted on flirting with her. She advised him that she was married and he said he was, too, and that it could be their secret. That's why he was hogtied in the backyard now. "Don't...worry...this will be our secret."

****

Sun never took his personal phone along on family business trips. Instead, he left it home with his wife. She had the green light to answer it but never did. To her surprise, there weren't women calling it day and night, except one, that is. The same name kept popping up on the screen so Bryonna finally become curious.

"Chardonay. Where do they come up with these names?" she laughed to herself at the name on the screen. She decided to call Shyne for advice. After all, she had been married for over a year now and that made her a relationship expert. Maybe not, but she did know her brother better than anyone on the planet.

"Sup, yo?" Shyne barked, out of breath. "Make it quick, the baby sleep and I'm trying to get mine!"

"Um...okay. Well...okay...how 'bout some chick named Chardonay keeps calling Sun's phone!"

"And? What she say?" Shyne wanted to know.

"I'on know. I haven't answered it," Bryonna shrugged as if Shyne could see her.

"I wish a bish would call my husband. I would answer it!"

"You don't have to worry about Asad! But Sun...Sun is...well, Sun," she sighed.

"Sun is the second best man I know. Yeah, he strung you along for as long as you let him. You see he stepped up and wifed you, though, when you finally put your foot down. I know my brother, he loves you. You have nothing to worry about," Shyne assured her. It wasn't just lip service, either. Their parents had raised them with dignity and morals. With Sun, it just took longer for it to stick.

"So, I guess your dad is number one, huh?" Bryonna asked.

"My dad! Hell naw, he ain't shit!" Shyne admitted. She loved him death and still turned into a five-year-old in his presence but she also accepted him for who he was. She knew it was his woman juggling that had cost her mother her life. "Okay, gotta go! Time for round three!"

Bryonna sat back and basked in relief of Shyne's words. Sun had been a great husband so far and had given her no reason to doubt anything he said or did. That's why he left his phone with her. He'd told his old women that he was married and to never call him again. They had all respected that and moved on. All except Chardonay, that is. She didn't respect herself so why would she respect someone else's bonds of matrimony? She called again, so Bryonna called Shyne once more.

"Bruh, why you keep calling me! I'm tryna get my groove on and you keep calling me!" Shyne whined.

"Cuz, she called again!" she said, matching her whiny tone.

"Go...answer it! Just don't call me NO more tonight!"

"I..." was all Bryonna got out before getting hung up on. Chardonay called again so she answered it. "Can I hel-"

"Put Sun on the phone!" the ghetto girl demanded, popping her gum and tapping her foot impatiently.

"I'm fine, thanks for asking! And how are you?" she quipped.

"Bitch, ain't nobody axe you how you feel! Now put Sun on the damn phone!" she said, clapping her hands with each word. "Who is you, his mama?"

"Wife, I'm his wife. You know, to have and to hold, for better or worse, sickness..."

"Bitch, a bitch don't care nothing 'bout no wife! Now quit playing on the man's phone. I fuck married niggas err'day and you playing!"

"Hold on, please," Bryonna said courteously and put her on hold. She checked her own phone for the number Sun called from last and dialed it on conference.

"Sup, B, everything okay?" Sun asked with a tone of concern that made her warm inside. She could also hear a tinge of confusion due to her calling from his line.

"Yes, dear, all is well. A friend of yours would like to speak with you," she said and connected the three-way. "Chardonay?"

"Bitch, put Sun on the phone!" the tramp spat.

"The fuck! A-yo, why you on the phone with my wife?" Sun asked, really confused.

"Hey, Sun, when we gon' hook up?" Chardonay sang seductively.

"What? We're not! I told you I was getting married before I even asked her to marry me. Why would I wanna hook up?"

"Boy, you know you wanna hit this! Quit playing!"

"B, hang up on that broad," Sun ordered and she complied.

"You and yo' damn hoodrats," Bryonna said, shaking her head.

"I never touched that...thot! We met in a club, exchanged numbers and that's it. We never hooked up cuz I been gone with my dad."

"What exactly is it that you and your father actually do?" Bryonna asked for the hundredth time.

"Family business," he replied as if that explained it. It didn't but it was all she had coming. The silent shrug she gave meant she knew it. Whatever it was paid well and he called home every night.

"Well, I...hold on. This chick just sent a text. A picture of her...ewww!" Bryonna shrieked and slung the phone.

"What? What? Bryonna what's wrong?" Sun shouted in concern.

"She just sent a picture of her vagina! Honey needs an OB-GYN ASAP! It looks like a baked potato!"

"A-yo, just ignore the broad. I'll change the number when I get home. Love you, see you in a couple of days," Sun said, making his wife cheese from ear to ear.

"Love you, too!" she proclaimed and clicked off.

Chapter 45

"Damn, I'm iced the fuck out!" Igloo cheered as he admired his reflection in the full length mirror. He was right, too, with a diamond necklace hanging down to an iced out belt buckle. A diamond crusted igloo the size of softball hung from the chain. His ears, wrists and fingers held more diamonds suspended in platinum.

"Yeah, you are!" his hype man/security agreed, because that's what hype men do.

The large man went by the initials BK. It was short for Beef Killer since that's what he did. Whenever the crew had beef, he killed. His name was about to be put to the test because they had more beef than they knew what to do with. Killa and sons were about to bring the whole cow.

"Let's get this money," Igloo said. They had a new connect from New York with great prices on blow.

"This shit better be what they say it is," BK growled. Fifteen grand a kilo was almost too good to be true. At that price, they could lockdown a new market without the Mob even knowing about it.

"If it is, we gon' put the press down," Igloo said of his plans.

"If it ain't, I'm gon' splat they ass," BK vowed. He set the GPS to follow the directions to the secluded cabin in the mountains. It was just perfect for their planned double-cross. They weren't the only ones plotting.

****

"A-yo, these shits look legit!" Rico cheered at his own handiwork. He'd made up fake kilos, laced with a liner of real coke that would allow them to be tested and pass. The twenty kilos at fifteen grand each represented three hundred thousand dollars.

"Yeah, they do," Sun said as he inspected one. Unlike his brother, he hadn't come up selling drugs but it looked real enough to him.

"Good job," Killa said when they passed his test. "Well, let me go assume my position."

Rico and Sun watched their father sling the sniper rifle over his shoulder and exit the cabin. More and more, he let his sons take the lead. Killing is a young man's game so he played the background and offered support.

"Sheesh," Killa sighed when he reached his destination. He looked up at the tree stand and shook his head. He knew it wouldn't come down and get him so he began to climb. By the time he reached the hunting platform, he felt his age. He got comfortable and peered through the scope. He could clearly see inside the cabin; especially exactly where the table sat where the deal would take place. He saw the lights turn down the long driveway and hit his walkie-talkie.

"Showtime," Sun announced and poured the drinks.

"Stinks out here," Igloo said, frowning up when the unusual smell assaulted his senses.

"Yeah, it do, but this is perfect!" BK said as he made the mistake of turning all the way around. Killa saw him and turned to see what he was looking for.

"Sho-nuff?' he said when he saw a car load of goons turn down the driveway behind them with its lights out. The irony brought a smile to his face. 'Lights out.'

"Sup?" Rico greeted as he stepped out on the porch and waved.

"What's good, yo? Stinks out here!" Igloo griped as he got out.

"Pigs," Rico explained as if that it explained it. He shook both of their hands and led them inside. "That's my brother, Sun."

"Peace," Igloo said, despite his malicious intentions. He smiled at the bricks on the table and went over.

"Have a drink while I count and you test," Sun offered. He held up a bottle to show it was the good shit and made their heads nod. Sun and Rico smiled internally when the men took sips of the spiked liquor.

"Whoa! This that dope, dope!" BK said when the first key proved to be 99.98 percent pure. He moved on to the next one while Sun continued counting the cash.

Meanwhile, outside...

"That's it. Everybody out," Killa whispered to himself as he watched the four men exit the second car. They all carried guns as they began their silent creep towards the cabin.

"Shush," the lead goon whispered when someone stepped on a twig. They all paused and looked towards the cabin. Nothing happened, so they resumed their creeping. That's what creeps do.

'Pst, pst' the silencer equipped rifle whispered as it dropped the two men in the rear. The second to the front heard the two thuds and spun around. Another 'pst' and his body made the third thud.

"What the hell y'all niggas doing?" the leader demanded through clenched teeth. A second look around showed the blood and brains oozing from his friend's heads. He opened his mouth to sound the alert but Killa fired at his tonsils, killing both him and the sound.

"Yeah, you nig...aaah...excuse me," Igloo yawned deeply as the sedative kicked in. "Need to get down with our movement."

"Fo' real tho', aaah," BK added with a deep yawn of his own. He turned to the front door, wondering why it hadn't flown open yet.

"They not coming," Sun said nonchalantly as he continued counting.

"Who?" Igloo asked. He, of course, knew but didn't know how they could.

"Whoever your man keep looking to the door for. Trust me, they ain't coming."

"Pops done sent them to the Upper Room!" Rico laughed. He and Sun couldn't help but belt out a few lines of the old gospel song.

"A-yo! Aaah, these niggas done slipped us a mickey!" BK announced between nods. He made a move towards the door but Rico hit him so hard that he was asleep before he hit the floor.

Igloo stood up and got knocked the fuck out, too. The brothers worked quickly to strip and tie up the two men.

"Yo, I got a guy in Harlem that'll break this shit down for us," Rico said as he relieved Igloo of his Igloo and other trinkets.

"Word. I can get something made for my wife," Sun said since she stayed on his mind. And to think, he'd almost let her get away.

"Make something for my lady, too," Killa said as he came in. He was out of breath and bloody from moving the four men.

"A-yo, I'ma need these, too," Rico said of Igloo's mouthful of platinum and diamonds. He turned the man's head to the side and politely kicked them all out.

"Showtime!" Killa said, opening the back door. His sons dragged the men out next to their dead homies. The hogs were already going hog wild from the smell of blood. They grunted loudly as they tried to get into the enclosure. Sun reached for the button that would set them free but Killa stopped him. "Wait! It's much more fun when they're awake."

"Well, let's wake 'em up then!" Rico said while getting ice water from the fridge and hitting them with it.

"The fuck!" BK barked and jumped to his feet. Igloo sat up just in time to see the pigs rushing out. As much as he liked pigs' feet, what could he say when a hog ate his? A young one bit it off and ran into a corner to enjoy it. The rest of the hogs ran out and joined the feast.

"Pigs!" Killa spat in disgust as they devoured their meal. His son's shook their heads at the corny pun. "What?"

"Anyway, Pops," Sun said, sliding an equal pile of money across the table at him.

"Nah, I'm good. I do it for the love, not for the money," he declined.

"Well, I do it for the love of money," Rico said, splitting the pile into two and sliding one to his brother while keeping the other.

The room went silent at the fact that they knew that money was the root of all evil. Like they say, what's understood doesn't need to be explained.

Chapter 46

Chardonay never said no nor did she take no for an answer, so she continued to text, call and send pictures of her beat up vagina every day. Sometimes Bryonna would take the call to amuse herself and other times she'd ignore them. She actually felt sorry for the girl. No girl aspires to be a hoe when she grows up.

It's a quantum leap from pigtails to blow jobs and back shots. The weed, music and desire to turn up had altered her direction in life. Now she was content with whatever she got. Married men didn't mind breaking bread for her to do things that their wives wouldn't

"What the heck?" Shyne laughed at the 'Bitch Betta' Have My Money' ringtone when it began to play from Sun's phone.

"Girl, that's that damn Chardonay chick again. Sending more pictures of that nasty box between her legs," Bryonna sighed, shaking her head in sorrow.

Shyne picked up the phone and grimaced at the picture. "Which way...is...up?" she asked, twisting the phone around and trying to make sense of the community coochie on the screen.

"What are you doing?" Bryonna asked as Shyne began to type a reply. The devious little smirk on her face proved she was up to no good.

"Oh, just setting a little date for my brother...for eleven tonight," she replied while reading her reply.

"But, Sun won't be home until tomorrow," she stated, slightly confused.

"Guess you and I will have to go in his place. We gone beat her home wrecking ass. Yesss!" Shyne cheered, pumping her fist. "It's on!"

****

"I don't know about this," Bryonna said nervously when they pulled into the dark park on the Westside of Atlanta. Mosely Park wasn't dangerous as Shyne, though, so it was all good.

"That's cuz you a punk," Shyne snickered. She had brought along a dainty .40 caliber Glock, but didn't plan on killing the girl. She planned to whoop her ass really good for disrespecting her friend's home.

"I'm far from a punk. I just feel like this is unnecessary. Fighting never solves anything!"

"Fighting, no, but a good ass whooping works every time! That's her, let's go!" Shyne said, seeing Chardonay's thot mobile pull up to a darkened pavilion.

Bryonna let out a deep sigh and got out behind Shyne. She had to jog slightly to keep up with her long, marching stride. A minute later, they were face-to-face with the homewrecker.

"Oh hell! You done went in the man's phone and came to cock block," Chardonay announced, already knowing what had happened since it wasn't the first time that it had. "Let me see, you must be his wife, cuz she's too plain."

"No, actually I'm his wife!" Bryonna said indignantly as she stepped forward. She should have put up her dukes, too, because Chardonay attacked.

Shyne watched from the sidelines for a few minutes as they went at it. After all, it was Bryonna's fight, and fight she did. The ghetto girl had a mean fight game and had a slight edge. Had, until Shyne jumped in. The tables quickly turned and Chardonay took a beating. She tried to run but Shyne clipped her. The two friends stomped and kicked all the weave, make-up and lip gloss of her face.

"That's enough," Shyne said once the girl curled up into a fetal position.

"Un uh! Just...a...little...more!" Bryonna grunted and gave her a little more. A lot more, actually, until Shyne had to pull her off.

"Come on! Let's bounce!" she said, snatching her away from the beaten woman. Shyne pulled her back to the car and pushed her inside. "Wait here. I dropped my watch."

Chardonay had just sat up when Shyne came back. She tried to get to her feet the defend herself but Shyne was too quick. Her life flashed before her eyes when Shyne pulled the pistol.

"Argh!" Chardonay grunted when the gun barrel reached her tonsils.

"Bitch, if you ever call my brother again, I'll blow your damn brains out! Do you understand me?"

"Un-huh," Chardonay said, nodding up and down with the gun still in her mouth. Shyne removed the gun from the girl's throat and went back to the car.

"Find it?" Bryonna asked when she returned.

"Nah, I'm tripping. I didn't even wear it. Wanna get some ice cream?"

"No, I want some food! I'm starving!" she replied.

"You know what? Me too! Let's stop at Waffle Shack," Shyne said as they pulled away from the park.

There are Waffle Shacks on practically every corner of Atlanta but Shyne chose the one closest to the condo's building. Sun had moved down the hall with Bryonna once they were married since it was cleaner. The couple was looking for houses in the same suburban county Asad and Shyne lived in.

"Eww, all that pork!" Shyne grimaced as the smell of bacon, sausage and ham frying on the grill filled her nostrils.

"Ugh!" Bryonna agreed. Being from New York, they didn't eat pork growing up. Now Shyne was married to a Muslim and Bryonna was almost a doctor so they wouldn't be eating any now.

"Girl, you turning green!" Shyne said, pointing at Bryonna's face.

"Me? You are, too," she shot back. She felt that taste of a salty fluid in her mouth. In her defense, she did try to get up and run to the bathroom, but didn't make it.

"Eww!" Shyne shouted when her friend threw up on the counter. She really couldn't talk since she threw up a second later.

"Really?" the waitress said, shaking her head as vomit spread on the counter. The patrons had to jump up and run to avoid getting hit with it.

"I'm...so...so..." Bryonna tried to say but threw up again. Her and Shyne took turns throwing up until their heaves turned dry.

"They must be pregnant," an elderly lady suggested. "Fast ass gals!"

"Fast, my ass," Bryonna said, holding up the ring finger of her left hand to show off her wedding set.

"Bam!" Shyne shouted and showed off her diamonds as well. Both girls held their heads high as they marched out. It would have been really dope if they didn't have vomit all over them.

****

"You think she right? You think we're really pregnant?" Bryonna asked once they got back to the car.

"Wouldn't surprise me the way...never mind. We 'bout to find out," Shyne said and whipped the car into a 24-hour pharmacy. They rushed inside and quickly found the aisle containing the pregnancy tests.

"This one!" Bryonna said, snatching a pink box form the shelf.

"They use it at the hospital?" Shyne asked. Since Bryonna was an intern, she assumed that she'd based her selection on medical knowledge.

"No, I just like pink," she said and rushed to the counter. She paid for hers as well as the blue one that Shyne picked.

Once they got inside the condo, they raced to the bathrooms. Both peed on the sticks, their fingers and the seats before looking at their watches. Five minutes later, they both emerged and met in the hallway.

"Well?" Shyne asked, holding her results behind her back.

"You're going to be an aunt!" Bryonna said, cracking a smile in the corner of her mouth.

"So are you!" Shyne cheered and held up her test. The girls hugged and bounced around happily, despite having pee on their hands.

****

The Killa clan gathered at Asad and Shyne's house for a welcome home barbecue. The trip to Philly had been a successful one for Killa and sons and Clayton and Sons Funeral Home, too. With the Black Mob eliminated, a violent turf war ensued for control of the city. One of those 'damned if you do, damned if you don't' type of situations.

Shyne and Bryonna decided to keep quiet about the good news until the family gathering. Rico and Killa were already at Shyne's house when Sun and Bryonna arrived. Rico and Sun joined Asad on the deck to smoke weed while he smoked a brisket.

"Here, Daddy!" Shyne said, pushing Malik to into his grandfather's arms so she and Bryonna could talk.

"Look at what my husband brought me!" Bryonna sang as she dangled her wrist to show off a platinum and diamond charm bracelet. It was nice and all but she really just liked saying the words 'my husband'. Who could blame her? It was an honorable term. A just reward for keeping herself chaste and being a good woman.

"Nice! Wait...are those...teeth?' Shyne asked, grabbing her arm for a closer look. Sure enough they were. They were Igloo's gold teeth, minus the actual teeth. His jewelry had netted another hundred thousand for the brothers, plus a few trinkets for their ladies.

"I...guess they are. Still pretty, though! My husband always brings me something nice when he comes home. What exactly does your family do?"

"Sanitation," Shyne replied quickly, then pressed her lips tightly. Bryonna knew enough to know that that was all that would be coming.

****

"So, how was the trip?" Asad asked as he tended to the grill full of steaks, turkey and lamb chops and chicken.

"Very rewarding," Rico said, plucking at the large diamond in his ear.

"We went to the Masjid!" Sun tossed in proudly. As expected, a smile spread on Asad's face. Sun left out the part about the violence that took place, but did inform him about the purse snatching thug who ended up becoming a Muslim after the Imam saved his life.

"I know Imam Mezan. Good dude. Anyway, food's ready," Asad said, loading up a tray. Good thing he didn't need any help because both Sun and Rico rushed inside to eat.

The family gathered around Shyne's fourteen-foot dining room table. It was so long that it looked like a conference table in a Wall Street boardroom. They didn't get to use it often but today they did since almost the entire family was present.

Bryonna and Shyne shared glances and giggles over dinner. When the time was right, Shyne gave the nod and Bryonna stood.

"Excuse me," she said, clinking her butter knife against her glass. "I...we...me and Shyne that is, have an announcement..."

"Which is...?" Sun said, urging his wife on. The words seem to have gotten trapped behind her smile until he spoke up.

"Oh! Well, Mr. Forrest, you are gonna to be a dad!" she bounced and clapped. Sun twisted his lips in confusion for a second until the words made sense.

"Wow! I'm going to be a father!" he said once he got it. He ran around the table and scooped her up in the air. Shyne let them have their moment before she stood.

"Um, me, too. Congrats, baby," she said and kissed her husband. The next few minutes were filled with cheer and celebration.

After dinner and dessert, Rico was the first to depart. He was single, handsome and had a pocket full of money. It was only right that he hit a club. Sun and Bryonna were next to leave, to make the drive back to downtown Atlanta.

"Walk me to my car," Killa said so he could have his daughter to himself for a minute. Daddy's get spoiled, too, and it's hard to share.

"You scared, Dad?" Shyne asked, wide eyed and broke into a giggle. "Don't worry, Big Mama got you."

"Anyway," Killa laughed, "I just wanted you to know how happy and proud I am of you and for you. I couldn't ask for anything more for you."

"Thank you, Daddy. I'm blessed. Asad is a good, God fearing man. I have a nice house, my car is crazy, my son is..." she went on and on counting her blessings. She could have gone on for a hundred years and still not been able to count them all. Truth be told, none of us can identify all of God's favors to be able to count them. How many sights, sounds, breaths and heartbeats do we take for granted?

"Well, you won't be upset about missing the convention," Killa said, seizing the opportunity to exclude her. "You definitely can't go pregnant!"

"What convention, Daddy?" she pleaded.

Killa let out a sigh and then filled her in. "And, no, you can't!" he insisted once he laid out the next chapter of Family Business.

"Aww, man! Why I gotta keep missing all the action?" Shyne stomped and pouted. It worked like a charm when she was five, but now her father just laughed.

"Yeah, right! Shyne, you forgot to fill the flame thrower back up after your visit to that drug company CEO," he reminded.

"Oh yeah!" she giggled. "Still, child molesters...I want in!"

"No! I mean it, Shyne. You stay here!" Killa said firmly, putting his foot down. He kissed her forehead and got into his car to leave.

She was still pouting with her arms crossed when he pulled away.

Chapter 47

The Children's Expo was the largest gathering of child molesters, pedophiles and sick fucks since...the one Killa blow up in *Killa Season*. This year, it was being held in scenic Salt Lake City, Utah.

An amazing array of toy and candy manufacturers came to shop their wares. Any and everything needed to entice a minor would be on display. According to the program, there would be a live auction held for children. Not if Killa could help it.

"I never been to Salt Lake," Rico said as they reached the airport.

"Me neither," Sun replied.

"I have. Pretty nice out there. They have great skiing, mountains, food and...Shyne!"

"Shyne, what?" Sun asked when his father went suddenly silent.

"Shyne, there!" he said, pointing his finger. Rico and Sun turned in the direction of his finger and saw what he was pointing at. Who he was pointing at, actually.

"Sup, guys!" Shyne said so cheerfully one might think she was welcome.

"What are you doing here?" Sun demanded big brotherly. "I thought Pops told you to stay home?"

"He did! But, no way I'm missing out on this. I'm a mother. One of these sickos could get my kids one day! I want in!"

"Shyne, Shyne, Shyne," Killa said, shaking his head. What else could he do, he'd already put his foot down. "Well, I'm not paying for your ticket!"

"Don't have to. I got my own," she said smugly, showing off her boarding pass.

"Fligh' fi'-fo'-fo'-ni' is now finna board at gate ni'."

"I do declare, I believe that's us," Shyne said, fanning herself like a Southern Belle. The woman was definitely *Gone with the Wind*.

As usual, Killa stopped in first class and took a seat next to an attractive forty-something-year-old. She smiled and batted her eyes in invitation for conversation. They began to chat while his kids went down the aisle to coach. Sun found his seat number next to a pretty brown lady. She, too, smiled and flirted until Shyne spoke up.

"He married, to my best friend, who's pregnant and I'll beat yo' ass about him and her, so that's two ass whoopings instead of one, and..."

"Chill, Shyne," Rico laughed. "Come on, Sun, trade seats."

Ironically, the girl flirted with him, too, when he sat down. A good man is hard to find but easy to spot. It was clear from first glance that the Forrest men were good men. Sun sat next to a middle aged white man and read over his shoulder.

"Just nasty!" Shyne hissed as her father led the woman to the bathroom. The stewardess had just announced that seat belts could be removed before they rushed by. A minute later, Killa removed her panties and pulled out a condom.

****

"Festivities start at noon tomorrow. What's the plan?" Killa asked once they were all settled in his suite. Shyne would have to sleep there since every other room in the city was booked.

"Well, I can rig the sprinklers to spray gas like I did the funeral home," Shyne offered. The men went silently as they mulled over the gruesome murder. One by one, heads shook side to side for different reasons.

Killa now knew punishment by fire was God's domain and should be left to Him. Rico wanted to be sure no one got away and Sun just wanted to get his hands dirty. Pedophiles are the lowest of the low and deserved the worst of the worst.

"Nah, the kids might be on-site. First priority is saving those kids," Killa reminded. "Priority two is David Smith. He's the organizer of the event. Tonight is his last night on earth. He dies tomorrow."

"Who?!" Sun barked to the knock on the door. The family was totally unarmed but still dangerous. He couldn't make out the muffled response through the door so he repeated, "Who?"

"That's Bubba. Let him in," Killa directed.

"Bubba?" Shyne giggled as her brother opened the door.

In walked a huge white man with a huge belly and a huge beard, wearing some overalls and carrying a huge duffle bag. He looked just like a Bubba should look.

"Bubba!" Killa greeted and threw his arms open. He clenched his teeth and braced himself for the violent greeting he knew was coming.

"My man, Killa!" Bubba shouted. He dropped the bag with a loud thud and crossed the room.

"Ugh!" Killa grunted as the man scooped him up and spun him around.

"He hug like grandma!" Rico laughed. Sun and Shyne both nodded in agreement. No one said it out loud but they all made instant plans to go visit the woman.

"I got your stuff," Bubba said, looking around urgently. Killa knew just what he was looking for and passed him an empty soda can.

"Thank ya!" he said after spitting brown tobacco juice into it. A line of the saliva clung to his brown beard.

"Eww," Shyne frowned in disgust. She had her stink face on until her father opened the bag. "Ooh! Guns!"

"And lots of them," Killa said as he pulled them from the bag. The order didn't include Shyne but there were enough to share. He began to announce each weapon as he pulled it out. "MP-5, Glock 40..."

"What the heck is that?" Shyne demanded when he pulled out a shiny gold crown.

"A crown for King Pedophile David West," he smiled wickedly once he confirmed that everything was present. Bubba prepared to leave. That, of course, meant a good-bye hug that nearly crushed Killa.

"Damn, Pops, you know people everywhere!" Rico exclaimed. He was amazed how much juice he had, even way out West with rednecks named Bubba.

"Not everywhere. If I ever get to the moon, I'm on my own."

****

Breakfast the next morning was stoic and tense as malice and murder consumed their thoughts. Shyne was eating for two but still ate lightly. She had no idea what they might see and didn't want to throw up. Sun and Rico smashed piles of pancakes while their dad had a bagel and coffee. The killer kids got out of the booth and walked off once the waitress brought the bill over.

"No, I got it. Thanks guys," he called sarcastically after them. He caught up with them and they returned to the hotel. It was show time.

"You make a good cop," Rico snickered at Sun in his security guard uniform. It came with a large badge and hat, but no gun. It didn't matter because they had plenty of guns.

"Ha, ha, janitor boy. Clean-up on aisle three," Sun shot back. There was about to be a clean-up on every aisle once they got there.

"Ready?" Killa asked, coming out of his room. The crisp suit and tie he wore made him look like the professional film maker he was posing as.

"Ready!" Shyne announced. She was posing as a daycare owner to gain access. Last minute tickets had cost a thousand dollars each.

"See you guys inside," Sun announced before he and Rico left.

They rode over to the convention hall together but entered separately. Rico loaded his tool boxes on a pull cart and pulled them inside. Meanwhile, Sun eased in and took a post like he worked there. "Damn!" Rico said out loud when he saw how full the place was. What shocked him most was how normal and regular most of them looked. They looked nothing like the three-headed monsters he was expecting. They were mothers, fathers, preachers and teachers. Rappers, singers, actors and authors. Oh, and a killer and his daughter.

Shyne wore a look of disgust when she walked in and saw how many people were present. Meanwhile, Killa wore a satisfied smirk since he knew what was coming. Shyne saw a daycare display and ambled over.

"Well, hello there!" a pudgy black woman greeted cheerfully. "Are you a provider?"

"A what?" Shyne snapped. She saw a sign about registered childcare providers and relaxed a little. As much as one on the cusp of a mass murder could relax. "Oh, um, yes."

"Great! Did you submit a contester? The finals are coming soon!" she reminded. Shyne had no idea what she was talking about, but played along.

"Not yet. I hope I can make it. Did you?" she inquired.

"I sure did! I have a three-year-old who can whip a grown man! Would you like to see a clip?" the woman asked excitedly.

"Um, sure," Shyne said unsurely. After all, you can't un-see something once you've seen it. She held her breath when the woman pulled up a video on her phone. A distinctive nursery school rhyme played as an intro before a voice announced, *Toddler Fight Club.* Shyne looked up and saw little kids fighting each other while grown folks cheered and placed bets.

"I told you he was a beast!" the woman said proudly.

"So am I. See you in a bit," Shyne said and left quickly. Another second and she would've attacked. That would have fucked up the whole plan.

"Everyone, please gather around the main stage," an announcer announced. "Mr. David Smith is about to speak!"

"Showtime!" Killa, Sun, Shyne and Rico all said to themselves when they heard their cue.

Rico opened the tool box and began handing out the tools. Killa tucked a submachine gun under his suit jacket and grabbed the crown. Shyne took two pistols with extended clips and got into position. That left the MP-5s for the brothers. Rico and Sun began to chain and lock all the doors. No one was leaving there alive, except for the family of killers. Pedophiles checked in, but they wouldn't be checking out.

"Thank you, thank you!" David Smith said as he took the stage. He had to pause until the thunderous rounds of applause stopped. "It's a pleasure to see so many like-minded people in one place!"

"Yeah, it is," Killa laughed to himself. The total tally was just over two-hundred. He and the kids only had one-hundred and fifty rounds between them. The lucky ones would get shot and die quickly, if not instantly while the rest would be stabbed, beaten and stomped to death.

"Oh, a crown! I...um...wasn't expecting this," Smith frowned curiously as Killa approached as if awarding the crown. He looked to one of the organizers who didn't know either so he just shrugged. "Um...okay."

"This is what you've truly earned," Killa announced as he fit the crown upon his head. He made a couple of adjustments to make sure it fit just right, then hit the switch.

The modified crown had been fitted with the inner workings of the DC 2000, so instead of cutting his head off at the neck, it sliced through his forehead. The top of his head flipped onto the stage while he continued to stand there blinking. Finally, gravity kicked in and pulled him to the floor, too. His diseased brain fell out and rolled away. Killa kicked it into the stunned crowed and the killing began.

"Where are you?" Shyne growled as she shot her way through the crowd. It looked like an episode of *The Walking Dead* as she dropped pedophiles with one shot to the head. She finally found the Daycare Fight Club lady and shot her in her face.

"Twenty-four, twenty-five, twenty-six..." Sun said, keeping count of his tally as he went. He and Rico had two thirty-round clips each and they were quickly running out.

"Shit!" Rico fussed when his gun clicked empty. He'd only got forty-five bodies for his sixty shots.

A total of one-hundred and forty-five people lay dead when the Killa clan ran out of bullets. Fifty-something perverts ran around looking for a way out. Sun pulled out a machete and went in. Killa watched with an emotional mix of pride and elation along with a never felt before tinge of fear. He was now witnessing his son become who Karate Joe said he would one day be.

"Damn!" Shyne exclaimed as her twin hacked and chopped people who really needed to be hacked and chopped to death.

"Eat, Sun!" Rico cheered his brother on.

And eat Sun did. A man held up his hands to block the blade and lost them both. He lost his head, as well, with the next swing of the sling blade.

"Go, Sun, go, Sun! Uh-uh-uh!" Shyne cheered like a cheerleader. She even did a little dance to accompany her song.

"Wait! Wait! I'll show you where the kids are!" a scrawny white lady pleaded. She'd looked around and realized that she was the sole survivor and wanted to stay that way. It looked like she just might when Sun let the bloody machete slip from his hand.

"Where?!" he huffed, winded from the massacre. He was completely covered in blood from head to toe as she led him to the so-called green room. This was where the children waited to be bought and sold. She stuck the key in but Sun stopped her short of turning it. "Thank you," he said warmly, then politely picked her up and slammed her on her head. The sound of her neck breaking echoed throughout the now silent convention hall. The children looked at the blood soaked man in wonderment. "Don't be scared. I'm here to help you."

"Thank you, mister," a tired little girl said and reached for his bloody hand.

"He's ready," Killa sighed to himself. The maturation of his heir meant that he could retire, fall back and do what killers do when they get older. At least he would still have his 1-800-Killa site. After all, you can't just turn that killer shit off.

"Can I burn it down, Daddy?" Shyne asked with flames dancing in her pupils.

"Nah, let the police see all this evidence," he replied. Once they led the children safely outside, Killa placed a call to 9-1-1 before they made their departure. Later that night, they caught a news report on the massacre as they rode to the airport.

"In bizarre news, a death cult committed mass suicide at the Midtown Convention Center. Authorities say that at least two-hundred people killed each other and themselves..."

Chapter 48

"Won't be much longer now," Bryonna sighed as she drove. The baby in her belly seemed like it was either working out or break dancing.

"I know, right! What, two weeks?" Shyne replied from the passenger's seat. Their due dates were days apart and only weeks away.

"And then, right after that is Malik's first birthday!" her friend added with a goofy look on her face from trying not to laugh. It amused Bryonna to no end that Shyne got pregnant again six weeks after giving birth to her first child.

"Screw you!" she shot back. "Me and my husband be getting it in! I'ma have ten babies!"

"Yo, real talk, though," Bryonna said and paused to transition from playful banter to real talk. "Is it, is it gonna hurt?"

"Like hell! It feels like your entire insides are being ripped out! Like your vagina is being torn apart! Then they stitch you up with a big pirate's hook and..."

"It's amazing that we're still friends because you make me sick!"

"Girl, you know you love me!" Shyne snickered. She looked up and spotted their destination. "There it is!"

Bryonna pulled into the parking lot of The Little People Academy. The daycare center looked clean and professional enough on the outside for them to actually park and go inside. Shyne had decided that her son could benefit socially from being around other kids. It would also give her a break when the baby came, so the two had been looking at different daycare centers for weeks but hadn't found anything suitable.

"Welcome to The Little People Academy!" a pasty white lady sang as if the women were toddlers. It's a habit and hazard of the job people who spend all day speaking to children acquire.

Bryonna knew her sarcastic friend was about to say something sarcastic so she jumped in as soon as Shyne opened her sarcastic mouth. "Thank you. We're looking for a good daycare program for her son."

"Not quite ripe yet, is he?" the woman sang and placed both her hands on Shyne's belly.

Shyne flinched from the stranger's touch and barely managed to not karate chop her in her throat. "I have a one-year-old at home with his father," Shyne said through clenched teeth.

"Not quite one yet," Bryonna tossed in with a snicker.

"It's so good when the baby's daddy helps out. Rare with you people," the director said without a trace of malice. She actually didn't mean any harm; she just spoke the truth.

"Well, my husband...takes good care of his family!" Shyne growled.

"Husband! That's just great when you people get married!" she squealed and clapped her pudgy hands.

"You know what..."

"Oh, I just love you, Shyne!" Bryonna exclaimed and wrapped her arms around her, pinning her arms and preventing a karate chop to the throat.

"Why don't I call Camille to show you guys around, she's black, too!" the woman announced then called, "Camille!"

"Yes, ma'am?" The pretty yet plain girl replied as she came out front. She had a clean, fresh look about her with her hair pulled into a tasteful bun. Her loose fitting clothes couldn't fully conceal her curves but showed that she at least had tried to.

"Where do we know her from?" Shyne whispered as the director gave her instructions.

"I'on know. Somewhere," Bryonna replied, squinting at the girl as if that would help her remember. Kinda like shaking the mouse when the computer is moving slow. It doesn't help either.

"This way, ladies," Camille smiled and began the tour. The two missed most of what she said as she pointed out the activities and amenities of the facility. They were both too busy trying to place her face.

They would have been impressed by all the programs that were included. There were brain games, foreign languages, computer skills and etc. They did, however, notice that their guide seemed to love the children and that they loved her back.

"What's wrong, princess?" Camille pouted at a teary-eyed little girl. She squatted to be eye level with the girl, causing her shirt to rise in the back and reveal a tattoo. The tramp stamp read 'Chardonay'.

"Un-uh!" Shyne said, shaking her head in disbelief. No way was this sweet woman the disrespectful little ratchet girl they'd beat up.

"Uh-huh!" Bryonna said, nodding hers.

It was proof that you can knock sense into someone's head. After getting her ass whooped, Camille turned down in the streets and turned up in church. She'd suddenly remembered all the lessons and morals her grandmother had tried to instill in her. You can definitely change a hoe into a lady since she was a lady first. God doesn't make hoes, society does. But no one's going to rap, sing or write a book about that!

"Everything okay?" Camille asked when she stood from soothing the child. She didn't remember them either since they hadn't formally introduced themselves before beating her up.

"Um, yup. Just great!" Shyne smiled. Her treatment of the child sold her on The Little People Academy.

"Great! Let's go back to Miss Crabapple," she smiled and led the way. Bryonna and Shyne giggled at the funny name for the funny lady.

"What the..." Shyne fussed when she heard the familiar nursery school music coming from Miss Crabapple's office.

She was already suspicious but when the woman scrambled to turn off her phone when they appeared at her office door, it really piqued her curiosity. She had been watching something with a gleeful smile but had stopped suddenly.

"Oh! Um...well, what did you guys think?" she said, regaining her composure.

"We'se like it," Shyne exclaimed in a Black Sambo voice. She was about to break into a tap dance but Bryonna stopped her.

"Wonderful! Clean, friendly staff..." Bryonna said, singing their praises while Shyne looked around the office. She noticed quite a few pill bottles in her open purse.

"I have extremely high blood pressure," Miss Crabapple explained when she saw what Shyne was looking at. She didn't want her to get the wrong impression. "It's usually you people who suffer from high blood pressure. What's next, sickle cell?"

"Wow," Bryonna said as the woman cracked up at her own joke.

"Or AIDS, no...a baby daddy!" Shyne said, joining the laughter. "Bad credit, fried chicken..."

"Chill, Shyne," Bryonna cut in and cut her off. "Well, Miss Crabapple, we will certainly get back with you."

"Great, take my card," she exclaimed and handed both of them a card. Her face changed as she looked around her desk. "I seem to have misplaced my phone."

"I'm sure it will turn up," Shyne suggested and turned to leave. The woman began to search for it as they left the building.

"Shyne!" Bryonna screeched and swerved slightly. "Did you steal that woman's phone?"

"Borrowed. If you really want to get to know a person, go through their phone," she shot back. She was right, too. Women would be shocked to see how many men search for 'chicks with dicks'.

"You...are...too...much," she said, trying to drive and see what was on the phone. Shyne found what she was looking for and pressed play. The nursery rhyme began to play, twisting Shyne's face into a murderous sneer.

"I thought so," she growled when she saw it was episode of Toddler Fight Club.

"What the hell was that?" Bryonna said, craning her neck to see the screen.

"Nothing," Shyne said, shutting it off.

Miss Crabapple needed dead and she was about to get it. She went into the picture gallery for more evidence. The first picture looked like a ball of dough.

"What is that? Pizza dough?" Bryonna asked.

"Or busted biscuit cans," Shyne replied. She swiped to the next picture and saw pink lips on the dough and realized that it was a plump, shaved vagina. "Oh, she's a freak!"

"Let's see what's in your phone!" she shot back defensively.

"Hell no!" Shyne laughed and swiped the screen.

The next picture was of a tiny pink penis that pissed Shyne off. She was about to tell Bryonna to turn around and go back so she could hurt the woman until the next picture showed a grown man attached to the tiny dick.

"Aww, poor fellow!"

****

Once Shyne got home, she jumped online and did some research. By the time she finished, she was an expert on hypertension in general, strokes in particular. She was armed with information when she prepared to go back out.

"Where you headed?" Asad asked when she breezed by him.

"Um...downtown. I have to return this lady's phone," she said truthfully. It wasn't the whole story but it was true. "Gotta stop by the drug store, too. You need anything?"

"Nope. We're going to the park. See you later," he said. They shared a peck on the lips before she rushed back out.

Shyne stopped by a drug store and found what she needed. Once she got back into her car, she mixed the supplies together before she headed back over to The Little People Academy.

"If you people don't produce my property this instant, I will call the police!" Miss Crabapple was saying when Shyne walked in. Camille and the other workers all stood patiently while she berated them once again. Every day it was something else with the miserable woman.

"Um, excuse me. I think I accidently took your phone. It looks just like mine," Shyne offered apologetically. She even lowered her head submissively as she handed it over.

"My phone!" Miss Crabapple cheered. She rushed over and snatched her phone from Shyne's hand. She then let out an audible sigh of relief when she saw it was powered off.

"I brought an olive branch," Shyne said, holding up Starbucks. "And I would like to enroll my son."

"Come right this way! You people can get back to work," she said instead of a well-deserved apology. The sound of teeth sucking could be heard as the staff went back to work.

"Is mocha caramel okay?" Shyne asked, knowing good and damn well it was. The woman's trash can was full of empty cups of the stuff.

"My fave!" she replied and took a gulp. She produced the enrollment forms and sipped while Shyne took her sweet time filling them out. The director understood that 'those people' weren't strong readers and was patient. "Take your time. If there's anything you don't understand, just... oh my!"

"What's wrong?" Shyne asked as the woman got woozy. The pure sodium and other chemicals she'd put in her drink had sent her blood pressure through the roof. Her face drooped on one side with the onset of a stroke.

"I..." was her last word before she fell out of her chair. The sound of her hitting the floor brought the first of the workers to the door.

"I don't know what's wrong with her," Shyne said, sounding frustrated that she had an audience. The last thing she wanted was someone calling an ambulance and saving her miserable ass.

"She probably having a stroke. She has real bad high blood pressure," a woman said dryly. However, she didn't call for help, either. She just stood there and watched her wiggle and writhe in pain. She was joined by the others who also enjoyed the show.

"We need to call an ambulance," Camille suggest softly. She didn't care for the woman but she felt bad for her.

"Not yet," a Spanish lady said in her best English.

Camille turned and went back to the children. Shyne took the opportunity to ease out while Miss Crabapple had the floor, literally. The woman had needed dead and got it.

Chapter 49

"Just relax, breathe. Relax and breathe," Asad said soothingly as he drove Shyne to the hospital. Her water had broken and her contractions were coming five minutes apart.

"Relax! Breathe! Say it again! Tell me to relax again!" she said, about to take off her seatbelt and jump on him.

"Okay," Asad laughed and kept on driving. Their son was in the back looking back and forth, trying to figure out what was going on.

"Ooh, let me call Bryonna. I won!" she said and grabbed her phone. The two had bet on who would deliver first and it looked as if she'd won.

"Whoo-whoo-whoo, hel-lo? Whoo-whoo," Bryonna huffed as she took the call.

"Guess where I'm going?" she gloated.

"I...can't...whoo...talk right now. Whoo-whoo...I'm...in...labor! We on our...whoo...way to...whoo the hospital!"

"Step on it!" Shyne shouted to her husband as she hung up on her friend. Asad just shook his head at his crazy wife.

Sun and Asad pulled up to the emergency room entrance at the same time. Bryonna broke the tie by jumping out and running inside.

"Oh, no you don't!" Shyne said and did the same.

Sun and Asad just stared on in disbelief.

"We could leave now," Sun suggested. "Just take off and go."

"Nah," Asad replied after a moment of contemplation. His wife was a lovely little lunatic, but she was his lovely little lunatic.

****

"Arrrgh, Arrgh!" Shyne grunted and pushed inside the delivery room. Asad wisely decided to wait this one out in the waiting room. He would go in once he or she had made his or her appearance.

"Slow down, young lady. There's no rush," the doctor said from his stool between her legs.

"Yes, there is! I got a Coach bag on the line!" she shot back.

The doctor twisted his lips and looked to the nurse. She didn't get it either, so shrugged her shoulders. The same thing was happening over in the next delivery room with Bryonna and Sun.

"Slow down, ma'am. It's coming," her doctor advised.

"Please don't call my baby an it. He or she will be here any second, so you can wait to address it properly!" Bryonna demanded.

The doctor looked at Sun who just shook his head. He got back to work as the baby's head emerged. A slight twist made way for the shoulders and out it came. Excuse me, she.

"A girl!" Sun cheered genuinely. He honestly hadn't cared if they'd had a boy or a girl. A heathy baby was all he'd prayed for so he shot a silent 'thank you' to his Creator.

"Yolo," Bryonna said immediately. She looked to Sun for approval and watched a slow smile spread on his face. His head began to nod as well and their child was named.

"It's a girl," the nurse announced to Asad out in the waiting room. The wait was over so he went inside to meet his daughter. The first order of business was to softly chant the call to prayer in her ear. Her soft whimpers came to an abrupt end as he began.

"Amina Fatima Abdus-Salaam," Shyne said, causing Asad to nod in agreement. They had been going back and forth about both names so they settled on them both.

"Time of birth was 1:35," the doctor announced to all present. Shyne grabbed her phone to text Bryonna but saw a text pop in.

"*1:35, sucker!*" Bryonna texted along with a bunch of emojis that had nothing to do with nothing.

"I need to call Dad!" both Sun and Shyne said at the same time from different rooms.

****

"Hold on for one second if you don't mind," Killa said when both of his twins' ringtones chimed back to back. The man couldn't speak due to the gun in his mouth so nodded his head up and down.

The calls bought him a few more moments of life because Killa had come to kill him. After all, that is what he does. The child molester definitely had it coming, too. He had virtually imprisoned his own daughters as his sex slaves. He made the mistake of leaving his phone out and one of them had got online. She found 1-800-Killa and along came a Killa.

"She named her Yolo, Dad," Sun said, beaming with pride. His ear to ear smile could actually be heard through the phone.

"We name our daughter Amina," Shyne, who was also on the line, said in turn.

"Wow!" Killa sighed. "I'm in Pittsburgh right now but I'm on my way!"

"See ya soon," Shyne said for the both of them. Killa clicked off and turned back to the condemned man. He thought about sparing him but he hadn't spared his daughters, so... "Don't you know men are supposed to be the protectors and maintainers of women?" he asked as he picked up where he'd left off.

The man mumbled something but the gun barrel in his mouth made it impossible to understand. He wasn't talking about anything anyway so Killa went on.

"That doesn't just mean family, either. All men should protect and maintain all women! Not disrespect them, degrade them, call them bitches and definitely not rape them; especially your damn daughters!" he growled.

The man tried to mumble something else but the gun shot cut him off. His brain made a knockoff Picasso on the wall behind him when it left his head.

****

"They're beautiful!" Killa gushed as he looked down at his grand-daughters. He had one in each arm looking curiously up at him.

"Thank you," Shyne and Bryonna sang proudly. They'd each bought the other one a Coach bag to settle the bet. Neither needed it since their closets were stuffed with whatever their hearts desired.

Not that either was overly materialistic, but both had men, no, husbands who showered them with gifts. All Shyne had to do was say something was cute and it would be delivered. Likewise, if Bryonna looked twice at anything, Sun bought it. That's what they got for being good women.

Chapter 50

"Where you going now?" Little Rock's mother, Cynthia, protested as Bull walked out of the walk-in closet. She had just given him a killer blow job hoping to keep him in for the night but he was now fully dressed for a night out.

"Out," he said, feeling slightly sedated. A good blow job had the same effects as a glass of wine or a joint. Cynthia was a good looking fifty-year-old, but she wasn't fucking with the twenty-something-year-olds her man was fucking with.

"Bastard!" she growled and slung her glass of cognac at him.

"Bitch!" Bull said, looking at the brown liquor on his white shirt. He crossed the room in a flash and commenced to beating her up. The thuds of the heavy blows echoed in the room. "I'ma beat that ass again if this shit don't come out my shirt, too!"

Cynthia stayed in the defensive ball she'd curled into to take the beating for several minutes after he left. It had been like a classic Muhammad Ali 'Rope-a-Dope'. She took a big swig directly from the bottle to help her get up. She was wobbly from both the liquor and the ass whooping as she staggered to the bathroom. This wasn't the worse whooping she'd gotten but it would be the last. She looked at the knot on her head, her bloody nose and missing tooth and called her son.

"Sup, ma?" Little Rock asked, looking at his diamond watch as he took the call. It was past midnight so something had to be wrong for her to call this time of night. "You okay?"

"No! I need you to come over, right now!" she demanded.

"Okay, give me..." he said, pausing to gauge the speed of his side piece's head movement, "...'bout ten minutes."

His side piece heard his end of the conversation and switched gears. That cut the blow job length by half. Now it was Little Rock who was feeling relaxed as he drove to the house his dad had built. It had never sat well with him that Bull had moved in after his death.

"Back here!" Cynthia slurred when she heard her son enter the house. She sat alone in the darkened den working on a second bottle of liquor.

"Sup, Ma, why you sitting in the dark?" he asked and hit the light switch. Light filled the room and gave him his answer. "Where is he?!"

"Prob'ly up in some young bitch. He got a bunch of 'em! Guess I deserve it fo' double-crossing yo' daddy," she slurred. Alcohol is like truth serum and the truth finally came out.

"What you mean, Ma?" Little Rock asked. He'd heard rumors but this was as close to the truth as he'd ever gotten out of his mother. He knew that he had to go slow and gentle to ease it out.

"I let that bastard talk me into setting yo' father up. He knew that Yolo and Killa was on they asses, so he double-crossed him. Told me he was gone be the man, so I went along with it."

"So, Yolo and Killa killed my father and Bull set it up?" he asked slowly.

"Actually, yo' daddy kilt himself. He was such a pussy," she cackled like a witch. "I guess it's true, you are what you eat cuz that man could suck a pussy like nobody's business! Why you think you ain't got no brothers and sisters! He prob'ly sucked my ovaries out!"

"Killed himself?" the man asked, feeling crestfallen. All his life, he'd heard how much of a gangster and killer his dad was.

"Yup! That Yolo came in here with them gold fangs and brass knuckles, ain't even have a gun, said she was gon' beat him to death. Me and Bull left and soon as we got outside, here come yo' daddy out the window! Broke his fool neck."

"Hmp," Little Rock huffed and let it all sink in. Once he processed it all, he crossed the room to his mother.

She opened her arms for a hug but that's not what he brought. Cynthia took her second ass whooping of the night at the hands of her son. She had knots on top of knots when he was done.

****

"Hey, Cynt, where you at? I brung you some blue crabs!" Bull called out when he came in the next afternoon. He felt a little bad about putting the smack down last night. A load of B-more's best crab usually did the trick when he'd gone too far.

"In here," Cynthia moaned like someone with a broken jaw. Probably because it was broken, but Bull didn't do it. Her son did.

"You smokin' weed now?" he asked, frowning up when he smelled pungent smoke as he approached the den.

"Nah, that's me," Little Rock replied and exhaled a plume of grey smoke towards the ceiling. His mom was curled up on the floor in front of him.

"You smokin' weed up in my house?" Bull dared as he looked around at Little Rock's young thugs in the room. They had him down bad but he didn't have a shred of bitch in him.

"Yo' hou— Nigga, boy, you lucky I'm going to kill you anyway cuz you'd definitely die for that shit! This my daddy house!"

"It was until he jumped out the window," Bull laughed. "I took his bitch, his house and Baltimore! Now, let me pull my gun so we can bang it out! Unless you a bitch like yo' daddy."

"Guess so," Little Rock laughed and began shooting. Bull took the first few slugs standing until a thigh shot took him down. Little Rock's friends joined in and unloaded on the man.

"What about her?" C-C asked, nodding towards Cynthia.

"Nigga, that's my mama!" Little Rock spat and shot him, too. Blood is thicker than water after all.

Cynthia got up an hour or so after her son and his friends removed Bull's bullet riddled corpse. It easily sank to the bottom of the harbor with all those holes in it. She got on her laptop and went straight to 1-800-Killa.

Chapter 51

"So, err'thing good? Cuz I'm ready to get home to my husband!" Shyne asked as the doctor summed up her six-week check-up after the birth of her daughter.

"Um...yeah. Um...congratulations, once again," he said after double checking her results. "You're pregnant, again."

"Nuh uh!" Shyne couldn't help but laugh. Six weeks was a long time and she couldn't make it.

"Wow," was all Asad could think to say. It was about right because what else could be said? They were a young married couple doing what young married couples do. Shyne was his wife, not his baby mama.

"I guess, I'll have to wait until we get back from our trip before I tell my father," Shyne said when they were back in their vehicle headed home. She'd left out the part about him not letting her go if he knew she was with child. They were headed up to Detroit to cut the head off another Black Mob faction.

"I guess," he replied, knowing there was more to the story. There was always with Sun and Shyne.

****

"Want me to come, too?" Bryonna sang eagerly as Sun began to pack for the trip.

"Nah," he chuckled to himself. His wife always tried and pried for information about his frequent out of town trips. He always returned with gifts but always left with the same answer; Family Business.

"That's what I figured," she laughed. They spent some quality time with Yolo before he set off. A car horn out front was his cue to leave.

"How about some chocolate?" he asked on his way out.

"I would love some!" she cheered. Women love chocolate diamonds.

"Sup, Sun," Rico greeted with a pound as Sun slid into the passenger's seat. He stared at the outstretched blunt for a second before shaking his head.

"I'm good. I'm ready to get this dough. I hear this nigga Dog is sitting on a couple mil. That's a sweet lick," Sun cheered.

"The lick is extra, a cherry on top. The main goal is to destroy the mob," Rico reminded.

"True," Sun nodded in agreement. The rest of the ride was made in silent reflection. The radio was on but neither heard what was playing.

"Last, but not least," Killa quipped when his sons joined him and his daughter in one of the condos. Sun and Bryonna had recently moved out to the suburbs as well. Not to be outdone, Sun had purchased a million-dollar home in the same subdivision as Asad and Shyne. Now all he had to do was pay for it.

"His fault," Sun laughed, pointing at Rico. They took a seat and closed their mouths so that Killa could brief them.

"Okay, the Detroit faction of The Black Mob is run by a dog ass nigga called Dog. I can only assume he acquired the moniker from his treatment of women. He has at least twenty known baby mamas and is known to smack a hoe," he began.

"I got him," Shyne offered. "Dead beat dads need dead!"

"Yeah, but so do these ratchet ass mamas! All up in the club every day of the week! Different men in their kids' faces every day. I went home with this chick last week. When we got in the house, it was quiet. Woke up with a kid in the bed and five more running around. I asked if she ran a daycare and she said, 'No, these my kids!' All of looked like a UN delegation!" Rico ranted.

"You finished, son?" Killa asked with a chuckle.

"Uh, yeah. Just had to, um...yeah, please continue."

"Thank you. Anyway, his second in command is a three hundred and fifty-pound ex-football player called Cheese. You can catch him at any all-you-can-eat buffet eating all he can eat. He has to die along with Dog or he'll take over and nothing will change.

"I'll cut the cheese," Sun said and cracked up. "Get it? Cut...y'all wack!"

"Your jokes wack!" Shyne cackled. That set off a round of back and forth jokes causing their dead old dad to shake his head. This would be their last mission as a family. The last hoorah before he retired.

"Mind if I continue?" he asked but didn't wait for a reply. He didn't need one because all mouths snapped closed so he could continue. "Rico, you need to hit all his corners and traps as hard and fast as possible. I want them to think it's four hundred people at them instead of just four."

"I got it, Pops," he assured him. After the way Sun put on in Salt Lake City, he had some catching up to do.

"What about the money, Pops?" Sun asked. "We gots to have it!"

"He keeps a safe at his mother's house. She's not in on the action but is the only one he can trust. He treats his children's mothers like shit. I'll take care of his mom," Killa said. He left out the part about the forty-five-year-old woman being a sexy motherfucker. He planned to seduce his way into her and her house to get to the safe. "Shyne, I'm going to need a pupil and hand to get pass the biometric security."

"Which one? Left, right?" she asked as casually as if he'd asked her to pick up some bagels. Instead of cream cheese, they were talking body parts.

"Um...bring both, just to be on the safe side. Get it? Safe...side!" he joked.

Shyne made cricket noises while Sun and Rico shook their heads. At least they all knew where they got it from.

The Killa clan arrived at Atlanta's airport just in time to hear, *"Fligh' fi'-ni-ni-fo' to Detroit is finna board on gate ni."*

Killa moved like he knew exactly where he was going once they touched down in Detroit. As usual, a rental car awaited to take them to their hotel where four rooms and four more cars awaited. An order of guns and ammo were en route as well.

"Welp, I'll see you guys in the morning," Shyne exclaimed once she had her room key. She took off like a shot and headed up to her room to call her husband. She wasn't the only one either.

"Yeah, I..." Sun said and yawned for effect. "Guess I'll turn in myself."

Killa and Rico twisted their lips dubiously as they watched him walk away. As soon as he got into his room, he pulled out his spare phone and called home.

"I see you made it safely," Bryonna said with relief audible in her tone. "You just missed your daughter, she's sleep now."

"That's okay, now I have you all to myself," he replied. Not to mention the baby couldn't talk anyway. She did make a gummy smile when she heard her daddy's voice on the phone, though.

"You know you don't have to do this," Bryonna advised.

"Do what?" he frowned curiously.

"Stay on the phone with me all night every time you go out of town. I trust you. Even if I have no idea what you guys actually do, I still trust you."

"I know. I do it because I love and miss you. I started missing you the second I left the house."

Chapter 52

Sun and Shyne may have planned to spend the night boo-loving on the phone, but not Killa and Rico. They were trying to go fuck something.

The night on the town wasn't just about sampling some out of town pussy. It had a lot to do with it but it was also a surveillance mission. Dog owned and operated several clubs in and around Detroit. They generated more than enough income for him to leave the streets alone but he couldn't. That street shit is addictive, it's hard to just turn it off.

Rico ended up at The Dog House. The trendy club catered to the city's twenty-something crowd. There were also a few thirty-something-year-olds in attendance who liked to turn up. Inevitably, there were a couple of forty-something-year-olds in the house in search of young flesh.

"Oh yeah," Rico said to himself as he walked inside. He may have come in alone but judging by the looks he was getting, he wouldn't be leaving alone. He stood way out in his New York clothes and his New York swag. Several women made beelines toward him as he headed to the bar. A pretty brown thing named Simone beat the crowd and posted up next to him.

"Sup, Ma?" Rico greeted with the killer smile he'd inherited from his father.

"Oh, a New Yorker!" she exclaimed with a smile of her own. "Let me buy you a drink to welcome you to Detroit."

"Only one, the next one is on me," he agreed.

"Fair exchange ain't no robbery. I do you, you do me," Simone said, hoping that they could swap head later. She had no problem going down on a stranger and hoped he didn't either.

"Indeed," he replied, licking his lips to show he understood and was with it. He was a male THOT just like his father. That's why he kept a dental dam in his wallet right next to condom.

****

Killa ended up in a dimly lit jazz club dubbed Doggy Style. He blinked rapidly as he stepped in so his eyes could adjust. Once they did, he scanned the bar, tables and booths. He thought he'd spotted his target and pulled out his phone to double check.

"Yup," he agreed and made his way over. He stared straight ahead while watching her watch him from his peripheral vision. He did a fake glance then a double take. "Deborah?"

"Yes?!" she replied eagerly. She strained her pretty facial features trying to recall his name. She would never get it since they'd never met.

"Xavier. Wow, you don't remember me," he said, sounding wounded. Killa had definitely missed his calling as an actor. "We met last time I was in town. Sorry I didn't call but I lost my wallet."

"Oh yeah! That's okay, I...shit! Quick, sit down!" she said urgently and pulled Killa into the booth next to her. He wondered what was going but didn't have to wait long for the answer.

"What's up, Deborah!" a flashy pimp type announced when he reached the booth. He stomped his foot to bring attention to his green gator boots and grimaced to show off his gold teeth.

"Oh, hey, Harold," she replied with an exasperated sigh. It was body language for 'beat it' but obviously he didn't speak that.

"Let's get up outta here and go somewhere and chill," he suggested as if the woman was alone.

"I'm with my friend. Xavier, meet Harold. Harold, Xavier," she introduced.

"How you doing, Harold?" Killa said cordially and extended his hand like a gentleman.

"Whatever, nigga," the pimp said, knocking his hand away like he was a chump. Killa was neither a gentleman nor a chump. He was a killer and Harold had just gotten himself killed. "Anyway, call me."

"Yeah, okay," she said since that got him to leave. She turned to her guest as he retreated. "I'm so sorry about that. Gave that man some twenty-years-ago and he been sniffing my ass ever since."

"Twenty-years-ago!" Killa reeled. "Damn, it must be good!"

"Good? No, it's great! It get so wet!" she giggled, "I'm sorry. I like to play."

"No problem. I like to play, too," he said. "This is a nice place. I'll have to come back next time I'm in town."

"My son owns it," she said proudly. "I named it, though. After my favorite position."

"Mine, too," he said and stared into her eyes. She leaned in for a kiss and he let her. Killa reached under her short skirt but she clamped her thighs closed on it. Another kiss and they began to part.

"Mmm," Deborah moaned as Killa played in her kitty. She got all wet and squishy then left a puddle in his palm when she came.

"Let's get out of here," he said and slid out of the booth. His erection was clearly visible through his slacks and sealed the deal.

"Let's!" she agreed and slid out after him. Once they got into the car, she graciously freed his erection from its confines. She spat on it and worked it in with hands as he drove.

"How much further?" he asked, feeling the tingles of an orgasm building.

"Turn right, blue house," she replied. She leaned in and kissed the swollen head before tucking it back in his pants.

Killa followed her into the modest house out in the suburbs. She led him straight to her bedroom and began to strip. Killa watched the show and was quite pleased with what he saw. The forty-five-year-old could put some twenty-five-year-olds to shame. Her breasts were still firm and stomach flat. Womanly hips spread around to a nice, fat ass. His dick stood straight out when he removed his pants. He rolled a condom on as she climbed to the center of the bed.

"You can get either hole you want," she purred and stuck her ass in the air.

"Thanks," he said, sliding into the right one. He slid his thumb into the other, making her cum instantly. This was supposed to be business and not pleasure, so he made it his business to give her pleasure. In other words, he gave her the business.

"Shit! Shit! Shit!" Deborah cussed as she had orgasm after orgasm. She felt like she came with every stroke. She finally couldn't take it anymore. One last nut and she fell face first on the bed.

Killa fell with her and kept on stroking. It didn't take long until he grunted and filled up the condom. Now, it was time for pillow talk.

****

"Shit! Shit! Shit!" Simone fussed as Rico fucked her to yet another orgasm. He sat straight up while she rode him so they were face-to-face.

"You like that, huh?" he bragged. He grabbed her ass cheeks and grinded her on him.

"I love it!" she confessed and clamped her vagina walls tight. Now it was his turn to curse and cum.

"Shit, you got...some...good...ass...pussy!" Rico exclaimed.

"Yup!" she said knowingly and fell off his dick. She cuddled up beside him to bask in post orgasmic bliss. "So, how long you gon' be here? When you coming back?"

"Not sure, don't know," he replied and kissed her forehead. "I gotta catch up with my partner, Dog and..."

"Psh," she sucked her teeth. "That nigga got time for err'body else 'cept his damn kids! Our daughter turned five and he ain't even show up. Bet his ass be at the car show tomorrow, though!"

"Sho' nuff," Rico comforted. He kissed her softly and rubbed her gently as she gave up all the goods on her baby's daddy.

Chapter 53

When the alarms began to chirp, chime and vibrate the next morning, it was a time to kill. Each Killa had an agenda and a plan to set in motion.

Shyne called home to listen to Asad pray then set out on her mission. Her father had all the props and supplies she needed to euthanize Dog. That meant: put to sleep.

Likewise, Sun got ready to trail Cheese. The moment he got the word, he was going to turn him into Swiss cheese with a tech nine.

Meanwhile, Rico was armed to the teeth. He had grenades, machine guns and a shit load of ammo. He mapped out a crisscross plan of attack that would keep the crew off balance.

Killa woke up next to Deborah and fucked her again. She cooked breakfast for him and begged him to spend his last day in town inside of her. He agreed since he couldn't open the safe while she slept. It had retinal scan and fingerprint security so he had to wait on Shyne.

****

"Bullshit!" Dog grumbled when a police car threw its lights on behind him. He glanced down and saw that he was doing close to a hundred miles per hour. The new V-12 Audi refused to do anything less. He knew he could get arrested at that speed so he pulled out a wad of cash when he stopped.

"Uh oh! A lady cop, and she cute!" he said as the female officer approached. He decided to further entice her and pulled his dick out. It lay on his lap when she arrived.

"License and registration!" she barked, ignoring both cash and cock.

"I'm kinda in a hurry, so take this and I'll give you this, later," he replied, offering the cash now and his cock for later.

"Step out of the car!" she demanded. One hand went on her sidearm and the other opened the car door.

"You must be new. You must not know who I am," Dog spat as he complied. His car was clean so he wasn't worried about the stop. If worse came to worse, he'd have to take a ride to the precinct and pay a bond on speeding violation.

"Mmhm," was her reply as she pulled out a shiny pair of hand-cuffs.

"Man, what about my car!" Dog whined while he was cuffed. The cop pulled out another shiny circular ring and slipped it over his head. Dog frowned at the unknown contraption as she led him to the police car. "What the hell is that?"

"It's called the DC 2000. It was my mom's but I had the cuffs made myself," Officer Shyne replied. She knew he would have more questions in that nasty high pitched voice black men used when in trouble. She didn't have the stomach for either so she hit the switch-es. His head fell onto the floor of the car while his hands dropped behind him. She put them all in a bag and left him in the back of the squad car. "I'll drop your car off at your mom's."

****

"Show time," Both Sun and Rico announced when Shyne's text came through. Leave it to her to send a picture of one of Dog's hands giving a thumbs up. What they didn't see was her giving it a high-five before she put it back in the bag.

Rico was parked near a bustling Black Mob corner. Young dealers were pushing coke, dope, weed and pills to the neighbors, aunts, un-cles and mamas. He took a deep breath, got out of the car and went in.

"Oh shit!" a young thug yelled when the man with a chopper opened fire. Those words could go on his head stone because they were his last.

Rico gunned down everything and everyone standing on or near the corner. A couple of junkies got killed along with the bad guys. They weren't exactly good guys anyway, so it was cool. By the time the shots stopped and the smoke cleared, Rico was gone. Off to the next Black Mob spot to turn red. For the next hour, he did drive-bys and walk-ups until the crew was laid down.

"Now that's some get down or lay down shit!" he told a room full of dead people before leaving with their cash.

****

"What! What? When? Who?" Cheese barked as news of the multiple massacres reached him. He was stuffing his face at the Chinese buffet when his phone began blowing up.

"Man, I don't know!" Eddie shot back. It would be the only shooting he would do since he was speeding out of town. "Might be Little Rock's people! Did y'all pay them?"

"Where's Dog?" Cheese asked. However, he didn't wait for an answer before hanging up and calling him himself. Dead people don't talk so he didn't get an answer. Shit, Dog didn't have hands to answer the phone, anyway.

"Sup, yo?" Sun greeted casually as he walked up to his table.

"What?" Cheese snapped with a mean mug on his face.

Sun lifted the 357 Bulldog and fired it twice. It erased his face like a magic trick. "I said, sup, yo," Sun repeated, turned and left. His mission was accomplished so he met up with Rico back at the hotel. Now all they had to do was wait on Shyne and Killa.

****

"Let me tie you up?" Killa asked seductively as he played in Deborah's box. He made sure she was on the steep cliff of a deep orgasm before asking. His fingers stopped while he waited for an answer.

"No, don't stop!" she pleaded while grinding and bucking her hips against his hand. "Tie me up. I don't care!"

Killa resumed playing in her puddle as he secured her wrists, then ankles to her bed. He wondered if he had enough time to smash once more. The doorbell rang, answering the question for him.

"Who the hell could that be?" Deborah asked, since no one came over without calling first. She lived too far off the beaten path for anyone to claim that they were in the area.

"That's Shyne, my daughter," he replied and went to open the door.

"Your daughter? Why would she come home? How does she know where I leave?" she called after him but he didn't stop to answer.

"In the closet," Killa told Shyne as he led her back into the bedroom.

"You so nasty," Shyne said, shaking her head at the naked woman tied to the bed.

"Yes, I am," he agreed. Why lie? He was.

"Oh my God!" Deborah screamed when her son's head came out of the bag. The murderous father and daughter ignored her cries and questions as they used Dog's body parts to open the safe.

"Damn!" Shyne said at the sight of all the cash. Her husband had a couple of million in the bank but it looked different on paper than in paper.

"Damn is right!" Killa agreed and began loading the cash.

"I'll take care of her," Shyne said and walked out of the walk-in closet.

Killa didn't pay any attention to what she had said until he saw her wrap a cord around her neck. "Wait!" Killa shouted before Shyne could choke the life out of her. Now, anyone who says good pussy can't save your life is a damn lie. "Leave her."

Shyne shrugged and let her live. She carted the first satchel of cash out to the car and came back for another. Killa picked up the last one and prepared to leave.

"Wait!" Deborah pleaded. She lifted her ample ass up and wiggled it. "At least hit once more? You ain't even gotta untie me!"

"You can't be serious," Killa chuckled and walked out of the house. He put the last bag into Dog's car and told Shyne, "Go 'head. I'll meet you back at the room."

Killa went back and hit that one last time and he didn't untie her.

Chapter 54

"Hmp..." Killa huffed while reading 1-800-Killa messages. His sons were busy counting the cash to split while Shyne talked to Asad on the phone.

The message from a Baltimore mother beaten up by her son caught his attention. The before and after pictures sealed the deal. The once pretty woman looked like she'd caught a case of Elephantitis. She had lumps and bruises everywhere. A footprint could even be clearly seen on her forehead.

"One point three hundred!" Sun exclaimed at the final count. Shyne twisted her lips since she didn't want any of the dirty money. What could she do with it, anyway? She did, however, baby talk her husband into buying her a V-12 Audi like the one Dog had. Shyne gets what Shyne wants.

"Yo, that's over six apiece!" Rico exclaimed since he knew that their father didn't want any of the money either. He was still caked up from the hits he'd done years ago.

"We'll split it up when we get home. Our flight leaves in an hour," Shyne said in her pouty voice. The wife and mother was ready to get home to her husband and kids.

****

"You guys go 'head. I'll see you in Atlanta in a few days," Killa announced after the flight to Atlanta was announced. Shyne frowned at his not say 'God willing' when speaking of future plans.

Both he and her husband had taught her to never say what she would do in the future without saying God willing. After all, it's not up to you. What makes people think there will even be a tomorrow if God doesn't will it?

"Bet!" Sun said and gave him a pound and hug.

"Where you going?" Shyne asked with her stink face on.

"Baltimore," he said and kissed her cheek. Rico rushed over for a pound and hug before boarding the plane.

Several hours later, Killa landed in Baltimore. A smile spread on his face as he entered the same hotel he and Yolo had stayed in when they'd come to kill Big Rock. He fondly recalled the way she rode him while he was tied to the bed. Then the memory of the maid came back and fucked it up. *No policia.*

****

After breakfast the following day, he set out to verify the claim. If true, he was going to murder the son. Paradise lies at the feet of mothers. That means keep your fucking hands off of them.

He saw Cynthia fresh off another beating from her son. She walked with a slight limp from a departing kick in the ass when he sent her for blue crabs. To add insult to injury, he made her walk the whole way.

"Can I give you a ride?" Killa asked as he pulled alongside the wounded woman. She looked around fearfully before nodding a reply. Not seeing her son in sight, she got in gingerly from the foot in the ass.

"Thanks," she said through her wired jaw. Tears streamed down her face, mixing with the sweat from walking in the sweltering heat.

"What's your name?" Killa asked to be personable.

"Kathy," she grunted passed her surgically clenched teeth.

"Did your son do this to you?" he asked. Her head began to nod up and down along with more tears. "When can I meet him?"

Cynthia heard the violence in his tone and grabbed a pen and paper from the center console. She wrote a time and place and handed it over. The trap was set.

****

"Wish her mouth wasn't wired," Killa mused to himself as he looked at her before picture. The pretty woman definitely could get it. He swiped over to the after picture and got pissed off. He was parked outside the condo Cynthia said he would be at when she said he would be there. Next, Cynthia limped up to the entrance. He needed her to gain access to the secured building, so he rushed over to catch up. "Here I am."

"Whew, I thought you'd changed your mind," she sighed in relief.

"Nah, I'm here. You might wanna stay outside. This will be messy," he replied. He was right, too, because a 40 Cal is known to make a mess.

"NO! I wanna watch," she insisted and led the way. After a quick elevator ride, they got out on the fifth floor. Again, he followed until she reached the unit.

"Wait," Killa whispered urgently. He gently pressed his ear against the door. The sounds of jazz and fucking crept through it and he knew he'd caught him with his pants down. "Okay."

Cynthia opened the door slowly as Killa pulled his pistol. They stepped quietly inside the dark apartment and closed the door. The sexual sounds sounded as if they were coming from a back room so he inched forward. Two steps later, the lights came on.

"Surprise!" the room full of gunmen cheered. Killa quickly ascertained that he was outnumbered and outgunned. He snatched Cynthia to use as a human shield and raised his gun.

"We can all live, or we can all die," Killa said to the man he assumed to be Little Rock. He was the only man sitting with his gun on the coffee table.

"So you're the great Killa, huh?" Little Rock remarked as he stood. He picked up his gun and drew nearer.

"Easy, or I'll blow her head clean off," Killa warned and raised the gun to her temple. "Another step and your mom dies."

"So!" Little Rock shrugged. He took that other step and fired a round into his mother's torso. She stumbled a few steps and fell, so he shot her again.

"So be it," Killa sighed. He set if off and the room erupted in gunfire.

Chapter 55

"Daddy," little Malik said when Asad entered the kitchen. Shyne stopped feeding him to smile at him.

"I love you, too," he replied since he knew what the look meant. He then grabbed the baby bottle he'd come for and patted his son on the head before he went to fed his sister.

"Yup, that's your daddy!" Shyne said proudly. Her demeanor quickly changed as her own daddy came to mind. He hadn't called or texted, and that was unusual. He didn't answer his phone when she called, either, but Sun answered his.

"Sup, yo?" Sun greeted and questioned at the same time. She usually called Bryonna and relayed messages through her. The only time she called him directly was when they had family business.

"You heard from yo' father?" she asked sarcastically, hoping it would mask her worry. It didn't and put him on high alert.

"Nah, not since yesterday. I'm 'bout to call him now!"

Sun's call went unanswered as well so he made a few more calls. He clicked on Baltimore's news cast online and heard the grim report.

"The bodies of several men and one woman were found inside a Harbor Front condo last night. Five were pronounced dead on the scene while two survivors are at Midtown Medical in critical condition. Police say over a hundred rounds were exchanged in the unit. No names have been released..."

"What?" Bryonna asked softly as her husband sank slowly to the floor. She had never seen him this way and it shook her to her core.

"...Eh...uh," he said, clearing his throat after his first attempt come up empty. "I have to go to Baltimore. Tell Shyne I'll call her later."

****

"Is my father dead?" Shyne demanded when she finally heard from Sun later that night.

"No," he replied in such a grim tone that it sounded like it couldn't be good news. "It's bad, though. He's in a coma."

"I'm on my way!" She shot back ready to catch the first thing smoking.

"Nah, don't come. You can't see him, anyway. They ran his prints. They know who he is. Police are guarding the room," he explained.

"I'm coming anyway!" she insisted and hung up on him before he could reply.

"I know. That's why I got you a room," he said mainly to himself.

Sun tortured enough people to get the whole story of the set up. There were no one to take it out on since Killa had killed them all. Only he and Little Rock had survived the shoot-out. Killa was in a coma but Little Rock was expected to make a full recovery. In a stroke of luck, he'd turned his head quick enough that Killa's first shot had entered his mouth and came out his cheek. Another collapsed his lung but he would be fine. Killa had gotten hit nine times and it was touch and go.

****

"Sup, Shyne?" Sun greeted and hugged his sister. Each tried and failed to remember the last time they felt any fear as they hugged. Neither could recall a time, and let each other go.

"Where's Rico?" she asked, looking around the hotel suit.

"He's with some nurse he bagged at the hospital," he replied.

"Our father clinging to his life and he out chasing ass?" she frowned.

"Nah, yo, she's our eyes and ears inside," he explained.

Shyne nodded in agreement since it was a smart idea. "Guess he gotta take one for the team."

****

Rico indeed was taking one for the team, even if Nurse Shonda was bad chick. He was so worried about his father that he could barely concentrate on the good, creamy vagina she had.

"I'm cumming!" she announced loud enough for him to mentally rejoin her in the room. His hips had been on autopilot, thrusting in and out on their own.

"Me, too," he lied and faked an orgasm along with her real one. She was now Team Killa, too. She was their way inside.

****

"Mmph! Look at this one!" one of the police officers guarding Killa's room exclaimed as a sexy nurse sashayed in their direction.

"Time for his meds," she said, seeking access to the patient's handcuffed to the bed.

"Yeah, take good care of that one. His ass is going to jail the minute he wakes up!" the other cop vowed. Both looked at the panty lines through her dress as she went in.

"Nah, I'ma kill y'all both and break him out the second he wakes up," Shyne corrected to herself as she went inside. She could feel eyes on her ass so couldn't lean in and kiss her dad. Instead, she shot a syringe full of saline in his IV. "Love you, Dad. See you soon."

"Damn, she got a sweet ass," a cop said as she left. Shyne stopped, turned and smiled. She made a gun with her finger and pretended to shoot them both in their foreheads.

Little Rock wasn't under guard since the condo was in his name. His story was that Killa broke in and tried to rob him. Then killed his mom and his men in the process.

"Mmph!" Little Rock said when the same sexy nurse entered. He would have said more if not for getting shot in his mouth.

"Medication time," Shyne sang as she injected a syringe into his IV line as well. However, this one contained drain cleaner. His whole body seized as the burning liquid spread through his blood stream.

His was going to be an extremely painful death so she quickly hit up her brothers on video chat so they could watch. The killer clan watched as he writhed in agony. Death was a relief when it came ten minutes later. Shyne quickly exited the hospital and went back to the hotel.

"Shonda said we shouldn't expect any change for a while. His body will need to heal from all the trauma before he can wake up," Rico explained.

"Then we'll be right here!" Shyne proclaimed. She knew Asad would be by her side as soon as she called him.

"No. You guys have families. I'll stay. Shonda can keep me filled in," he replied.

"Mmhm, and I'm sure you'll keep her 'filled in' as well!" Shyne quipped, making quotation signs with her fingers.

"But of course!" he admitted.

They shared a group hug before Rico took the twins to the airport. They boarded a plane back to Atlanta and that was...

The End.

Epilogue

"You okay?" Asad asked once again when he found Shyne curled up on the sectional sofa in the family room.

"No, but I'm sure I will be," she replied. A week had passed and her father was still in a coma.

"Come to bed," he suggested and stretched his hand to her.

"Go 'head. I'm gonna stay up and read," she replied, holding up a small book.

"Cool. What is that?" he asked.

"My mom's diary. I'm finally ready to read it."

Asad leaned in and kissed her goodnight. She watched him walk away until he was out of sight. She took a deep breath and opened the book.

Dear diary, my name is Yolo Jackson and I just killed someone...

Yolo 4, Diary of a Mad Woman....
Coming next!

?

Prologue

"Shyne, wake up!"

"I'm not sleep!" Shyne shot back. She was slightly perturbed at the interruption. She quickly realized who she was speaking to and softened her tone accordingly. "I was reading, Bae."

"Huh?" Asad asked with his face twisted into a question mark. "I didn't say anything."

"You didn't just tell me... Never mind," the fussy little diva shot back and went back to reading.

The small book had become a big distraction from the huge problems her family faced. Her beloved father was still in a bullet-induced coma up in Baltimore. The doctors said he had a fifty-fifty chance of survival. So did they because Shyne had vowed to kill each and every doctor, nurse and candy striper at the hospital if he died. No, it wouldn't be their faults, but they would get the blame.

The diary gave Shyne a chance to finally get to know her long lost mother better. What better way to get to know a person than through their own thoughts written in their own words? She traced her mother's words with her finger before starting to read. When she started to read, it was like she could her hear mother's voice ringing clearly in her mind.

"Dear Diary, I just killed someone..."

"Dang, Ma!" Shyne exclaimed and giggled at the end of reading about how a seven-year-old Yolo had strangled her playmate. She'd obviously forgotten about setting a fire that had killed four people when she was just nine herself.